IN THE BALLROOM

A fiercely addictive crime thriller

CATHERINE MOLONEY

Detective Markham Mystery Book 9

JOFFE BOOKS

First published in Great Britain 2020
Joffe Books, London
www.joffebooks.com

Join our mailing list for free Kindle books and new releases.

We love to hear from our readers! Please email any feedback you have to: feedback@joffebooks.com

ISBN 978-1-78931-456-4

For Ma and Percy.

PROLOGUE

Bluebell! What kind of daft la-di-da name is that?

As she plodded grumpily down Bromgrove Rise on the morning of Saturday, 4 January, Natalie Noakes's thoughts were none too pleasant.

It was a cold bright day with a sharp tang in the air, but she was too focused on her internal monologue to take in the heathery beauty of the Rise, which offered a scenic shortcut into the town centre and the bustling amenities of the high street.

She must have been mad telling her dad she was hooked on *Strictly Come Dancing*. Mad or trolleyed. That was all it took for him to shoot off and buy her a course of lessons at this crummy little outfit where he and Mum used to go when they were (shudder) going steady. Christmas present sorted!

Obviously, her policeman father DS George Noakes was a long way from suspecting the main attraction of *Strictly* was that snake-hipped soap star whose sizzling samba had made everyone sit up. She'd fallen madly in lust, along with half the female population, and thereafter tuned in religiously to follow her idol's progress. It was strange. He'd been a right ugly git when he played Kevin on *Elm Tree Farm* — real serial-killer material — and now look at him. Totally ripped . . . a real babe magnet.

For a moment, Natalie lost herself in a pleasurable reverie. Then her sense of grievance reasserted itself.

Fat chance of meeting any buff guys at this Bluebell place. More likely it'd be wall-to-wall coffin dodgers doing the foxtrot or whatever cos the doctor said exercise was good for them and they couldn't be arsed playing bowls.

Worst of all, her dad said his boss's girlfriend would be taking dance lessons too. DI Gilbert 'Gil' Markham was dreamy. Well, for an older guy at any rate. He had to be in his late thirties, but he was tall, dark and handsome with it. And he was always respectful, even after that incident at the Krazyhouse when he could have dobbed her in. Not like DI Carstairs with his knowing smirk . . .

Yeah, Markham was all right. But Olivia Mullen was another matter, with all that red hair flying about and the arty-fartiness. Natalie and her mother Muriel rarely saw eye to eye. But they were united in their dislike of Markham's girlfriend, a feeling only increased by the fact that, in George Noakes's eyes, she was practically perfect. Her father's 'weak spot', Muriel called it, her words heavy with meaning.

Anyway, Olivia Mullen was bound to take to the waltzing and all the other stuff like she'd been *born* to it, thought Natalie sourly. The woman never seemed to put on an ounce whereas Natalie herself only had to *look* at a sodding mince pie for it to show on her hips. Mind you — she glanced down complacently at her spray-tanned Cheddar Gorge of cleavage — at least she had curves in all the right places whereas the other had no figure to speak of. With Olivia as a partner, it'd be like dancing with a stepladder.

Her voucher thingy specified ballroom, but if she was lucky, she might be able to swap it for street or freestyle. She just couldn't imagine herself doing the kind of *Downton Abbey* crip-crap her parents favoured. Fishtails, pivots and reverse spins . . . *FFS*! She'd look a right wazzock if she tried any of that in Bromgrove's nightclubs . . .

It wouldn't surprise her if her parents were in this together, she thought darkly. All part of some grand plan to stop her seeing 'Jakey Jake' and the rest of them at the Krazyhouse. Deep down, she knew they were disappointed she hadn't gone to university (big yawn to that) and that she'd settled for her job as a beautician (*with prospects,* she reminded herself). So, mixing with the DI's girlfriend and other grade-A misfits probably represented a step up in their eyes. God, she could almost hear her mother at the Women's Guild. *Of course, Natalie and Gilbert Markham's partner are like* that. Yuck.

Natalie had now reached the bottom of the Rise where she took the shortcut through Badgers Copse to the town centre. The exercise had done something to alleviate her ill humour and her scowl softened as she felt the warmth of the sun's rays through her Calvin Klein puffer jacket (the real thing, mind, cos she didn't do knock offs). It was unusually mild for winter.

If this is climate change, bring it on. Greta Whasserface and that Attenborough bloke don't know they're born!

The town centre was quiet, but then Bromgrove wasn't exactly a retail hotspot and most folk were likely sleeping off their hangovers from the night before. Since Natalie and her latest romantic interest had split up in a noisy recrimination-fest two days earlier, she had spent a moody New Year's Eve with her parents and the neighbours, inwardly vowing this would be the year she bought her own place and showed Cazza and the rest of them a thing or two.

Feeling better for this laudable resolution, she turned her footsteps towards Heathfield Close, a few streets behind the high street.

And there on the corner, set well back from the road with a neat tarmacadamed forecourt, was the Bluebell Dance Studio.

In a former incarnation, the dance school had been a red-brick Victorian church and still possessed something of an ecclesiastical air. Needless to say, this did nothing to recommend the place to Natalie, whose prejudice against the studio was deepening by the minute.

It had the Hansel and Gretel, lumbago-ridden look of such buildings, with wonky gables and walls that seemed almost to bulge with damp. A two-storey annexe at the back gave onto a long garden. This at least had a certain overgrown charm, with rustic stone birdbaths and little arbours counteracting the overall neglect.

Altogether, it wasn't a prospect to make youthful spirits soar. But at least there was a Costa around the corner, so she had somewhere to hide if things got too bad.

She'd expected the interior to be dark and mildewed, but on passing through the front door, she found herself in a light bright reception area with sun streaming through a skylight. Double glass doors showed a vista of well-polished parquet flooring with more doors on either side.

There was nobody at the front desk and she couldn't see anyone in the corridor beyond the glass doors. Mind you, it wasn't nine o'clock yet. She'd deliberately arrived a full forty minutes early, promising herself she'd scarper if she got an attack of the willies.

All the same, there was something oppressive, almost unnatural about the heavy silence.

Surely *someone* should be around to . . . well, *welcome* people. It was customer-service values, she told herself with a smug consciousness of the well-oiled routines at Tanfastic.

Suddenly, a woman burst through a side door to the right of the front desk. There was nothing glamorous about her, Natalie noted sourly with a self-conscious toss of her own peroxide blonde mane. Just a middle-aged brown smudge of a woman with an unbecoming pudding-bowl haircut and slightly buck teeth.

But then she noticed the woman's fringe was plastered to her forehead with sweat and her face was a strange shade of greenish-white.

Despite her obsession with looking like a Love Islander, Natalie Noakes had a good heart and she could see something was terribly amiss.

She put out a steadying hand. 'What's wrong, luv?'

'It's Shirley.' The other clutched at her convulsively. '*My mum.*'

WTF? Natalie's mind began to race. 'You mean, your mum's had a turn?'

Wouldn't you just know it. Five minutes in the place and some wrinkly was having a heart attack. Too much bleeding cha-cha-cha, like as not.

The woman looked a sight, her face streaked with tears and snot.

Natalie tried again. 'Have you called an ambulance?'

'No, you don't understand,' the other gasped. 'She's *dead.*'

Little swimming curls of fear spiralled down Natalie's back. She turned icy cold, then the instincts of a policeman's daughter took over.

'Show me,' she said.

They went through the side door into a narrow sort of conservatory or lean-to. Above them, the flat Perspex roof appeared to run the length of the premises. At the far end was another door which opened onto some cement steps leading to the garden.

Natalie couldn't see anyone collapsed on the ground, or anyone at all for that matter.

But then, following her companion's gaze down to the bottom of the steps and just to the left, she saw an ornamental barrel or water butt with — *oh fuck* — a body protruding out of the top.

It was a woman's body, the lower portion clad in a long dark skirt and the feet shod in black low-heeled sandals with strap fastenings. A dance teacher's practice shoes, thought Natalie. Most eerie of all, it seemed to her that the feet were flexed in first position.

'Don't touch her,' she said hoarsely. 'We need to call 999.'

With clumsy hands, she found her mobile and made the call.

What came to be known as the Bluebell Case had begun.

1. SLOW BEGINNINGS

DI Gilbert Markham had a higher opinion of eco-warriors like Greta Thunberg and their Cassandra-like prophecies than Natalie Noakes. But even so, he was not averse to enjoying the unseasonably mild weather.

The morning of Sunday, 5 January found him walking meditatively in St Chad's, the terraced graveyard which overlooked the back of Bromgrove Police Station. As he strolled up and down, he felt a sense of new life stirring, of nature putting out shoots and tendrils in all directions, as though mysteriously eager to heal the broken-hearted and comfort those who mourned the dead.

He pulled a wry face at the thought of DCI Sidney's likely reaction to such philosophizing. His superior officer (known to the troops as 'Slimy Sid') had no patience with what he was wont to dismiss as 'Markham's ESP'. At his last appraisal, indeed, 'feyness' had featured high on the bill of indictment. 'Don't want senior officers going all wobbly, do we?' the DCI had pronounced, 'wobbliness' presumably covering a multitude of sins including any subversive challenge to Sidney's diktats.

Markham sensed there would be a tussle with Sidney over this Bluebell case. His thoughts turned to the events of the previous afternoon . . .

For all her blonde pulchritude, Natalie Noakes had shown herself to be no airhead and somehow restrained the victim's distraught daughter from trampling all over the crime scene.

Crime scene. Was that what it was?

The pathologist Doug 'Dimples' Davidson carried out the usual rituals with customary phlegm, his hearty countryman's face giving little away.

'I'd say she'd had one over the eight, went wandering . . . somehow toppled in and drowned. We'll know more once I get her on the table.'

'But there's only a few inches of water in that . . . *thing*.' Clearly DS George Noakes had no very high opinion of the Bluebell's horticultural equipment.

'If she got it in her lungs, an inch, a gallon, an ocean — the effect would be the same.' Dimples was trenchant. 'Easiest thing in the world. You could commit suicide by sticking your head in a bucket of water if it came to it.'

'Right little ray of sunshine, ain't he?' Noakes muttered disgustedly as they watched the doctor marshalling the stretcher party towards the lean-to. 'D'you think that was it, then . . . ? The poor cow had New Year blues or summat, got blotto an' decided to end it all?' He gazed after the sad little procession and observed almost plaintively, 'She looked kind of peaceful . . .'

It was quite true. With her long dark hair, wet blouse and cardigan clinging to her like a shroud, Shirley Bastin — for that was the woman's name — looked the picture of tranquillity itself. Her face was smooth as an onyx cameo, the features bearing no look of misery or desperation.

Suicide.

And yet, standing in respectful silence as the body was borne away, Markham felt an upsurge of uneasiness . . . of *suspicion*.

And he felt the presence of evil, too, in that nondescript little corner with its funny ornamental barrel. Felt it very strongly, as though something malign were oozing up through the concrete flags that paved the patio.

A memory of long-ago history lessons came to him. They *drowned* witches, didn't they? Called it 'ordeal by water' or some such. Trussed women up and chucked them in the river, or sealed them in a barrel and sent it out to sea. If they managed to work themselves free, that meant they were innocent of wrongdoing.

Was there a hidden message in the manner of Shirley Bastin's demise? Was she accused of some unknown malefaction? Was her drowning intended as retribution for some ancient sin?

Noakes's imagination was troubled by no such lively apprehension.

'S'pose that musta been it . . . got stuck into the vino, felt depressed an' decided it was a good idea to check out.' Then, struck by Markham's absorbed expression, 'What . . . You're not buying it, guv?'

'There were bruises on her arms, Sergeant. Recent from the look of them. As though someone had gripped her tightly . . . held her pinioned.'

Noakes's hangdog features contracted in a thoughtful scowl.

'Yeah, but Dimples thought she'd likely bashed into things — y'know, crashed into the furniture an' whatnot. It'd make sense if she was pissed. Or mebbe she took pills or summat to get the party started.'

'Hmmm . . . The daughter — Cathy Gould — she was adamant her mother wasn't a drinker and insisted she wasn't depressed or on medication. Got hysterical when one of the uniforms asked if there was any chance she could have taken something. They shared a flat, so the daughter would have known.'

Noakes assumed a look of impenetrable gravity. 'Denial, guv, *denial*. 'S only natural . . . wanting to show the best side of your own mum.'

'I'm not so sure about that.' Markham had been struck by the vehemence of Cathy's reaction to the idea of her mother succumbing to a mid-life alky crisis.

'Why'd they have different names?' Noakes liked everything cut and dried. 'Gould and Bastin . . . How come? Is the daughter married?' His tone suggested he thought it unlikely.

'Shirley owns — owned the dance school. Proprietor and principal as I understand it. Ex-dancer, so she used her maiden name for professional purposes. She was formerly Mrs Gould but got divorced a while back.'

'*Right*, I'm with you now.' Noakes turned these new facts over in his mind. 'That Cathy doesn't take after her mum.' He blushed as though aware he might be guilty of bad taste. 'I mean, Shirley was prob'ly a good-looking woman . . . when she were alive . . . but she didn't pass it on. What I'm saying is—'

Before the DS could tie himself in further knots, Markham interjected. 'It's okay, Noakes, I get it. You're right, Cathy Gould didn't inherit those dancer's genes.' She was a plain woman, stocky and thick set, whereas Shirley Bastin retained a certain coltish grace and sinuousness even in death.

Clearly relieved, Noakes pursued his cogitations. 'Well, if you're thinking foul play, guv . . . nine times out of ten it's family.'

'Indeed.' The DI's keen gaze raked the building behind them. 'Which is why we'll have to tread very carefully on this one if the forensics are inconclusive.'

Noakes scratched his chin. 'Dimples seemed pretty sure it was an accident. Elderly woman knocked herself out and ended up in that birdbath thingy. Or, worst-case scenario, she topped herself during a binge.'

'It seems that way admittedly, Sergeant.' Again, Markham looked down the long, overgrown garden, bordered on its left-hand side by the dance studio's two-storey modern annexe, which abutted a kind of ha-ha before dropping to a lower lawn. Again, he had that curious sense of evil . . . of something fermenting and festering unseen, waiting to be brought into the light.

'I want a rush on Ms Bastin's PM,' he said decisively. 'Dimples has done his own initial tests, but I need the full report. There's something here just doesn't *feel* right, Noakes.'

His rugged DS had the resigned look of a faithful Saint Bernard.

'Let's have a briefing tomorrow morning,' Markham continued. 'With it being Sunday, we should have CID to ourselves.' No need to point out that there was every chance the DCI would be on the golf course and thus unlikely to nobble proceedings.

They headed back into the main building, Noakes leading the way.

'By the by, Sergeant, full marks to Natalie . . . I thought she kept her cool very well.'

His previous encounters with the pneumatic Natalie having been largely confined to fishing her out of Bromgrove's more insalubrious nightclubs, Markham was pleased at being able to utter this sincere tribute.

Noakes visibly swelled with paternal pride.

'Got her head screwed on right has my Nat,' he replied gruffly.

'How did she happen to be here . . . is she a dance student?'

'Gave her a course of lessons for Crimbo,' the DS said happily. 'What with her being into *Strictly* an' all that.'

'Ah, I see.' And Markham did. All too well.

'Plus there's your Olivia being so keen an' all.' The tips of Noakes's ears turned pink as he said her name. 'They c'n encourage each other . . . sort of new kids on the block.'

Markham suspected that Noakes's rapture at the prospect of Olivia and his daughter becoming bosom pals far exceeded Natalie's. But he wisely kept his own counsel. 'Nothing like the New Year for new beginnings.'

''Xactly what my missus said.'

And with that the two detectives found themselves back in the front lobby where paper-suited SOCOs were already setting up.

The noisy chirruping of two magpies skirmishing on a nearby tomb recalled Markham to the present.

Thinking back over it all, he resolved to stay with this Bluebell business and see where it led. Call it 'copper's nose' or a 'hunch' or whatever, he couldn't shake the feeling that there was more to it than how it appeared on the surface. The DCI wouldn't like it, but he'd cross that bridge when he came to it.

He cast one last wistful look round the quiet graveyard. Over in the lee of the old stone church some wildflowers clustered shyly next to a sunken headstone. Not bluebells, surely — it was far too early for them to bloom. But the sight felt like an omen, a blessing on his decision to follow his instincts. Squaring his shoulders, the DI headed for the steps which led back to the world.

* * *

The outer office in CID was deserted as he passed through it to his own sanctum, with its unrivalled view of the station car park. The absence of personnel only highlighted the department's tired-looking fixtures and fittings. As he contemplated the sea of grey and beige (enlivened only by a sad Christmas poinsettia expiring of terminal neglect), Markham toyed with fantasies of a corporate makeover then, sighing, gave it up as a lost cause.

Oh God.

There on his desk, confronting him balefully, was a file headed *DS G. Noakes: Interim Appraisal.*

He'd forgotten about Noakesy's appraisal, but he was willing to bet the DCI hadn't.

The DS had proved stubbornly impervious to hints about it being 'carriage clock time' or 'the Costa del Sol waiting now he'd done his thirty'. Clearly the gold-braid mob had decided the situation called for drastic measures.

But Markham had no intention of giving up George Noakes, though he was well aware the retention of his wingman counted heavily against him.

How to explain what Noakes meant to him? The big lumbering sergeant had no filter, delivering his distinctly un-woke views with cheerful indifference to the sensibilities of others and, in particular, the 'clipboard johnnies' who ran CID.

But, dammit, Noakes *suited* Markham. The DS's unvarnished honesty and tactlessness were just so refreshing by comparison with the right-on PC double-speak that literally made his teeth ache.

There was a humanity about the man. A sureness of touch when dealing with the vulnerable and disenfranchised that so few of the shiny new recruits, with their 'interpersonal skills' and 'empathy', genuinely possessed. Without a word on the subject having ever passed between them, Markham knew his sergeant had guessed the trauma of his early years — his stepfather's abusive behaviour, which had for many years made his emotional life a wasteland.

Noakes was shrewd, too, with an inbuilt bullshit-detector that had proved invaluable time and time again. And he had no compunction when it came to pointing out inconvenient facts that Markham did not care to hear. You could not put a price on that kind of integrity. It was the more precious because his meteoric rise through the ranks as Bromgrove Police's wunderkind had made him a target for flatterers and brown-nosers.

He could hear Sidney now, droning away like a malevolent Greek Chorus. 'It doesn't do to be sentimental, Markham . . . time to move on . . . embrace the zeitgeist . . . look to the future . . . modern policing . . . no room for backward attitudes . . . diversity . . . minorities . . . customer-facing values . . .' He could write the script in his sleep.

The DI's jaw set and his expression became flinty. Noakes was going nowhere and that was that. And anyway, he'd be lost without the job. Muriel, or She Who Must Be Obeyed as Olivia had christened her, would likely banish her husband to the garden shed to avoid him 'getting under her feet'. It would be death by a thousand cuts, the cruellest being a requirement for his heightened participation in the provincial 'social scene'.

Noakes was practically family, given the sympathy that had sprung up between himself and Olivia. How it came about that the slobbish policeman and Markham's highly strung intellectual girlfriend had gelled was something of a mystery to the DI, but they were devoted to each other, Noakes regarding her with the reverential attitude of a medieval troubadour and Olivia drawing him out with her teasing and quips in a way that nobody else quite managed. Small wonder that Muriel was so prickly about it.

Actually, it occurred to him that Muriel's insight might possibly be useful in this case. Unlikely as it seemed, she and her husband were champion ballroom performers who demonstrated a near miraculous synergy on the dance floor. While Markham had never quite fathomed the chemistry between Noakes and his overbearing, snobbish wife, the DS was touchingly proud of 'the missus' and convinced of her essential superiority to the rest of womankind. With the one mysterious exception of Olivia, of course.

Talking of miracles, the DI knew he would have to box clever if he was to circumvent this 'interim appraisal' wheeze. He'd get Chris Carstairs on it. See if the junior DI could wangle a sympathetic senior officer or help Markham to somehow ventriloquize Noakes through the process. At least the DS had passed his latest physical and had cut down on junk food after the previous year's health scare. If they could just fix it so he bluffed his way through this damned mumbo jumbo . . .

Kate Burton would be a useful ally, he knew. The smart-as-paint young DS and the old-timer had started out at daggers drawn, Noakes classifying her as 'one of the liberal mob'. And while it was true that her earnest millennial puritanism and eager-beaver ways were an acquired taste, she had mellowed to the point where she could fight her corner with good humour and, on occasion, guile. Burton's path into the force had not been strewn with roses, since her parents considered it a waste of a good degree (in psychology) and unsuitable in every way ('no job for a woman' as her father put it). But she had persisted and risen to become a valued member of the DI's tight-knit team, demonstrating an indefatigable commitment and unswerving loyalty to Markham. This alone had earned her the grudging respect of contemporaries who had never made it into Markham's inner circle. It bothered him that she appeared to have put her inspector's exams on the backburner, and he had heard rumours her relationship with that boringly stolid DS in Fraud was on the rocks. So he would have to find a way to get her to open up. He knew she envied his camaraderie with Noakes — the understanding that somehow existed between them without the need for words — whereas her own interactions with Markham were almost painfully proper. Capable of soaring, her confidence needed a boost and the DI mentally vowed to miss no opportunity for demonstrating that she had his trust.

At least all appeared to be well with DC Doyle, the final member of the unit. Gangling and ginger-haired, he was enjoying his distance-learning degree in criminal law and itching to take his sergeant's exams. Noakes was his mentor in matters of the heart and football punditry alike, the two men enjoying an easy friendship which revolved round their beloved Bromgrove Rovers and their shared passion for real ale. Occasionally they tolerated Kate Burton as a third wheel, but she tended to steer well clear of carousing in the pub.

He heard voices in the outer office.

'There's no brown sauce on my bacon butty.'

'Sorry, sarge, that dopey cow must've forgot.'

The next moment, Noakes and Doyle hove into view, preceded by a pungent whiff of grease.

Clearly any New Year's resolutions about healthy eating had bitten the dust already.

Markham cranked the sash window open as far as it would go and regarded his colleagues with long-suffering fortitude as they settled down with their picnic on the other side of his desk.

A polite tap and Kate Burton joined the party. 'Happy New Year, sir.'

'And to you, Kate.'

The other two grunted amicably in her direction through mouthfuls of toast.

With a thin smile, she slipped into the third chair, setting her soy-milk latte primly in front of her.

There might be 'trouble at t'mill' as Noakes put it, but Burton looked immaculate as ever in bootleg trousers, skinny-rib roll-neck and hacking jacket. Her neat chestnut bob gleamed, and the alert brown eyes held their usual expression of hopeful candour. Perhaps there was a hint of shadows under those eyes, but out came the reading glasses to conceal any ravages.

Noakes's ensemble was simply horrendous. Granted it was the weekend, so they were all in civvies, but he was giving a passable impersonation of a down-and-out, the mismatched fisherman's jumper and straining cords giving the impression of having been pitchforked on in the dark. Muriel had long since abandoned the battle to inculcate some kind of sartorial finesse in her husband, digging her heels in only when it came to church and occasions where there was the risk of social disgrace, but Markham devoutly hoped he could induce her to enter the fray once more in the interests of eliminating at least one cause for complaint before Noakes's appraisal. Otherwise, CID's very own Worzel Gummidge would be wearing a target on his back.

With a sensation of relief, the DI took in Doyle's dapper appearance. He might have the complexion and loose-limbed ranginess of a farm-boy, but his dress sense was all that could be desired. Today it was neatly pressed dark blue jeans and striped button-down shirt.

Markham supposed two out of three wasn't bad . . .

'So, what about this Bluebell malarkey then, guv? Are we going after it or what?' Having swallowed every last crumb and licked his fingers with a vigour that made Kate Burton wince, Noakes was ready to hear the boss's assessment.

Disconcertingly, his fellow DS now had her pocketbook out, pen poised like an executive secretary.

'Dimples says Shirley Bastin probably died sometime between midnight and one o'clock,' Markham began. 'He's done some initial tests and there was alcohol in her blood but no sign of drugs.'

'An' he's sticking to her having drowned, yeah?'

'Correct, Noakes.'

Burton was watching him closely. 'You're not convinced, sir?'

'Her arms and the back of her neck had bruises on them.' Restlessly, Markham twirled a fountain pen between his fingers. 'But she was a dance teacher . . . and her daughter says that was nothing unusual, especially if she'd been working through routines.' With a wry smile, he added, 'Apparently, you wouldn't believe how performers suffer for their art.'

'*I* would,' Burton observed with feeling. 'Remember the Baranov case, sir? Those ballerinas were covered in bruises from head to toe. And as for the state of their feet . . .'

It was true, recalled Markham, casting his mind back to their investigation of Bromgrove Ballet at the Royal Court.

'Well, there you go then,' Noakes said magisterially. 'Case closed . . . She drowned her sorrows an' then did a swan dive into that bucket.'

'Water butt,' Burton amended punctiliously.

'Whatever.' The pug-like features were intent. 'The point is she got plastered an' was prob'ly staggering all over the shop . . . could even have fallen over a few times . . . an' then ended up keeling over. Either that or she tried to end it all by sticking her head under water . . .'

Watching his subordinate's contumacious expression, it occurred to Markham that his sergeant would be happy to see this one squared away as accidental death — on Natalie's account, perhaps? Was Noakes fearful that his daughter might be caught up in a fully fledged murder investigation with its attendant danger?

Gently but firmly, he said, 'I want to take a closer look at the Bluebell Dance Studio. For my own peace of mind.'

Noakes sighed gustily, causing Burton to shift uncomfortably as her nostrils were assailed by the aroma of greasy spoon.

'Sidney won't like it,' Noakes said. 'Specially if Dimples won't play ball.'

'Leave Dimples to me.' The DI smiled at them. 'There's not much on at the moment, so we can afford to check this out.'

Noakes was now wearing his martyr-at-the-stake face, but the DI ploughed gamely on.

'Here's our *dramatis personae*, for want of a better word.' He handed each of them a piece of paper with what appeared to be briefing notes. 'Basically, a list of key staff and people we need to speak to . . . Feel free to see what else you can google before we make a start tomorrow morning. Let's meet here at eight sharp and divvy up the interviews between us. We can start with the family — Ms Bastin lived with her daughter and elderly mother — and take it from there. The studio will be closed to students all this week, but the English Language College next door has agreed we can meet staff there.'

'When's the PM?' Doyle looked somewhat apprehensive.

Markham turned to Noakes.

'Tomorrow afternoon, guv. Dr Death's bumped it up the list.'

Burton piped up. 'I'll take that, sir.'

Doyle visibly sagged with relief, thanking God for Burton. Medical textbooks were her idea of light reading, so at least he didn't have to feel too guilty about ducking out of it.

'Are you sure, Kate?' Markham wanted to be certain. 'You did more than your fair share of PMs last year.' His gaze rested lightly on Doyle who squirmed self-consciously. 'So let me know if you change your mind.'

'Righto, sir,' came the stoic response.

‘So it’s spangles an’ sequins.’ Noakes scratched his bristly chin. ‘Talk about bleeding déjà vu . . . It’ll be like them poofy ballet folk all over again.’

‘Oh, I had the feeling you were quite into all that by the end, sarge,’ Burton rejoined with a sly twinkle. ‘Rattling off the lingo with the best of them.’

‘Yeah well . . .’ Noakes looked embarrassed and shuffled his feet as Burton and Doyle grinned at each other knowingly. Markham was pleased to see the moment of amused complicity between them. He refrained from pointing out that his DS was a proficient ballroom dancer, sensing that such a reminder would not be welcome. Cultural philistinism was the order of the day in CID, so Noakes generally kept his extracurricular pursuits well under wraps.

‘Right,’ the DI said. ‘That’s it for now. Go and enjoy the rest of your weekend.’

He noticed Burton dragged her feet as she left the room.

‘Looks like she’s lost a pound and found a penny that one,’ Noakes opined.

The old warhorse knew his colleague’s relationship was in trouble. And he guessed that her longstanding crush on Markham had something to do with it. It was a source of never-ending amazement to him that the DI hadn’t twigged, but then for all his sophistication and book-learning the man was curiously unperceptive about women. On the other hand, Noakes had recently caught Markham looking solicitously at Burton, which suggested he might have some inkling. He knew Olivia had figured it out but would keep shtum. Best to keep his mouth shut, too — unless of course Burton availed herself of his superior wisdom in such matters.

‘See you tomorrow, guv,’ he said. He waved his sheet of notes, which was already looking crumpled and dog-eared. ‘Happen the missus’ll know all about this lot.’

‘I’m counting on it,’ came the reply.

2. A DIFFERENCE OF OPINION

'The place has been going for donkey's years,' Noakes pronounced on Monday morning at the briefing. 'They offer everything. Classes in tap, ballet, ballroom, musical theatre — you name it, they do it. Toddlers right through to codgers.' He chuckled. 'Y'know, one, two, three — *ooh, me back* — four, five, six.'

Burton was wearing, what Doyle privately termed, her prune face, but Noakes was cheerfully oblivious.

'Got a good reputation.' He drew himself up proudly. 'Quite exclusive, like . . . That's why we got our Nat a set of lessons there.' His face fell. 'Though now she'll have to wait till it opens again.'

The DI suspected Natalie wouldn't exactly be devastated to learn of this development. 'A pleasure deferred, I'm sure,' he murmured tactfully.

Burton had her notebook and fountain pen out.

'There's just six permanent members of staff,' she said briskly. 'Shirley and Dave Gould—'

'Weird that . . . working with her ex,' interjected Noakes.

'The divorce was amicable, and they were on good terms apparently.' Burton found her place once more. 'Both former professionals. Then we've got Clay Clifton—'

'Where do they get them daft names?' Noakes rolled his eyes. 'Like summat out of *Dallas* . . .'

'He and Anton Bhaer,' this time it was Doyle who raised his eyes to heaven, 'are the senior instructors. And under them there's Robyn DiAngelo and Vivienne Sansom.' Burton scanned the jotter. 'DiAngelo — that's a woman by the way, Robyn with a "y" — came to them by way of the exhibition circuit. Vivienne was a former student . . . had all her RAD and LAMDA qualifications,' Burton was never happier than when she was rattling off acronyms, 'but got herself injured, which meant she went into teaching instead of going professional.'

'An injury?' Markham said quickly. 'Something that happened at Bluebell?'

'Well, she was one of Shirley's pupils,' Burton said thoughtfully, 'and reading between the lines it sounds like maybe they let her dance when they shouldn't have . . .'

'What was up with her?' Noakes asked curiously.

'Torn ligaments, crepitus, something like that.' Burton frowned. 'It's all a bit vague really, but dancing with that lot most likely caused permanent damage . . . I'm just going by what's online.'

'Negligence, then?' Doyle's law student antennae were twitching.

'Could be . . . But they must have settled it between themselves, with her ending up on the staff.'

'Very cosy.' Distrust was written all over Noakes's face. 'Better'n having to buy her off.'

'Let's not make any assumptions until we know the facts,' the DI said. 'Plenty of cases are settled without any aggro.'

'If her career went down the Swanee cos Shirl ballsed it up, then that's a big fat reason to hate the boss.'

Markham was amused to see how quickly Noakes shifted gear into homicide mode once he caught a whiff of potential skulduggery. 'It's certainly something to bear in mind,' the DI said smoothly. 'Anything else, Kate? Anything on Ms Bastin's personal life?'

It was noticeable that the DI rarely used first names when referring to the deceased. As though to restore the dignity stripped away by violent death. He had a notoriously low threshold for anything approaching gallows humour, which led junior colleagues who had been quenched by his freezing hauteur to dub him 'that narky bastard Markham'. But Kate Burton understood where he was coming from and respected him for it.

'This one's not on the list, sir, but he was an on-off boyfriend . . . Name of Fred Stroud . . . Drama teacher at Hope Academy.'

'Oh, *gimme a break*. Not that place again.' Noakes's groan was heartfelt and Burton grimaced sympathetically, a recent case of theirs having reached a shocking denouement on the school premises.

'It's just the boyfriend works there, sarge,' she said soothingly before her colleague could burst a blood vessel. 'No other overlap with Hope.'

Fingers crossed, she said to herself.

'Hmm . . . Stroud,' mused Markham. 'I've heard that name before . . . If he's in drama, then Olivia will be able to fill me in.' His lover taught English at Hope Academy and he always enjoyed her descriptions of battles between staff and 'the Stasi', as she categorized the school's managers. Recalling the horrific notoriety achieved by Hope in previous murder investigations, he could only pray that this time round Olivia would not be imperilled. From the way Noakes's expression had darkened, it was clear the DS was thinking along similar lines. Where Olivia was concerned, his knight-like errantry was always at full throttle.

'That pretty much covers it in terms of key personnel, sir,' Burton continued hastily. 'There's some sort of PTA—'

'Eh?' Noakes couldn't be doing with all the abbreviations.

'Parent Teacher Association,' she explained patiently.

'Oh aye . . . So where do they fit in?'

'The parents help with performances, fundraising, that kind of thing.' An odd little smile quirked the corners of her mouth. 'Bit of a coven, really. The chief witch is one Aline Hosking . . . Got a daughter on one of the competition teams . . . Mum doesn't hold back when it comes to mouthing off about favouritism. You know, talented kids not getting the breaks . . .'

'Sounds like you've been busy sleuthing, Kate.'

There was a strangled sound from Noakes, and the usual exasperated semaphore passed between himself and Doyle.

Burton blushed. 'Oh, it's just from stuff like Mumsnet and some of the local chat sites. It's surprising how indiscreet people can be, especially pushy parents.' Another reminiscent smile. 'I had ballet lessons at primary school . . . No talent . . . Mum always said I had two left feet and the other kids called me Nelly the Elephant cos I was podgy.' She blinked as though suddenly recalling where she was. 'Anyway, there were always folk who kicked off about nepotism and that kind of thing.'

'Yeah.' Confirmation came from an unexpected quarter. 'It were like that with my Nat's lessons when she was little. The missus said the way some parents carried on was freaking unbelievable.' Muriel Noakes being no shrinking violet, Markham had difficulty imagining what type of behaviour qualified as being beyond the pale. ''S like that programme, *Child Genius*, innit?' Noakes was now warming to his theme. 'Y'know, the quiz show for freaky kids with massive IQs . . . there's allus some parent squawking that their sprog was distracted or penalized when they shouldn't have been.' He shook his head more in sorrow than in anger. 'Bloody awful . . . Makes you wonder how they'll cope when Little Einstein brings his first girlfriend home . . .'

Despite this welcome outbreak of amity, the DI felt they were in danger of being side-tracked.

'So, we need to bear parents in mind too,' Markham said decisively. 'And check out the studio's finances.'

'It seemed to be doing well, sir.' Burton again. 'Apparently there'd been an offer from a potential buyer . . .

Doug Callaghan wanted to develop the site and turn it into chi-chi apartments, but Shirley turned him down.'

'As in *Mister Councillor Callaghan*?' Noakes's mouth was well turned down at the corners. 'I mighta known.' He was no fan of Bromgrove's elected representatives and loathed Councillor Penny Callaghan, the other half of the town's 'power couple'.

'The plot thickens.' Markham spoke lightly but was feeling somewhat dismayed. How many more of them with an axe to grind?

'That's the lot, boss.' Burton tapped her pearly whites with the fountain pen. 'Apart from Cathy Gould and the grandmother.'

'What grandmother?' demanded Noakes rudely. 'Nobody said owt about a grannie.'

Burton rewound the reel.

'Remember, the boss mentioned yesterday that Shirley's mum Enid lived with her,' she said patiently. 'They were very close apparently . . . the *Gazette* did a mother-and-daughter feature on them a few years back.' She consulted her notes again. 'There's a basement flat leading off the main building . . . all quite separate, so they had their privacy.'

'Is she bed-bound or doddery or what?'

'She's got some form of Parkinson's, so pretty much an invalid. There's a care package in place . . . apart from that, Shirley and Cathy seem to have managed things between them.'

'Cathy's the daughter, right?' Doyle clearly felt it was time he brought something to the party. 'Is she a dancer too?'

'Drudge more like,' Burton said with some asperity. 'She's front desk and all-round dogsbody. Wanted to train to be a dancer but,' she shrugged her shoulders, 'it never happened. So she ended up as the receptionist.'

'She'd never've made it,' Noakes pronounced with the sublime assurance of a natural-born Diaghilev. 'A real thunder-thighs an' one of them rabbity faces.' He thought for a minute. 'Her mum looked the business, though . . . like the other Shirley . . .'

'*Other* Shirley? Sorry, Sergeant, you've lost me.'

'Shirley *Ballas*.' As much as to say, *keep up at the back*. 'The head judge on *Strictly* . . . The classy one with the black hair.'

'Ah yes, I'm with you now.' Markham smiled. 'It's true, heredity didn't count for much in Cathy's case.' His tone reflective, he added, 'It sounds as though she was somewhat "under the cosh" . . . But,' with a meaningful glance at Noakes, 'let's not jump to any conclusions.' Family dynamics were complex, and you never knew what went on behind closed doors.

'Any other instructors or staff we need to know about?' he asked Burton.

'Only the permanent people had their own keys. There's a couple of supply instructors come in from Medway Stage School as and when they're needed. And they use Fresh as a Daisy Cleaning to look after the building. But in terms of ready access, we're only talking the ones on your list, sir.'

'We'll need to check all the casuals,' the DI said heavily. 'But hopefully we can rule them out early on.'

'Are we really going with this then, guv?' Noakes burst out. '*Murder?*'

'I've done an initial report for the DCI and will be speaking to him tomorrow morning once the PM's out of the way and I've had another word with Dimples.' He sighed. 'Obviously, there'll be an inquest in due course, and as things stand it looks like the forensics are going to be inconclusive. So—'

'We jus' have to see if the killer tries again.'

'Correct, Noakes.'

Such was the universe they inhabited, he told himself ruefully. A world where their best chance of solving a murder was to hope that the predator they were hunting would slip up.

A uniquely unpleasant perspective.

'D'you think he will, guv — try again?'

'Something tells me yes, Sergeant.'

How to convey what he had felt standing in that corner at the back of the dance studio? That sense of evil . . . and something else too . . . the feeling of there being a cold spot in that angle between studio and garden where they had found Shirley Bastin's body.

'Bad vibes, boss?' enquired Noakes eyeing him shrewdly, always surprisingly sensitive to what their superiors dismissed as 'Markham's mystical streak'.

'Something like that,' the DI admitted. 'Though I doubt it'll be enough for the DCI . . . at least, not unless I can dig up some criminal antecedents.' He paused, struck by the other's sudden expression of unusual absorption. 'What is it, Noakesy?'

'*Ackshually*, guv . . . now I come ter think of it, there was summat went on with a dance school way back . . .' He rumpled his salt-and-pepper thatch so that it stood on end, giving him the look of a startled porcupine. 'Dunno if it was the Bluebell though.'

Burton and Doyle looked at him expectantly.

After a few minutes' cogitation, the DS thumped Markham's desk, making them jump.

'Got it!' He patted his paunch complacently. 'Mickey Willett,' he said gnomically.

Doyle leaned forward eagerly. 'Who's he?'

'Missing teenager . . . Did a vanishing act long before your time, lad. Giggsy from the cold-case team was talking about it in the canteen the other day. It's one of the unsolveds . . . They're bringing Jim McLeod out of retirement as senior review officer on Willett an' there'll be three under him.'

'What's the connection with a dance school?' the young DC pressed him.

'Willett fancied himself a bit of a twinkle toes,' Noakes leered in the fashion of a pantomime villain. 'Or at any rate, he tried to cop off with lasses who went to the Saturday Night Hops . . . Did some deejaying down at the Astoria when it was still in business . . . Hung round various joints with a bunch of ravers.' It was clear from his tone that George Noakes had never been a headbanger.

Markham felt a faint hope flare. 'Was the Bluebell on his patch then?'

'Yeah that's right, guv. Last sighting was somewhere round Heathfield Close. One of his mates reckoned he was going steady with a bird who went there for dance classes — well, tap or drama, summat like that. Heathfield must mean the Bluebell, right?'

'Yeees,' the DI answered slowly. 'But this must have been well before Shirley's time.'

Burton volunteered, 'That was likely when her Aunt Rose was running the studio.' She frowned. 'Rose is dead now . . . cancer, about ten years ago. So, no way of checking with her.' She fell silent for a moment then brightened. 'But there'll be the case files for Willett . . . Rose will have been interviewed as part of the investigation.'

'Aunt Rose.' Markham mulled it over. 'The Bluebell's a real family affair then.'

'Yes, sir. What you might call a dance dynasty . . . A cousin ran it before Rose, and they go quite a way back . . . bought the old church from Bromgrove Diocese in the thirties and they've been making a go of it ever since.'

The DI turned to Noakes.

'They turn up anything that tied Mr Willett to the Bluebell?'

More head scratching.

'Not that I recall, boss.' Momentarily, he looked downcast but then rallied. 'But you c'n sell it to Sidney as going joint dibs on McLeod's review — a 'new angle' or a 'fresh pair of eyes' — some bollocks like that.' 'Bollocks' being Noakes's shorthand for corporate-speak.

Markham suppressed a smile. You just couldn't keep a seasoned copper down. His wingman had the resilience of an India-rubber ball. All the Sidneys in the world couldn't squelch him.

'Worth a try,' he agreed.

'So, what's the plan, sir?' As ever, Kate Burton was raring to go.

'I want you and Doyle to visit the family . . . That's Cathy, Enid and the ex-husband Dave Gould. Kid gloves, mind.'

'How much do we tell them, boss?' The DC sounded anxious.

'As little as possible.' Markham's mouth twisted. 'It goes against the grain not to be frank, but so far all we've got is what looks like a tragic accident. I'll be along shortly, but in the meantime, I want you to get the lie of the land . . . see what you make of the background . . . check out any undercurrents . . . any domestic ill feeling.' He smiled reassuringly. 'I have great faith in your instincts.' At this, the gangling DC Doyle sat up straighter in his chair and Burton too looked like she had received a welcome shot in the arm.

'I've got police liaison meetings this afternoon,' the DI added. 'Hopefully I can call on the family once they're out of the way.'

Two minutes later, Markham and Noakes had the DI's office to themselves.

'What about Dimples?' the DS asked bluntly. 'You know what that one's like when he digs his heels in. Won't like us second-guessing him.'

'Leave the doc to me, Noakesy. I'll make it all right with him. The PM's not till later today, so we don't know what may turn up.'

His wingman grunted.

'Whatcha want me to do about Willett? Hook up with Big Jim an' come up with summat to knock the socks off Sidney?'

The DI raised a quizzical eyebrow. 'I doubt we'll manage that . . . But there may be enough for the DCI to give us a few days' grace.'

He got up and strode across to the window, looking towards the town centre where cash tills were no doubt ringing as the New Year sales got underway. His idea of hell, though Olivia assured him he was underestimating the benefits of 'retail therapy'.

Noakes sat contentedly, accustomed to the DI's moments of brooding introspection. He could tell this Bluebell thing had gotten under Markham's skin. He reckoned the boss was haunted by the carnage of that last investigation. Probably imagining another line of ghosts congaing behind him like he was some kind of bloody Pied Piper . . .

The DI came back to his desk.

'Look up DS Giggs and the DCI,' Markham was careful to accord retired Jim McCleod his full title, 'and get me some preliminary on Mr Willett,' he said. 'But be discreet about it . . . No treading on anyone's toes and no suggestion we're trying to outflank Sidney.' Even though they were.

'I'll sweet talk Dimples,' he continued, reaching for the telephone on his desk.

'You c'n allus go for the sympathy vote, guv.'

'How so?'

'Let Dimples think you're still . . . er, *traumatized* or whatnot over them killings in New College Close. Not so you get occy health pitching in or owt like that,' Noakes qualified hastily, 'but nuff to make it look like you're dead set on covering all the angles for this one. Y'know, kinda like it's *therapy* . . .'

For such a blunderbuss of a policeman, the DS possessed surprising reserves of guile. Enough to make Noakes's boss overlook the DS's latest sartorial atrocity, which consisted of baggy sweater, crumpled chinos and a string tie knotted somewhere under his left armpit.

'Excellent advice, Sergeant. It shall be attended to.'

The other man heaved himself up, hitched up his trousers and headed for the door.

'Y'know me, boss.' He turned at the threshold and tapped the side of his nose conspiratorially. 'There's nowt gets past George Noakes . . . Give it the violins with ole Dimples an' he'll be putty in your hands.'

* * *

Shirley Bastin's private quarters at the Bluebell Dance Studio were situated at the rear of the converted Victorian church which formed the main building. A staircase leading down from the Wardrobe Room gave access to her basement flat.

The upside-down layout meant that the living room and Enid's en suite were on the flat's upper level with the other rooms beneath. Steps outside the living-room French windows led up to a minuscule low-walled courtyard with a gate that opened into the garden. So it looked like the apartment's residents could come and go without having to traipse through the school.

Kate Burton found the flat pleasant enough, albeit distinctly old-fashioned, with swirly patterned carpets whose psychedelic vibrancy harked back to the seventies. Plain wooden flooring would have opened up the space, she reflected.

Everywhere was clean and tidy with none of the bohemian squalor she had been half expecting. Full marks to Cathy Gould then, since she looked to be the most likely candidate for getting out the marigolds. Everywhere was stiflingly hot, perhaps owing to Enid's invalid status. Looking at DC Doyle, Burton could tell he was finding it thoroughly claustrophobic. *Too bad*, she thought grimly, we've got a job to do here . . .

In the end, however, it was what Noakes would have called 'slim pickings', the three family members appearing shell-shocked to the point of muteness — or could it be they were on their guard? At any rate, it felt like pulling teeth. No, they couldn't think of anyone with a grudge against Shirley. No, she hadn't seemed unusually depressed or as if there was anything on her mind. No, there was no one she'd been rowing with lately.

Dave Gould appeared to be in his late sixties. A mild-looking man with what looked like dyed hair, a drooping moustache and an air of the world being too much for him. His eyes were bloodshot but for all they knew, Burton reflected with a twinge of self-loathing, it could have been from booze as much as grief.

He explained that he and his ex-wife should never have gotten married. 'But it often happens that way when you're on the circuit with someone . . . what with the long hours and partnering being so intimate, folk kind of fall into it . . . easier all round.'

Not the world's greatest romantic then, Kate noted. But there was a certain candour about his admission.

'We got along miles better after the divorce,' Dave concluded.

Cathy Gould seemed close to her father, confirming what he said between hiccoughs and sniffles. There was something off-putting about the woman and Burton felt an instinctive revulsion at the sight of her without understanding why. Then it hit her. Cathy Gould reminded her of one of the civilian clerks back at the station. *Totty*, that was her name, the sly one who listened at doors and was always dropping people in it with the top brass.

Easy, she told herself. *The woman's had a tough time of it, so a bit of compassion wouldn't go amiss*. On the other hand, she wouldn't take anything for granted. Those unprepossessing looks and the fact that she'd spent her life as her mother's slavey could have stoked who knew what hidden fires. Even Cathy's passionate insistence that Shirley's death 'didn't make any sense' could be a double bluff. Whenever Burton thought back to the team's last case and the New College Close murders, she never failed to remind herself that evil was often hiding in plain sight . . . The killer who had brought terror to that innocuous suburban street had been the very last person in the world anyone would have suspected. A fearful reminder never to judge by appearances.

Grandmother Enid was clearly not all there. Beshawled in an armchair, with her orange and grey streaked hair, and her habit of emitting the occasional manic cackle, she resembled a bedraggled parakeet. Most disconcerting of all, was the way she kept repeating, 'I knew you'd be along soon enough . . . couldn't keep it hidden forever . . . these things always come out in the end . . .'

'What things, ma'am?' Doyle tried to coax a coherent response out of her.

'She's having one of her bad days,' Cathy Gould hissed out of the corner of her mouth.

The old lady looked medicated up to the eyeballs and Burton resolved to follow up with the family GP. If they could catch her in a lucid interval, she might have something for them. Burton could swear there was a look of something like supplication in the rheumy depths of Enid's eyes. As if there was something she wanted to communicate, if only she could find the words to do so. There was no appearance of abuse or neglect, and she seemed comfortable enough round her family, but there was definitely something not quite right about the woman . . .

Cathy beckoned them out and gently closed the living-room door, leaving her father to settle the old lady, whose querulous ramblings rose and fell in a babbling stream.

'We can go into the kitchen if you like,' she said.

'No, you're okay.' Now Burton too was feeling a prickling claustrophobia as she stood on the narrow landing. 'Inspector Markham will be along later . . . to, er, pay his condolences personally.' That sounded all right. 'Really, we're just here to see you've got everything you need.' A useful catch-all.

The landing was dark even with the spot lighting.

'Where are we in relation to the annexe?' she asked, suddenly disorientated.

'That was built over the old cellars,' came the reply. 'There was a priest's house — a presbytery or whatever it's called — at the back of the church originally and the storerooms underneath were left intact when it was demolished. You can get to them from the annexe theatre — there's props and stage sets and other stuff down there — and they back onto this flat.'

'Is there any access to your flat from the annexe?'

'No. You can only get in from the Wardrobe Room in the main building or through our living-room doors.'

'And no access from the conservatory?' Burton probed, thinking of the lean-to or corridor along which Cathy Gould had led Natalie when Shirley Bastin's body was discovered.

'No . . . You see, that's over on the right of the building. Completely separate. We're on the left-hand side.'

Burton narrowed her eyes in the gloom, visualizing it . . . the paved corner area on the other side of the building basically replicating the flat's little courtyard.

'Mum always kept to her own side,' Cathy insisted, her eyes glittering with overwrought emotion. 'She was a stickler for that . . . Wanted to keep work and home separate.' Fiercely, she added, 'There was no reason for her to be round that side . . . None.'

'Maybe after a few drinks . . .' Doyle prompted delicately thinking about that alcohol reading. 'Maybe she was just trying to unwind . . .'

'No way. And that's another thing . . . Mum liked to be in control . . . hardly ever drank. Just ask my dad.'

* * *

'Phew!' Doyle exclaimed once they were outside, gratefully gulping down cold fresh air. 'Poor cow's not having any of it.'

His colleague glanced at her watch.

'I have to shoot off to the PM before long,' she said glumly.

The DC looked at her guiltily. 'C'mon, sarge,' he said. You've got time for a coffee, my shout. There's a Costa just round the corner.' She hesitated. 'Oh *c'mon*, sarge. We've earned it and anyway,' he added craftily, 'we can talk over the case.'

That settled it. 'Right you are,' she said.

Doyle smiled to himself. George Noakes wasn't his mentor for nothing.

3. SPOILED FOR CHOICE

At 8 a.m. on Tuesday, 7 January, Markham and Noakes sat closeted in the DI's office deferring the evil hour when they would have to beard the DCI in his lair.

Noakes's stubby fingers drummed on a slim manila folder on the desk between them.

'If we bung him this stuff on Willett, we should be okay for a bit, guv... give it the ole "joined-up policing" oojah ... inter-departmental cooperation... pooling our expertise an' all that jazz.'

Desperate straits called for desperate measures, and the DS was clearly prepared to spout whatever gobbledygook it took to allay Sidney's suspicions.

'Olivia tells me the Bluebell Studio's something of an institution in Bromgrove,' Markham said thoughtfully. 'And according to DI Carstairs, half the top brass have connections with the place one way or another — either their children went there for classes and competitions, or the wives did sponsored bakes to raise funds . . . or they mix with the cha-cha-cha set.' He gave an exasperated laugh. 'You could call the place a "community hub". And, just to top it off, apparently Sidney's lady wife swears by Clay Clifton's rumba lessons!'

'Christ, she's built like a Sherman tank.' Noakes was suitably awe-struck. 'Reckon that'd be worth seeing.'

'Yes, well—'

'*Houston, we have a problem.*'

'Quite. And after the New College Close investigation—'

'Sidney'll tell us to Foxtrot Oscar if we go snooping round Bluebell.'

'Precisely.'

'Wants us to focus on ringers an' shoplifters 'stead of the pointy-toe brigade.'

'Got it in one.'

The two men contemplated each other gloomily before Noakes fell to playing with the executive pendulum toy on Markham's desk, smacking the LED-light balls so hard it seemed he would sweep them from their cradle.

Eventually the DS came to a halt.

'Bugger Sidney,' he said. Then, 'Any joy with Dimples?'

'He's hedged his bets in the PM report. "Cause of death not established pending further examination", the usual pack drill.'

'I s'pose that's summat at any rate.'

Markham flashed his rare charming smile. 'I softened him up like you suggested, Noakesy. It was a good strategy . . . I reckon he was busy diagnosing overachievement disorder by the time we finished talking.'

Highly gratified, Noakes cradled his paunch in the manner of a Confucian philosopher.

'Well, if Dimples is on-side, that's gotta carry some weight.' He tapped the manila folder emphatically. 'As for Willett, Jimbo McLeod was never happy with the way Bretherton steered 'em away from the Bluebell.'

It came as no surprise to learn that Blethering Bretherton (now Superintendent Bretherton) had tap danced away from offending the respectable burghers of Bromgrove.

'What, pray, was Bretherton's theory?' Markham enquired wearily.

Noakes grinned evilly. 'Drug feud . . . Tried to pin it on Nick Carter who went down for a load of other stuff. Only problem being, Nick coughed to any number of TICs 'cept Willett . . . Wouldn't be budged, so they left that off in the end . . . couldn't make it stick an' the CPS were having none of it.'

'Remarkable,' the DI observed drily, 'given the way they usually fall over themselves to go after hopeless cases.'

'Willett was a scrote an' no mistake. Clever an' good-looking, too, by all accounts — a real Flash Harry. Could've had his fingers in all sorts of pies . . . but he hung round that dance school all right, though no one was sure which bird he was banging.'

'When *was* all this, Noakes? What about dates?'

'Nineteen ninety-nine, guv. Willett was nineteen . . . I was new in CID an' Bretherton was SIO,' he scowled, 'givin' it large.'

'What about Jim McLeod?'

'DI same as Bretherton . . . He was the senior DI, but you wouldn't have known it from the way Bretherton muscled in.'

'Did Mr McLeod find anything to place Willett on the premises — as in, actual physical evidence *in* the dance school?'

'Not in the building,' Noakes admitted, 'but some of the local kids placed him outside . . . One of the oldies from the ballroom classes thought he looked familiar an' a part-time teacher recognized him too, but they're both dead now an' Bretherton stuck to the party line that it was nowt to do with Glitterball Central.'

Nothing changes, Markham thought, suppressing an almost hysterical desire to laugh.

He got to his feet. 'Come on, let's get it over with,' he said, adding with a wry smile, 'Afterwards, we can treat ourselves to a fry up downstairs and work out next steps.'

Noakes beamed at this unwonted concession to his need for refuelling.

'Champion. Doris allus saves me the crispy bits.'

'A girl in every canteen, that's you, Sergeant.'

* * *

Twenty minutes later, they sat opposite each other in the rather dreary station canteen. Not that the uninspiring ambience troubled Noakes, who savoured his fried egg, sausage, hash browns and baked beans with something akin to ecstasy while Markham tackled a bacon and cheese toastie with coffee.

'Could've been worse,' the DS mumbled through a mouthful of egg. 'That Gavin Conors did us a favour for once.'

It was true, thought Markham. The *Gazette*'s recent denunciation of the local force for its obsession with 'woke' hate crimes as opposed to 'traditional policing' was currently preoccupying Sidney to the exclusion of all else, so the anticipated thunderbolts never came.

When they arrived in the Holy of Holies, he noticed the DCI's eczema had flared up, detracting somewhat from the executive charisma of his buzz cut and goatee (why was it that baldies so often cultivated beards?). Irritably tugging at the latter, Sidney appeared distracted, his gaze passing restlessly from his glossy paperless desk (adorned with framed studio portraits of Mrs Valkyrie Sidney and the couple's assorted well-scrubbed offspring) to the photomontage which covered one wall and was irreverently known among the hoi polloi as 'the Hall of Fame'. No doubt the DCI was planning which of his celebrity cronies could be called on to assist with a PR counterstrike and mitigate the bad press being dealt out by Conors. The dreaded cross-examination about Bluebell failed to materialize, and even the presence of Noakes — whom Sidney regarded as little better than the village idiot — elicited no more than the usual automatic glower.

Of course, the DI knew this was merely a temporary reprieve and they had gotten off lightly. There was the usual mini-lecture about the perils of relying on 'flair' and 'getting carried away', but that was pretty much par for the course with Sidney whose resentment of his fastidious, self-contained subordinate's meteoric rise was poorly concealed. There was a sticky moment when the subject of Shirley Bastin's PM came up, but Markham flannelled on about 'further tests' and 'second opinions', and the moment passed.

Finally, 'There's to be no re-run of New College Close,' Sidney admonished in his disagreeably nasal honk. 'No persecuting pillars of the community.' Somehow managing to refrain from pointing out that nothing of the sort had occurred and Bromgrove's chattering classes were not magically immune from criminal impulses, Markham murmured the deferential nothings that were the surest guarantee of emerging unscathed. Noakes said nothing but watched admiringly from the side-lines. You really had to hand it to the guvnor, he thought. He managed to be polite while making Sidney look a total knobhead. *Priceless.*

Even the long-suffering Miss Peabody, the great man's PA, looked less oppressed than usual. Guiltily stuffing a copy of the *Gazette* under some files as the two men emerged from Sidney's office, the staid little secretary — who looked more like *Father Brown*'s housekeeper than a lean, mean typing machine — turned pink as Noakes joshed her.

'What's new with *News of the Screws*, luv? C'mon, give us the goss.'

Fingering her pearls, she eyed the open door nervously.

'Don't worry — your secret's safe with us, Miss P,' Noakes winked as they made their escape.

Now the DS marvelled, 'Sidney didn't even mention my appraisal.'

'Oh, he will, Sergeant, he will,' Markham replied grimly. 'Which is why we'll keep our heads below the parapet for the time being . . . Tact and discretion should be the watchwords when we're interviewing Bluebell staff, okay?'

'Sure thing, guv. Pass the ketchup, will you?'

The DI stifled a sigh and pushed his unfinished bacon sandwich away.

'Did Kate and Doyle come up with anything yesterday while I was tied up at the Town Hall?' He frowned at the recollection of the utter tedium of the previous afternoon's police liaison meetings. Another four hours of his life he would never get back. Worse still, it meant his visit of condolence to Shirley Bastin's grieving family was postponed to later that afternoon.

'Not specially, guv. Burton's done a report.' Noakes wrinkled his nose dismissively. 'Drawn you a diagram thingy as well . . . Bastin's flat was separate from the school. Jus' her, the daughter an' gran. Nice enough but pokey . . . a whiff of care home about the place if you get me.' Markham was willing to bet that his sergeant was quoting Doyle, since Kate Burton's summaries were invariably punctiliously correct.

'What about the ex — Dave Gould?'

''S got a flat in Orrell Terrace, but seems like he helps out with Enid an' stays over sometimes . . . Apparently, they all got on . . . daughter said deffo no way her mum would've gone on a bender.'

'Hmmm . . . So, nothing useful from the family?'

'Well, Gran kept burbling 'bout how she knew we'd come . . . stuff being hidden an' you couldn't keep everything under wraps forever.'

'Was she wandering?'

'Couldn't say for sure . . . Burton's gonna follow up with the GP in case there's any chance of talking with her when she's not doped up . . . had the feeling there was summat the old girl wanted to tell her.'

'Good idea.' Markham thought hard. It occurred to him Enid Bastin might not talk freely if her family were around. 'Let's get something fixed up with the nursing team . . . see if we can have a word in private.'

'With Parkinson's, there's delusions an' paranoia, boss.' Kate Burton had clearly imparted some medical knowledge. 'So, most like she's imagining stuff.'

'You're probably right, Noakes.'

But still . . . *knowing the police would come . . . stuff being hidden . . . you couldn't keep everything under wraps* . . . The phrases reverberated in his mind. The old lady might not be lucid, but what if there was *something* lodged in her consciousness — some clue as to Shirley Bastin's fate . . . Markham recalled the creeping sensation of revulsion he had experienced standing behind the nondescript little dance school, his gut feeling that there was something wrong . . . something off-key. *Evil is banal*, he thought uneasily. Wasn't that why that crime writer had called his biography of Rose and Fred West *Happy Like Murderers*? On the surface, their lives were pleasant and commonplace and ordinary, but underneath a nest of maggots.

Over the years, despite Sidney's cavilling, he had learned to take notice of such feelings, trusting that his instincts would lead him to the truth before it was too late.

He became aware that the DS was watching him speculatively.

'Don't worry, Noakesy,' he said. 'I'm not going all telepathic on you.'

'That's okay,' came the surprising response. 'That psychic who told us things on the New College case . . . the one we called Mystic Meg . . . she got some stuff right.'

'Mrs Shaw. Yes, I remember,' Markham said slowly. She certainly hadn't been the stereotypical crystal-ball-gazing seer. Her appearance was almost boringly conventional, but the images she conjured up eerily prefigured developments in the case. 'I reckon we could do with her now,' he went on with a shaky laugh. 'To give us a paranormal nudge.'

'You didn't like that garden did you, guv?' the DS observed shrewdly. 'They dug it up, y'know, when Mickey Willett went missing.' A shake of the head. 'Nada.'

'It had a bad atmosphere.'

Only to Noakes could Markham make such a bald admission, it being a strange feature of their relationship that the older man respected his out-of-body communion with victims of violent death. Sidney might call it 'fey', but the DS never disparaged, never sniggered. Without the need for words, he knew his boss had been formed by haunting childhood experiences and carried that legacy down through the nights and days, wherever there were lost souls calling out for justice.

Now Noakes nodded. 'Mebbe there's summat there,' he said simply. 'Summat they missed first time round . . . When we're done with interviews, me an' Doyle c'n take a gander.'

'Right.' Markham gave himself a mental shake. 'Let's get over there.'

He needed to put the Willett case out of his mind for the time being and focus on the job in hand.

'Who've we got lined up?' he asked as Noakes hitched up his trousers with a last regretful glance at the canteen hot-plates where Doris and Co were preparing to dish up 'Stew of the Day'.

'Burton an' Doyle are doing that Viv bird . . . the one who got herself injured.'

'Oh yes . . . Vivienne Sansom. The one who had to go into teaching after an accident . . .'

'Yeah, her . . . An' Burton said they'd hook up with that bossy mum cos it sounded like she'd be happy to dish the dirt.'

'Aline Hosking . . . Excellent. So, who does that leave for us?'

'I said we'd do the woofters.'

'*Noakes*.' There was a world of meaning in the word.

'All right, all right, guv. But I mean, *Clay Clifton* an' *Anton Bhaer* . . . Like they're not gonna be a bit light in the loafers!'

They should have a fun time when it came to completing the *Diversity Objectives* section of Noakes's appraisal, his boss reflected with a sinking heart.

'If I catch you so much as looking sideways at them, Sergeant . . .'

The DS sniffed eloquently. 'No way was I leaving 'em to Burton. It'd be the usual yak-fest . . . her wanting to know 'bout being a dancer an' banging on like Melvyn Bragg.'

Markham grinned despite himself. There was no denying Kate Burton's sponge-like thirst for facts and knowledge.

Noakes put down his cutlery with a clatter. 'At least they won't try an' pull the wool with us.'

'That remains to be seen. Just those two, then?'

'The other teacher too. The Robyn woman with the wop surname.'

'You know, there *is* such a thing as a "stage name", Noakes. So for God's sake, don't go in there shouting the odds and being obnoxious.'

'Wouldn't dream of it, guv.'

'Yes, you bloody well would and *remember*, we need to keep Sidney sweet for the foreseeable — or at least till your appraisal's done and dusted.' The DI headed for the exit, trailed by his wingman. 'What about Doug Callaghan and Fred Stroud?' He recollected himself. 'No, never mind about those two for now. We'll make arrangements to interview them tomorrow.'

Curious eyes followed them as they left the canteen. The elegant chilly DI and his shambling sergeant. 'Batman and Robin.' But the words fell on empty air.

* * *

It was late afternoon by the time the team reassembled in the principal's office at Bromgrove English Language College in Heathfield Close. Quietly spoken and efficient, Mrs Seddon saw to it that they were comfortably settled with tea and biscuits then left them to review the 'events' of the day.

'More like *non-events*,' rumbled Noakes as the door closed behind her. 'Don' know about you,' he thrust his massive hand challengingly across the table at Burton and Doyle, 'but we got frigging *zilch*. Bill an' Ben were *useless*.'

'He means they were discreet,' Markham qualified wearily.

Clay Clifton and Anton Bhaer were attractive specimens of manhood, the first in his late forties, the other his late thirties.

Clifton was tall, dark and well-built with gelled hair, eyes like dark molasses and a retroussé nose that he admitted was the result of 'having work done'. He spoke with a drawl and was undeniably languid in manner, but there was nothing effeminate about him and Markham suspected the affected vowels and arch theatricality were a well-honed act that had come to fit him like a second skin.

His colleague was more of the David Niven type. Also dark, but slender and fine-boned where the other was burly, with clean-cut features, liquid black eyes, expressive hands and a sensitive mobile mouth. Although quieter and more restrained than Clifton, it was clear that the two men got on well. They even performed an impromptu soft-shoe shuffle for Markham that made Noakes's shaggy eyebrows rise as far as they could go.

'I notice you didn't mention your own dance credentials,' the DI observed afterwards.

'Didn't want to be there all night,' came the response, but it was clear his sergeant had been in no hurry to claim kinship with such an exotic pair.

They seemed genuinely upset about Shirley — no appearance of dissimulation or laying it on thick. 'She was a good boss,' Bhaer said, 'and a damned hard worker . . . The place was her life really.'

'Sure, she could be volatile sometimes,' his fellow instructor admitted. 'But all of us in the profession are a bit like that. It's the artistic temperament, *dah-ling*.'

Neither man would be drawn on drink or drugs, presenting a carefully blank facade to their questioning. 'You can hardly blame them,' Markham said now they were all together in the office. 'They've got their jobs to think about . . . blabbing might cost them dear if it got back to the management.'

'Who takes over the dance school, then?' asked Doyle.

Burton riffled through her notes. 'It's left to the ex and her daughter.'

'Musta rated him,' Noakes observed thoughtfully.

'Looks like it,' Burton concurred. Restlessly, she twiddled her pen. 'Did they say anything about squabbles or jealousy, sir? I mean, there's *bound* to have been the occasional tiff, surely? It's that kind of environment . . . everyone wanting to hog the spotlight.'

'The "odd spat" was all they would admit to. *Artistic differences . . .*'

'See what I mean, freaking *useless*.' Noakes's piggy eyes held a malevolent look that suggested he would happily have skewered Clifton and Bhaer on their own dance canes.

'What about alibis?' Burton asked. More riffling. 'Dimples says Shirley died in the small hours . . .'

'Both of 'em were tucked up in bed like good little boys.' Her colleague sounded disgusted, as though dancers might have been counted on for some nocturnal debauchery.

'Any luck with the other one . . . DiAngelo?' Doyle asked hopefully.

'Not really. Bit of a cat, though,' the DI replied.

There had indeed been something feline about Robyn DiAngelo with her narrow, rapacious face and scrawny frame. She'd looked at the guvnor like she wanted to gobble him up, Noakes told Doyle later over a pint. With her sharp gamine haircut, sultry eyes and drooping lids, she exuded sexuality with an undercurrent of danger.

'I could jus' see her bashing someone over the head if she got a cob on,' was Noakes's verdict.

'Like the other two, she says she was at home in bed, Sergeant,' Markham put in. 'And anyway what about motive?'

'Like you said, guv . . . *bitchy* . . . got her claws out about Shirl.'

'Well, there was no false modesty about her, that's for sure.'

'How come, sir?' Doyle was curious.

'Said she was the better dancer but didn't have Ms Bastin's luck with partners . . . or the financial support someone like Dave Gould could provide.'

'*Miaow*.'

'Quite, Constable. Plus, she implied Ms Bastin snaffled opportunities that should have been hers.'

'Jealous then,' Doyle concluded hopefully.

'The thing is, she didn't mind us knowing.'

Burton chipped in. 'Maybe she thought it'd come out somewhere along the line and decided to get it in first . . . otherwise her not having mentioned it would look fishy.'

'Yes, it could have been a pre-emptive strike, Kate . . .'

'Any chance she had her hooks in Dave Gould, boss?' Doyle asked.

'That's an angle worth checking out, Constable. See what you can get on his personal life.'

Markham thought about the brief visit he had made earlier to offer his condolences. On the face of it, they were simply another grieving family. He hadn't picked up on any vibes to suggest otherwise, but they would still need a fuller picture of Dave and Cathy Gould.

'*DiAngelo* . . . What a load of old cobblers!' Noakes exclaimed. 'She's no more Italian than I'm Brad Pitt!'

'From her colouring, I'd say there's Mediterranean blood somewhere in her background,' the DI surmised. He thought of the watchful way she had of looking out of the corners of her eyes without turning her head. Something about her made him uncomfortable, but he would be hard pressed to put his finger on precisely what.

'How old d'you reckon DiAngelo is?' Noakes asked. 'I mean, she looks like a stick insect, but them anorexic dancer types live on lettuce leaves.'

'Early fifties but very well preserved,' was Markham's verdict.

'Shirley was fifty-three,' Burton informed them.

'There you are then. She and Ms DiAngelo were contemporaries—'

'And rivals.'

'Indeed, Kate.'

The DI got up and walked over to the bay window of the principal's office. Outside, a semi-circular drive was bordered by a neat privet hedge precluding any view of the road beyond. The afternoon had turned dark and still, with just a faint hum of traffic in the distance. Briefly, his back to the others, he shut his eyes. For some reason, the image of those delicate wildflowers in St Chad's cemetery came into his mind. What were they — winter aconites, irises?

A rustling of papers interrupted his reverie. The others were growing restless.

'Right then.' Markham resumed his seat. 'How did you do with Vivienne Sansom and Aline Hosking?'

'The Hosking woman was *poisonous*!' Doyle burst out.

'Really?'

'Yeah, a real bitch on wheels.'

Markham raised his eyebrows interrogatively and turned to Burton.

'Ex-dancer, sir,' she said. 'Gave up when she got married and never went back to it. Well-to-do, pampered . . . One of those women who live through their children.'

'They call them "helicopter parents",' Doyle put in. 'Cos they're always hovering over the kids and smothering them.'

Burton nodded. 'She was convinced Shirley had it in for her Monica because she kept passing her over for shows and competitions, that kind of thing.'

'The reason being?'

'Who can say, boss?' Burton shrugged. 'Reading between the lines, I'd say the kid didn't have the talent and Mum took it personally.'

'Mmm.'

'I'll know more once I've tapped into the "Mummy Mafia".'

'Good. Doyle can help with that . . . perhaps his boyish charm will work its usual magic.'

Noakes made a noise that sounded very like someone blowing a raspberry.

'Anything else from our stage mom?'

'She threw out some dark hints all right. Said Shirley gave her teachers "a dog's life" and "flirted with anything in trousers"' — Burton air-quoted vigorously — 'but I think even Hosking felt awkward about having a mega-bitch, what with the poor woman's body being barely cold.'

'Sounds promising.' And distasteful.

'Yes, sir. I thought I'd let her sleep on it and then have another crack tomorrow.'

'Sounds like a plan.' Markham was pleased by her enthusiasm. 'What about Vivienne Sansom?'

'Ladylike and very pretty.'

'Reminded me of that Darcey Bussell,' Doyle added.

'Well, what did *Darce* have to say for herself?' Noakes was impatient. 'Or were you too busy checking out her vital statistics?'

The DC grinned lazily, too used to the old warhorse to rise to the bait.

'She seemed nice,' he said. 'No edge to her . . . Teaches the little ones . . . working towards some higher qualification or other.'

'What about the injury?' Noakes persisted. 'The one that was Shirley's fault?'

'It was an ankle injury,' Burton took over. 'She should have had physio and rested up, but Shirley persuaded her to take part in a matinee . . . Worst thing she could have done, apparently . . . put the mockers on her stage career.'

'So, it was down to Ms Bastin?'

'Well, it never went to court or anything like that . . . They "worked out a package"' — more air quotes — 'and she took a job at the dance school.'

'Bitter, would you say?'

'If she is, she hides it well, sir.' Burton thought for a moment. 'She said Dave Gould felt bad about it, cos she was his protégée, but not Shirley.'

All very interesting, thought Markham. No obvious connection with the Mickey Willett investigation, but certainly enough to reinforce his suspicions that someone had it in for Shirley Bastin.

Looking at their jaded faces, he decided it was time to call it a day.

'Well done, team. Noakes and I will chase up Doug Callaghan and Fred Stroud tomorrow morning, while Kate and Doyle crack on with the Goulds and the Mummy Mafia.'

Class dismissed!

* * *

It had been a tiring day.

Markham decided to reward himself with an outing to 'Doggie' Dickerson's Gym. And then home to Olivia.

As far as potential suspects went, it was beginning to look as though he would be spoiled for choice.

4. BREAKTHROUGH

Doggie Dickerson was an army veteran and the proud proprietor of Bromgrove Police Boxing Club, where Markham liked to go to unwind. As far as DCI Sidney was concerned, this predilection for Doggie's was yet another of the inspector's 'bizarre whims'.

'You do know half the villains in Bromgrove go there?' he had snapped in a recent encounter. 'And as for that character who runs the place . . . unsavoury in the extreme.' The man's infamous moniker was the least of it.

Doggie bore not the remotest resemblance to a member of the 'my-body-is-a-temple' brigade. Physically, he was quite alarming, thanks to his crooked jaw and tombstone teeth. Then there was his nicotine-hued leer, which made him Bromgrove's answer to Quasimodo. An eyepatch (covering a pupil-less eye, so the rumour went) and extraordinary horsehair wig did nothing to mitigate the sinister overall impression, though Markham suspected Doggie played it up for all he was worth.

It was also true his club was popular with criminals and coppers alike, the two sides declaring an unofficial armistice that allowed them to spar away together quite happily. It was actually part of the place's seedy glamour. The council frequently tried to dislodge Doggie under the pretext of health and safety, but he somehow always managed to save the day in the nick of time and keep his 'no frills' show on the road.

The DI kept on going to the place for the same reasons as he stuck by Noakes. He liked the lack of pretention and had become unaccountably fond of Doggie, with a sneaking admiration for the old reprobate's point-blank refusal to emulate the antiseptic spa culture that dominated elsewhere.

Even the euphemistically titled 'sauna' (in reality a locker room of dubious salubrity with showers in urgent need of regrouting) now felt like a 'home from home'. At times, he felt more comfortable there than in his own office.

DI Chris Carstairs from Vice now sat next to him on a rickety bench panting hard.

'I can always tell when you've had a barney with Sidney,' he observed, 'cos you get in that ring and pummel seven bells out of me.' He grinned resignedly. ''S like I'm a frigging *substitute* or something.'

'You said it!'

Markham stretched pleasurably, feeling muscles and tendons unknot.

'How come you get away with visiting this den of iniquity, Chris?' he asked. 'Sidney's always on at me about coming here . . . "sending the wrong message, bad example, dragging the force into disrepute," blah, blah.'

His fellow DI smirked. 'That's cos "We're the Sweeney, son, and we haven't had any dinner,"' he recited in affected Mockney.

'Oh, *I see* . . . All right for Vice and the Flying Squad but not the likes of me.'

'Something like that.' Carstairs chuckled. 'You're meant to be a posho, mate. *On the inside track. Destined for higher things*.' He began towelling himself off with cheerful vigour. 'Can't have you rubbing shoulders with lowlifes like Vinnie Macdonald and Johnnie Molloy.'

'Very funny.'

‘’Course it’s far more likely Sidney’s just shit-stirring cos he’s jealous.’

‘Hmm.’ Olivia shared the same opinion of his boss, invariably describing him as ‘first cousin to Judas Iscariot’.

The young DI eyed Markham shrewdly. ‘Word has it you’re sniffing round the Willett case,’ he said.

‘Ah, I take it Noakes has been making waves.’

‘Well, he wouldn’t be the only tec uneasy about that particular investigation.’ Carstairs’ tone was casual, but his glance was keen.

‘The one that got away — thanks to Bretherton,’ Markham said stonily.

‘You think maybe it’s got something to do with this death at the Bluebell?’

‘Early days, Chris, early days.’ Where different departments were involved, it paid to be circumspect.

‘Let me know if you need anything from my end.’ Carstairs was pulling on his clothes. ‘Willett was a scrote by all accounts, but him disappearing like that practically did for his mum . . . She was never the same afterwards. Died of a broken heart apparently.’ He flashed Markham a wolfish grin. ‘If Sidney runs true to form, I’m guessing he’ll cut up rough over anything that upsets the nice middle-class mummies and daddies.’

‘More than likely.’

‘In which case, you might want to bung him some intel about mispers in the late nineties . . . get him looking at the *broader picture*, yeah?’

‘Got you. Thanks, Chris.’ Markham smiled mischievously. ‘That’s pretty much what Noakes suggested. “Give it the ole joined-up policing bollocks,” or words to that effect.’

‘Christ, it’s a bad lookout when me and the old villain are on the same page!’ Carstairs whistled. ‘Talking of old villains . . .’

The club’s proprietor hove into view, preceded by the pungent aroma of Jack Daniel’s and wearing the weird permanent smile that was a consequence of his broken jaw ('an old war wound'), his lopsided ugliness more pronounced than ever.

'Gotta love you and leave you, Dogs.' Carstairs made good his escape.

Doggie greeted his 'fav'rite 'spector' with great affability, and Markham responded in kind.

'I see you've ditched the kaftan,' he observed after they'd exchanged the usual pleasantries.

The DI wondered if this portended trouble on the domestic front, since it was through Doggie's latest girlfriend Marlene (a bingo caller at the Pavillion, renowned for her stupendous cleavage) that he had become enamoured of the spiritual, to the point where he'd taken to wearing flowing cloaks — the likes of which Gandalf might have coveted.

'Marl said better keep it for when we're in private,' he said solemnly, ''case folk think I'm weird.'

Hmm. Pretty much a case of shutting the stable door after the horse had bolted.

'Fair enough . . . So you're still into astrology and all the rest of it?'

'Oh yes, Mr Markham.' He hitched up his grubby gansey. 'I'm wearing crystals next to my skin, see?'

'*Excellent.*' Frankly, Markham would have been happy to take this on trust.

'What else have you been up to?' he asked heartily, averting his eyes while Doggie readjusted himself.

'Well, Marl thinks I should branch out,' was the startling reply. 'Offer summat *extra* . . . classes, p'raps . . .' He trailed off uncertainly.

The DI boggled at the prospect of Bromgrove's yummy mummies rolling out their yoga mats alongside local villains like Vinnie Macdonald and Johnnie Molloy.

'That's interesting, Dogs.' He swallowed hard. 'Perhaps it might be worth doing some research first . . . see what kind of thing people want.'

'Marl can teach dance,' the other said with a kind of defiant pride that reminded Markham of Noakes's encomiums to 'the missus'.

'Indeed,' he said politely. 'You'll be off to a head start there then.'

'Yeah. She took lessons at the Bluebell back in the day. Didn't hit it off with the woman in charge, though. Said she were a snotty bitch . . . shouting at the teachers an' sucking up to anyone with a bit of money. That's when she wasn't flashing her bits at the fellas. Like one of them cheetahs.'

Doggie had worked himself into quite a state of virtuous indignation, though the DI presumed he meant *cougars*.

'Uh-huh.'

'Marl really liked some gay bloke with a daft name. But the boss woman was allus on his case . . . used to say he was drunk or had a hangover.'

And that was no impediment to doing one's job as far as Doggie was concerned.

Markham tutted sympathetically. It sounded as though working under Shirley had been anything but easy — despite what they had been told about the dead woman being all sweetness and light.

'Sounds like a bit of a perfectionist,' he said noncommittally.

'Marl said the husband and daughter got it in the neck too. But then' — Doggie shook his head sagely — 'it don' do to 'ave family on the payroll. Asking for trouble that is.'

All hail Doggie, Alan Sugar of Bromgrove's wellness sector, Markham thought with detached amusement. Clearly Doggie figured himself something of an industry insider.

'You may well be right,' he agreed, since some sort of affirmation was clearly required. 'But by all accounts, the place is doing well.'

'That's as may be, Mr Markham. But' — invoking the oracle again — 'Marl said it weren't a happy ship.' He sniffed self-righteously. 'An' you can't put a price on employee satisfaction, can you? All very well working 'em to the bone, but if they don' like you . . .'

Anything could happen. Maybe even murder.

'Artists are strange people,' the DI observed, feeling somewhat at a loss. 'Very sensitive, you know. Highly strung.'

'Like my Marl.' Doggie was smug. 'In tune with folks' chakras.'

Markham felt the conversation heading somewhere he didn't care to go.

'Let me know how it goes with the . . . er, classes,' he said kindly. 'I believe dance is all the rage these days.'

When Doggie heard about Shirley Bastin's demise, he would no doubt regard the news as irrefutable proof of Marlene's psychic instincts. At that moment, however, the DI felt it was a subject best left unexplored.

'Right, I should get dressed before I catch my death.'

That's if the resident bacteria didn't do for him.

'I'll be seeing you, Mr Markham,' said Doggie. 'Mr Carstairs ain't giving you nuff of a work-out these days. Reckon you're ready for the next level.'

God only knew what that would involve, but for the moment Markham was safe.

* * *

Later that evening, back in his apartment at the Sweepstakes, an upmarket complex off Bromgrove Avenue, Markham regaled Olivia with the events of the day as they sprawled on the living-room floor eating takeaway from the Lotus Garden. Outside it was raining steadily, but indoors all was cosy.

His lover enjoyed hearing about his visit to the boxing club.

'*Cheetahs!*' she chuckled. 'God, Doggie's malapropisms get better and better.'

'Is that what you call them?' He smiled affectionately as he watched her forking up her chow mein with gusto. 'I just think of him as coining a new language.'

Suddenly she stopped mid-laugh, the grey-green eyes clouding with compunction.

'Sorry, Gil. It doesn't feel right to be joking about it, what with the poor woman dying like that.'

She scooped back a hank of red-gold hair that was too heavy for the loosely pinned chignon.

'D'you really think she could've been *murdered*?'

'I honestly don't know, love.'

How to put into words the acute sense of foreboding he had experienced in that narrow corner at the back of the dance studio? He couldn't properly articulate it even to himself.

'There might be a connection with another case,' he said, pushing away the foil container of sweet-and-sour pork, appetite abruptly gone.

Olivia gazed at him attentively.

'So you think that whoever killed this Mickey Willett also murdered Shirley Bastin?'

'Assuming Mickey was murdered and didn't just drop off the radar, I think it's possible there might be some connection, yes.'

'Because Shirley knew something about what happened to him . . . or because she was involved in some way . . . ?'

'Who can say?' Markham tried to keep the hopelessness he felt out of his voice. 'The thing is, it means Sidney won't shut us down just yet.'

'*That man*!' Olivia speared a bean sprout as though she wished it were a tender portion of the DCI's anatomy. 'What a weasel . . . Grabs all the glory when you get it right while secretly hoping you fall flat on your face. *Yuk*!'

'Oh, Sidney's not the worst,' her lover rejoined mildly. 'Just nervous about treading on establishment toes.'

'More like trying to make sure you don't leapfrog him and make chief constable first!'

'I'd *hate* that, Liv. I'm not a bean counter.' He grinned. 'And besides, they'd never let me keep Noakesy.'

She burst out laughing. 'Can't see George schmoozing along the corridors of power, that's for sure!'

'He's a holy terror. Not best suited to handling our Bluebell suspects. You know what he's like round "poofy types". The hackles go up and he gives them *that look* . . . You know the one.'

'Mmm. Only too well.' She thought for a minute. 'Maybe he's over-compensating because of the ballroom dancing. You know, brandishing his macho credentials in case anyone thinks he's not one-hundred-percent raw male.'

'Well, he certainly got his point across,' Markham sighed. 'Those instructors at the Bluebell won't be in any doubt about which team *he* bats for!'

'What did you make of the set-up down at the Bluebell?'

'Difficult to say really.'

Crunching prawn crackers, his lover waited patiently.

'Everything *seemed* all right on the surface,' he said finally. 'But apparently there were tensions. Looks like Ms Bastin knew how to crack the whip and she alienated various folk. Took advantage of family too from the sound of it.' Another sigh. 'But whether it adds up to *murder* . . .'

'What does Dimples reckon?'

'Accidental death. Or suicide at a push.' A faint smile. 'Noakes told me to spin him a sob story about needing to dot the i's and cross the t's after what happened at New College Close . . . so he'd give us more time to check it out.'

'Crafty old devil.' Olivia too was smiling. 'And did it work, this guff about you needing *closure*?'

'Well, to the extent that Dimples' findings aren't cut and dried. Further tests and samples needed, etcetera.'

'Should help with Sidney, then.'

'Luckily for us, he's distracted by the *Gazette*'s campaign attacking the force for being wet and woke.'

'Oh yes. Gavin Conors' column, isn't it?' She opened another foil container. 'C'mon, Gil, you've got to help me with the spare ribs.'

To please her, Markham duly tucked in. The sticky barbecue sauce wasn't too bad, and the gypsy-style picnic was a novel diversion from their usual routine.

'I never thought I'd be grateful to the *Gazette*,' he said at last. 'But if this keeps Sidney's attention engaged elsewhere, then I hope Conors spins it out.'

'Maybe you should arrange for George to be interviewed,' Olivia suggested mischievously. 'Ten minutes with him should put paid to the idea of CID being super-woke and snowflaky.'

'Ah, that'd be the nuclear option, sweetheart.' Markham's expression lightened with genuine amusement. 'Can you imagine the impact of unvarnished Noakes? The DCI would be doing damage limitation till the cows came home.'

And no bad thing, Olivia thought to herself.

Aloud, she said, 'So what's your plan with the Bluebell?'

'Well, Kate and Doyle plan to look up some of the stage mums and see what the jungle drums are saying. Meanwhile, Noakes and I will pay Doug Callaghan a visit.'

'*Callaghan* . . .' she repeated ruminatively. 'Wasn't there a Callaghan involved in the New College case?'

'Yes, Councillor Penny Callaghan.' Markham frowned. 'A real juggernaut of a woman . . . Let's just say she and Noakes didn't exactly hit it off.'

'Figures.'

He grinned. 'This is the husband.'

'Another Doug to boot.'

'Yes . . . We call Dimples Good Doug and this one Bad Doug to distinguish them.'

Olivia's joyous, full-throated laugh invigorated him.

'He had his eye on the Bluebell for a property development, but Ms Bastin turned him down.' Absently, he began tidying the foil containers, stacking them one inside the other. 'We don't know of any other connection between them, but he's worth a look. Then there's an on-off boyfriend.' Markham chewed his lip guiltily. 'Sorry, love, I should have mentioned it earlier. He teaches at Hope, name of Fred Stroud.'

'*Fred*!' she was startled. Then, laying a hand softly on his, 'No need to feel bad, Gil. It's just a bit of a surprise.'

'What sort of man is he?' Markham probed gently.

'A gentle giant,' was the reply. 'Half American . . . still has the "twang" . . . Nice looking but quite shy. He comes out of his shell with the kids but never really lets anyone else get close.'

'It seems he made an exception for Shirley Bastin,' Markham observed grimly.

'Do her family know?'

'Stroud's name didn't come up when we spoke to them. One of the parents told Kate.'

'God, how awkward.'

'Well, it looks as if Shirley and the ex-husband were still pretty tight, so she could have been running the two men in tandem. If she was in some kind of love triangle, we'll have to get to the bottom of it.'

Markham's lean sensitive face was full of intense distaste at the prospect of airing this dirty laundry and dragging a dead woman's secrets into the light.

He held out his hands and helped Olivia to her feet. For a moment, they stood entwined.

'Maybe Dimples is right and it *was* an accident,' she whispered.

But she didn't sound as though she believed it.

* * *

Markham slept badly and was up very early the following morning, slipping quietly into his study so as not to wake Olivia.

Overlooking Bromgrove North Municipal Cemetery, his desk was as paperless as Sidney's, but that was where the resemblance ended. There was something almost monastic about the lack of furniture in Markham's room, its principal feature being a huge picture window which drew the eye to the cemetery beyond.

Sitting in the window seat with his coffee, Markham contemplated the graves. Tidy ranks of monuments and headstones amid wild, tussocky undergrowth.

All Passion Spent.

Was that why he never tired of the view, he wondered. Because of the ordered serenity and the contrast it offered with the tangled skeins and disordered lives it was his job to unravel?

His gaze wandered to the Wilderness Garden at the far side of the cemetery where it bordered Bromgrove Avenue. It was a corner of beauty and peace, with winter jasmine, snowdrops and larkspur showing bravely beneath a pale sky tinged with streaks of red.

Suddenly, he found himself thinking of that other garden at the rear of the Bluebell Dance Studio. What was it about the place that filled him with such disquiet?

They dug it up when Mickey Willett went missing . . . Nada.

So why had he seen it in his dreams, a shadow falling across the ground that might have been cast by an invisible watcher standing just out of sight?

Kate Burton's 'diagram thingy' showed a children's playground behind the garden, and next to that was Heathfield Primary School. No building works at the school to speak of in the last thirty years. So Mickey Willett's body was unlikely to have been buried there.

Outwardly, the Bluebell studio was the picture of suburban respectability. But, as though borne on an evil wind, he had picked up the stench of something rotten. Something that made him think of death and coffins and corruption.

His fingers tightened around the mug of coffee. No way could he start sounding off about 'premonitions' or 'funny feelings'. Nothing short of hard evidence would induce Sidney to let him run a fully fledged investigation into the Bluebell. And as yet they didn't have any.

At that moment, his mobile pinged. It was Noakes.

Bad Doug in meetings till 12. C u at Hope?

They could take Fred Stroud first, though from what Olivia had said, the drama teacher didn't sound a likely prospect.

On the other hand, as his wingman was wont to say, *still waters run deep*.

Reluctantly, he abandoned his window-seat vista and went to shave, deciding that he'd walk to Hope. Maybe that would clear his head.

* * *

'Watcha reckon to Yogi Bear then?' Noakes asked an hour later as they sat in his Fiesta outside the school.

It was an apt description, the big dark teacher with his transatlantic accent having something undeniably ursine about him.

Like Dave Gould, he was walrus-moustached (clearly Shirley Bastin favoured a particular 'type') but younger and brawnier.

Stroud had shown no visible signs of strain when he'd greeted them in the HR manager's office, the teacher readily admitting to a 'relationship' with the dead woman.

'I think it had run its course, though,' he said candidly. 'The spark had gone.' A flash of perfect teeth suggested the American fetish for cosmetic orthodontia had crossed the pond with him. 'She was onto the next thing.'

'The next thing?' Markham asked.

'Just a figure of speech, Inspector. I don't know if there was someone else on the scene. I kinda assumed there was.' His voice thickened as he added, 'We had some good times did me and Shirl, but it was never gonna end with a happily ever after.'

Not for her at any rate, Markham thought sadly.

'When did you see Ms Bastin last?'

'About a month ago. We watched *As Good as It Gets* in her flat and had a meal together. But I didn't stay over.' He met their eyes boldly. 'The sex fizzled out a while back, but we still met up from time to time . . . no hard feelings.'

'Would you have said she was the type to take her own life?'

'Hell, no.' He looked genuinely shocked. 'She was the up-and-at-'em type.' He smiled ruefully. 'A real firecracker.' Too fiery for him, was the subtext.

Noakes had stayed quiet for much of the interview. But now, ensconced in his Fiesta, he weighed it all up.

'So, she was onto the next stud muffin then, guv?'

The DI winced. His sergeant believed in calling a spade a spade.

'It would appear so.'

'Marlboro Man too laid-back for her.'

From the nicknames Noakes was bestowing on their interviewee, it appeared he liked him. Markham too had warmed to the genial teacher, but he knew better than to jump to conclusions. There had been a certain wariness in the man's eyes when asked if his late lover could be 'difficult', a tightening of the generous lips when the subject of her family came up.

'Didn't like ole Dave an' Cathy, did he?'

As ever, Noakes was on the DI's wavelength.

'I got the feeling he thought they were like leeches,' the DS continued. 'Hanging off her while she hustled to bring home the bacon.'

'Yes, it did sound like that. But depending on how you look at it, *she* was the one exploiting *them*.' Succinctly, Markham outlined what Doggie had vouchsafed the previous evening.

'Bit of a nag an' a nympho then.' The DS scowled ferociously as was his habit when thrashing out a problem. 'If she'd dumped lover boy, who was she shagging instead?'

'It's just possible she was embracing celibacy, Noakes.' The DI's tone was ironic. 'Though I believe they call it "self-partnered" these days.'

His wingman's eyes narrowed to slits. 'Sounds pervy.'

Moving on swiftly from sexual semiotics, Markham mused, 'Mickey Willett's name didn't produce a flicker.'

'Don' forget he's a *drama* teacher, guv. Them arty types know how to pull the wool.'

'True enough.'

'An' he's lived in Bromgrove most of his life, despite the Yank accent . . . Could've been on the scene the same time as Willett.'

'I'll get Matthew Sullivan to do some digging,' Markham said finally. The assistant head was an old friend and highly regarded by Noakes, whose politically incorrect view of the universe chimed with Sullivan's own distinctly subversive sense of humour. Having briefly fallen under suspicion in Hope's notorious Ashley Dean murder investigation, Sullivan had weathered the storm to become a well-respected member of the school community. The DI could rely on his tact and discretion.

At that moment, Markham's mobile trilled.

'Kate, how's it going?'

As the DI listened, his face darkened. Noakes, bulldog head on one side, watched him attentively.

'Whassup, boss?' he asked once Markham ended the call.

'Enid has disappeared.'

It took the DS a moment to remember. '*The grannie*? But, guv, she can't hardly walk, can she?'

'Start the engine, Noakesy. We need to get moving.'

'You don' think she's topped herself an' all, boss?'

'Oh no, Sergeant.' The DI's face was set. 'Do you remember saying we had to see if the killer would strike again? Well, you know what — he just has!'

5. AN END AND A BEGINNING

'Okay, luv, when did you last see your gran?'

The team was assembled in the kitchen of Shirley Bastin's upside-down apartment, perched on banquette stools around a white oak island-cum-dining table. Amtico-tiled with streamlined fittings, the kitchen had a light, airy feel at variance with the hothouse living room and Enid's en suite on the floor above. Two bedrooms plus a study and bathroom along the hardwood-floored corridor comprised the remainder of the living space, their windows all overlooking the indoor glass-ceilinged courtyard, which cleverly drew down natural light from above. With sliding glass doors, neatly raked gravel and rustic bench alongside a bonsai tree, there was something very peaceful and Zen about it all. Contemplating the indoor oasis that Shirley Bastin had created for herself, Burton felt a pang of genuine sorrow that the dead woman would never sit there again, nevermore savour the tranquillity of her little Japanese garden.

Noakes pushed the mug of well-sugared tea towards Cathy Gould and patiently repeated his question.

Shirley's daughter looked less than ever like the doyenne of a successful dance school, with her unbrushed hair and what appeared to be a bad case of rosacea.

'I checked on her last thing yesterday.'

'What time was that, luv?'

'Eleven-ish.'

'Was she in bed?'

'No, she usually watched television in the living room till quite late. Didn't like to be fussed, so I left her to it.'

'She didn't need help getting to bed?'

'No.' This was said with something of a defensive air. 'There were good days and bad, see.' The woman turned to Kate Burton. 'Monday when you saw Gran, she wasn't so lively. But yesterday was better.'

'She could move around on her own then, Ms Gould?' Markham tried to gauge Enid's level of mobility.

'Well, she wasn't always very steady on her feet, but on a good day, she was able to potter around.'

'If she . . . er, decided to take a walk or something . . . how far would she get?' Doyle was devoted to his own grandmother who was still a powerhouse of strength, ruling the family with a will of iron. But Enid hadn't struck him as a hardy specimen, and adding her Parkinson's into the mix, he couldn't imagine her going for a ramble.

'She hasn't been further than the bottom of Heathfield Close — that's where her chiropodist lives — in ages. The living room and bedroom's her world really.' Which explained the sharp contrast between the old-fashioned décor on the floor above them and the sleek minimalism of the downstairs area.

'When did you realize that she was missing, Ms Gould?'

Cathy Gould looked up into the grave, kind face of the tall inspector.

'I overslept, Inspector.' She gestured helplessly. 'What with the shock of finding Mum and everything that's happened, I didn't get up at my usual time.'

'That's completely understandable.' Markham smiled reassuringly. 'So you had a lie-in and then what?'

'I couldn't hear Gran moving around . . . figured she must've watched telly till very late and needed her sleep. But when I took a cup of tea up, there was no sign of her.'

'What time was this?'

'Quarter past ten. I remember because I'd just listened to the news on Radio 4.'

'Did you check the school buildings?'

'No.' Cathy Gould looked tremulous. If her distress was simulated, it was a convincing performance. 'I thought I ought to stay put . . . in case she suddenly came back and got frightened when I wasn't there. I rang Sergeant Burton's number so your people could start searching for her.'

'Very sensible.' Noakes didn't approve of civilians taking the initiative. They were just a bleeding nuisance half the time. He returned to the questioning. 'Could your gran have had a funny turn cos of her meds?' Smarty pants Burton wasn't the only one who knew medical stuff. Some old biddy in *Casualty* had gone walkabout and started imagining things after they got the dose wrong. 'Y'know, mebbe she thought someone was after her an' took off?' He screwed up his face to denote intellectual acumen. 'Kinda like a persecution complex.'

'Gran's GP adjusted her L-Dopa recently because it looked like she was having some side effects. But they had it under control and a nurse was coming from the medical centre today.' Cathy Gould's tone became mulish. 'She has a decent quality of life despite the illness.'

'I'm quite sure of it,' the DI replied soothingly. He looked round the smart, modern kitchen, taking in all the gadgets and appliances, including a top-of-the-range De'Longhi coffee machine.

'What's your security system like here, Ms Gould? I noticed an alarm box on the way in.'

She looked embarrassed.

'It's just a dummy, Inspector. The school buildings are alarmed, but Mum figured we didn't need anything fancy at our end cos most people don't even know there's a flat back here. Dad has his own keys, of course, but the only way in is through the French doors in the living room.'

'Didn't you say there's access from the Wardrobe Room in the main building?' Burton enquired alertly.

'Well, there's a staircase that leads from there to our downstairs bathroom.' She waved her hand vaguely in the direction of the corridor. 'There's another door in there next to the towel rails.'

Over her head, Markham's eyes met Noakes's.

'So far as I know, that door's always locked,' she said uncertainly. 'I don't remember ever seeing it open. No idea where the key is, though.' She frowned. 'Mum lost her keys a while back . . . She meant to get a new set cut but never got round to it.'

Another glance passed between the two men.

So there was a set of keys out there. Which meant someone would have been able to access Shirley Bastin's flat from the dance studio without anyone being any the wiser.

Cathy Gould sensed the change in atmosphere.

'The buildings are higgledy-piggledy,' she said in a rush. 'The school used to be a church, you see. It was my aunt got this flat done so she could live on site and keep an eye on the place . . . I think it was some sort of underground storeroom before she had it converted.'

'And there are cellars on the other side of you,' Burton said slowly, visualizing it.

'That's right. Under the new annexe. But there's no connecting door or anything like that, just a wall dividing our flat from the extension.'

The DS changed tack. 'Your gran seemed agitated about something when we were here on Monday,' she said.

'That's right.' Doyle backed Burton up. 'Enid said she'd been expecting the police . . . said there was something hidden that was going to be found out.'

Cathy Gould's expression was a perfect blank.

'Can't say I recall that,' she said. 'But the last forty-eight hours are pretty much a blur, to be honest with you.'

'No worries if you can't remember that part,' Burton reassured her. 'I just wonder if anything might have happened to spook Enid?'

Noakes took up the baton. 'Could she've seen someone up to no good, luv . . . casing the joint . . . or doing summat they oughtn't?'

'I remember Dad was here, helping Gran get settled . . . But he didn't mention anything like that. Just said she was a bit more wound up than usual and maybe we should adjust her meds again.' There was a bewildered note in her voice, but Markham had met some very plausible liars in his time and knew better than to take anything at face value.

'Look,' Cathy said finally, 'what sort of thing is Gran supposed to have seen when most of the time she's either glued to the telly or sound asleep?'

'We're just considering all the possibilities, Ms Gould,' Markham said calmly.

'Well, hadn't you better get out there and start looking for her?' She was truculent now.

'Uniformed officers are searching the school grounds as we speak,' Markham said with no alteration in manner. It was one of his greatest gifts, thought Burton, the ability to appear as though nothing was amiss when, in reality, his anxiety levels were being ratcheted up several notches.

A new thought struck the DI and he turned to look at the stumpy woman in front of him.

'How many people know the code for the school alarm?' he asked.

'Most people, I should imagine. Everyone who works in the office, the caretaker, all of them.'

'Do you think that's wise?'

'Well, we've never had any trouble . . . up till now.'

'You need to wake up an' smell the coffee, luv.' Noakes went into paternal mode. 'There's some real scuzzballs out there an' you're laying yourselves right open.'

'I'll get onto Securicor first thing.'

'You won't regret it.'

She looked at the DI.

'You think this is an inside job, don't you?' The facial redness looked almost painful now. 'But why pick on Gran? I mean, even if she *did* notice something, she'd be sure to forget about it the next minute . . . as if it never happened. She forgets short-term things, you see, but remembers all kinds of stuff from way back . . . To be honest, she's in a world of her own these days.'

But Markham wasn't so sure about that. From Kate Burton's report, he had formed a different impression of Enid. Burton had seen in her a spark that still flickered through the ravages of her illness. The old lady had apparently been napping when Markham paid his courtesy call on the family. He hadn't waited to see her — and now he regretted it. What if she'd rallied sufficiently to disclose what was weighing on her mind? There was always a chance.

'Did she confide in you about anything?' he asked. 'Hint there was something bothering her?'

'Not that I can think of.' Cathy picked a hangnail distractedly. 'She liked to have a natter about the old days, but most of her friends aren't around anymore.' Apologetically, she added, 'We should've made more time to listen. But work's been manic lately, and people are always looking for the next big thing. There's "Dance for All" and "*Barre* Fit" just opened in the town centre for starters.'

'It's a competitive market,' Burton said.

The other looked at her gratefully. 'Too right.'

At that moment, Noakes's mobile rang.

''Scuse me a mo.' The DS shambled out of the kitchen.

Markham had a bad feeling about the call. His wingman's rumble was faintly audible from the corridor. Then he broke off abruptly.

'I'm just going to step outside to see where we're up to with the search, Ms Gould,' he said levelly. His eyes telegraphed an urgent message to Burton and Doyle.

Bad news. The worst. Distract her. Keep her talking.

'You look like you could use another cuppa,' Doyle said easily to Cathy Gould. 'Why don't I get a brew on?'

Burton joined in, creating a bustle while Markham slipped out to join Noakes.

The DS jerked a thumb towards the little courtyard. Silently, Markham followed and drew the glass door behind them.

'They've found her body,' Noakes stated without preamble.

'Where?'

'The cellars.'

'But they're underneath the annexe, aren't they?' Markham sank onto the bench as if winded and looked up at his sergeant. 'How the hell did she end up down there?'

'The woodentop said it looks like she went wandering round the theatre or whatchamacallit an' fell down some stairs.'

'Oh, c'mon. Don't give me that.' The DI's brows knitted. '*No way is this a natural death. No way.*'

'Hey, don' shoot the messenger, guv.' But Noakes's face was troubled. 'I grant you, it looks a bit fishy.'

'*It stinks!*' The DI did not raise his voice, but it rang with conviction. 'Enid knew a secret that was a threat to someone here.' He brought his fist down on the bench with controlled violence. 'It was too risky to let her live.'

'Yeah, but she didn't have all her marbles, guv.' Markham's face darkened, but Noakes stuck to his guns. 'No disrespect, but she was away with the fairies most of the time an' who was gonna take her seriously? I mean, that Cathy more or less said they didn't have time to listen to her stories.'

'I'm sorry, Noakesy, you've got a point.'

The DS nodded pacifically at this as though to say, *That's me, the sweet voice of reason.*

'But look,' his boss continued, 'it's just too much of a coincidence that Shirley Bastin turns up dead and then her mother has an "accident" after talking about hidden secrets coming to light.'

'Musta been a bloody big secret for someone to clobber the old girl,' the DS mused.

'They were going to adjust Enid's meds, Sergeant. The killer couldn't take the chance of her having some sort of remission and people taking her seriously.'

'But if she fell downstairs, we ain't gonna make murder stick . . .'

'Let's get over there and see what Dimples has to say.' Markham glanced over at the kitchen door, which Burton had discreetly closed behind them. 'I don't want Cathy Gould anywhere near the other building until we know what we're dealing with.'

'No worries, guv. You know what Burton's like. She'll keep her yakety-yakking 'bout the dance scene an' all that . . . Remember how she went on during the Baranov case . . . like she'd swallowed a pile of ballet books.'

Poor old Doyle. He'd be sure to stand the lad an extra-large drink in the Grapes tonight. Likely he'd be needing it after all that arty-farty bullshit.

* * *

The theatre in the annexe consisted of a simple proscenium stage looking out onto a small auditorium with raked seating. The backstage area, filled with lighting, props and stage sets, was curtained off, but when Markham and Noakes arrived they could hear the hubbub of paramedics and SOCOs beyond the heavy drapes.

Pushing their way through, they were directed to a small trapdoor. A flight of stairs led down to the basement where the pathologist was waiting.

There was nothing particularly gothic about the former church cellars. It was simply an echoey space filled with theatrical impedimenta — clothes rails, painted canvases, hampers of costumes and more props.

Enid's body lay like a crumpled marionette at the foot of the steps, her neck twisted at an odd angle, face partially obscured by her strange orange-and-grey-striped hair. One eye was half-open, unfocused and filmy in death.

The two policemen contemplated the pathetic sight in silence.

Finally, Noakes asked, 'Did she know owt about it, Dimples?'

'No, the end would have been mercifully quick.' Davidson cleared his throat awkwardly. 'As you can see, she died of a broken neck, but I reckon she was helped on her way.'

'You mean—'

'Yes, Markham. I think someone gave her a karate chop to the throat which made her pass out . . . then an almighty shove finished the job.'

'Can you prove it, Dimples?' The DI's voice was hoarse with suppressed emotion.

The other nodded slowly.

'Yes, I think so.' His honest countryman's gaze met Markham's. 'There's soft-tissue trauma that points to it.' He regarded the pitiful remains compassionately. 'And she's got a broken clavicle too.'

'Why didn't he just push her downstairs?' Noakes was puzzled. 'That way there'd be no questions. Broken neck. End of story.'

Davidson's lips were set in a grim line.

'That was most likely the plan, Sergeant.' Bending down, with gloved hands he tenderly adjusted the nightdress that had ridden up over the poor legs twisted with arthritis. 'But at the last minute something happened . . . She realized something was wrong . . . fought back.'

'So he went to plan B.' Noakes's expression boded ill for the murderer whenever they found him. '*The bastard.*'

'How'd he get her over here, Dimples?' Markham wanted to know.

'Well, that's more your department than mine.' The pathologist pursed his lips pensively. 'She lived on site, yes?' At the DI's confirmatory nod, he continued, 'Coaxed out on some cockamamie pretext or other . . . Or she was slipped something to make her compliant.'

'Enid suffered from some combination of Parkinson's and Alzheimer's but' — Markham's voice held a world of anger — 'she wasn't finished by a long way . . . still had a life.'

'God love her.'

It was highly unusual for Dimples to let emotion get the better of him on such occasions, but his bluff features were working. Then he was in control once more.

'With all the meds she was on, abducting her was probably a piece of cake.'

'She were a bit befuddled all right,' Noakes said. 'Lived in the past a lot according to the family.'

'In that case, she wouldn't have realized the danger until it was too late,' Markham observed.

And then, face to face with a killer, he reflected, there was that sudden 'lightning before death' and she was catapulted into eternity.

When Markham had called at the flat to offer his condolences, Dave Gould had told him Enid couldn't fully take in the fact of Shirley's death. Markham now found himself praying that the veil had been lifted between mother and daughter, and there were no more secrets.

Noakes too, that Christmas-and-Easter churchgoer, bowed his head as the paramedics closed in around the body, preparing to move it from the scene.

There's a special place in hell waiting for the piece of shit who did this to you, luv. And we're going to book him a one-way ticket there.

Dimples nodded to the two men. 'I'll be off now. PM results as soon as I can get them to you.' At the foot of the stairs, he turned back to the DI. 'This puts a new complexion on the other death,' he said with a look of frank respect. 'I'd say you were right all along, Markham . . . Looks like you're dealing with a double homicide.'

* * *

Two hours later, the team sat huddled round Markham's desk in the station.

Outside the weather had turned wintry. Freezing mist furled between leafless trees, rolling up to the windows of CID like an invisible cohort of wraiths.

The DI flicked on his heater since the radiators were, as usual, on the blink.

Doyle distributed drinks from a polystyrene tray. 'Black espresso for you, sir. Flat white for me. Cappuccino with extra sugar for you, sarge. And a soy latte.' Burton accepted the last with gratitude and even took a chocolate muffin from the bag that the DC handed round.

'That was *awful*,' she said once they were settled with their snacks.

Cathy Gould had become hysterical when they finally broke the news of her grandmother's death to her. So much so, that her GP had to come and administer a sedative.

Noakes grunted sympathetically. 'You never get used to telling the rellies,' he said. 'An' we haven't even said it's murder yet.'

'Is that what it is, sir — *murder*?' Doyle was torn between horror at what had happened to Enid and the tingling exhilaration that always attended a homicide investigation.

'Yes, I believe so, Constable.' The DI understood what the younger man was feeling — shared his half-guilty relish for a new challenge. 'Dimples reckons there was a blow to the throat, hard enough to knock her out before she was thrown downstairs.' Markham's expression was sombre. 'Were it not for the signs of trauma to the neck, we could easily have written this one off as an accidental death.'

'How d'you reckon it happened, sir?' Burton had been primly nibbling her muffin in a manner normally guaranteed to drive her colleagues — who'd wolfed theirs in a couple of bites — round the bend. But apart from a few expressive glances, they refrained from overt disapproval today.

You gotta make allowances, Noakes telegraphed to his younger colleague. *She's all shook up after the caterwauling an' carry-on back there.*

'You mean, how did the killer get to Enid?' Markham smoothed the blotter on his desk with careful precision. 'I think he most likely came in via that door in the bathroom—'

'The one they kept locked cos there were stairs on the other side connecting the flat to the dance school?' Burton asked.

'Correct, Kate.' More thoughtful stroking of the blotter in what Noakes recognized as the guvnor's version of displacement activity. 'The only other way was via the French doors in the living room, but he'd have had to break the glass.'

'An' Cathy said her mum had lost a set of keys but didn't bother to get new ones cut.'

'Right, Noakes. Nothing easier than to slip into the flat in the small hours via that interconnecting door.' He shivered involuntarily. 'Maybe it wasn't the first time he'd used it to gain access.'

'An' then up to Enid's bedroom . . .' Noakes added.

'Yes.' Another shiver. 'This is all conjecture, but I imagine she was confused and — what was it you said earlier, Sergeant? — *befuddled* . . . Maybe she even thought she was dreaming.'

The DI's gaze was remote as he mentally transported himself to the old woman's bedroom.

'P'raps he gave her summat,' Noakes said. 'Y'know, so she'd do as she was told.'

'It's possible. But with the amount of medication she'd been prescribed, he wouldn't have met with much resistance.' Markham's brooding expression turned even darker. 'He may even have sold her a line, so she was willing to go with him.'

'What sort of thing?' Doyle was intrigued.

'Well, there was that secret she kept talking about . . . something that had been "kept under wraps", remember. Maybe he promised to tell her more about what had happened.'

'*Lured* her on.'

'Exactly.'

The DI turned to Kate Burton.

'Ms Gould said her grandmother liked to have a natter about the old days but not many of her friends were still around.' Markham's keen eyes were filled with intent. 'Did she mention any names? Anyone Enid used to talk about?'

Burton took out her pocketbook and flipped through its pages.

'There was a Mrs Carmichael from the post office in Carnaby Street . . . A Miss O'Dowd whose niece gave her a terrible time.' A wry grin. '"No better than she ought to be," apparently.' The DS squinted at another name. 'Oh yes, and there was a neighbour called Mrs Heron . . . no, sorry, Hernan. Then there was Mrs—'

'Hold on a mo. Reel it back. Did you say *Hernan*?' Noakes's cappuccino was halfway to his mouth.

'That's right, sarge. Does it ring a bell?'

They were struck by the animation in Noakes's eyes.

''Appen it does.' With careful deliberation, Noakes set down the paper cup and regarded his colleagues with the air of a conjuror about to produce his rabbit from an empty hat. 'You're not gonna believe this, but Mickey Willett's mum called herself Hernan.'

'How come?'

'Two relationships, see.' The DS leaned forward eagerly. 'She split from Mickey's dad on account of he liked to use his fists . . . put her in hospital more'n once. Dunno if they ever got divorced, but later she moved in with Jack Hernan — he owned a bookie's in Medway — an' was allus "Mrs Hernan" after that.' He thumped the desk. 'If she an' Enid were mates, there's *gotta* be a connection with the Willett case, guv. Stands to reason.'

'It's an interesting coincidence, certainly, and as you know, I—'

'Don' like coincidences.'

'Quite, Noakes.'

‘So where does it leave us, sir?’ Burton looked at him anxiously.

Markham walked over to the window, looking across the car park to the town centre, whose neon glow struggled against the stealthily encroaching fog. Somewhere out there, he thought, was a double killer, a demi-devil holding his breath . . . waiting to see if the police were on his track. He could almost imagine hate-filled eyes, luridly yellow like the streetlamps, staring back at him across the misty cityscape where unseen shadows lurked.

He turned back to his team.

‘We need to re-interview everyone from the Bluebell starting with Cathy and Dave Gould,’ he said. ‘See what we can dredge up about the connection between Enid and Mrs Hernan, for one thing.’

Burton was scribbling away like a woman possessed, oblivious of her colleagues’ pained expressions.

‘Check with the nurses from the medical centre. Find out if Enid said anything to them. If she liked to talk about the old days, then it’s possible she let something slip.’ Markham resumed his seat, long elegant fingers drumming the blotter as he marshalled his thoughts. ‘Try the GP too. Maybe with a bit of prodding something will come back to them . . . something they didn’t realize was important at the time.’

‘Do we say it’s murder, boss?’

‘Not yet, Doyle.’ He reflected a moment. ‘You can talk about “sudden death” and “unexplained circumstances” . . . Let them think social services want us to rule out domestic violence or anything sinister . . . medical negligence, perhaps.’

‘Could be difficult to do that without folk kicking off, sir.’

‘Oh, you’re a mistress of the dark arts, Kate. I’m sure you’ll come up with something to put people off the scent.’

She was visibly pleased at the compliment.

‘I’ll do my best, sir.’

Noakes regarded this exchange with a jaundiced eye. No wonder swot-face didn't want to take her inspector's exams while there was a chance of staying near the guvnor. At some point, someone would need to set the lass straight and he had a horrible feeling it was going to have to be him.

'What about the Mickey Willett investigation, guv?' Noakes asked. 'If we hook up with Jim McLeod an' the cold-case mob, then it's legit, right?'

'Well, we've got grounds to liaise with them, Noakes. But remember,' Markham's voice held a warning note, 'even if Dimples comes up trumps with Enid's PM, the Willett connection's pretty thin as things stand. An elderly lady with Alzheimer's said something about a secret and it turns out she was friends with Mickey Willett's mother . . . Doesn't necessarily *mean* anything.'

'There *must* be summat to link the Bluebell an' Willett, guv.'

'I certainly hope so, but let's not go in all guns blazing. You know how it is with Sidney.'

'He's too busy willy waving wi' Gavin Conors to notice,' Noakes persisted stubbornly.

Markham smiled thinly. 'I fear the "willy waving", as you call it, is merely a temporary diversion. If the DCI gets a whiff of any joint investigation that might tarnish the Bluebell's reputation, he'll be all over us like a rash.'

A particularly nasty one, the DI thought grimly.

'We c'n at least speak to Jimbo, yeah?'

'He works from home Thursdays, doesn't he? We'll go out to Calder Vale tomorrow, that'll be more discreet than meeting in the office.'

No names, no pack drill. From Noakes's expression, it was clear this decision suited him down to the ground.

'Sounds like a plan, guv.'

'What about Doug Callaghan, sir?' Burton enquired.

The search for Enid had put paid to their meeting with the local businessman.

'I'd forgotten all about him, Kate, but he needs checking out too . . . See if you can get to the bottom of his commercial proposal to Shirley. And we need to see the studio's accounts—'

He broke off. 'It strikes me I'm fairly loading you with tasks.'

'I don't mind, sir,' she replied stoutly.

Noakes had a variety of faces he reserved for outbreaks of Burton's lovesick masochism. But on this occasion, he merely relieved his feelings by slurping the dregs of his cappuccino with unnecessary vigour.

'So, the Milkybar Kids cover the Bluebell while you an' me take Jimbo,' he said laconically.

The Milkybar Kids! Kate Burton bridled.

'Sorry, Burton. Only joking.'

But it was clear from the unrepentant grin her fellow DS flashed at Doyle that he meant nothing of the kind.

Nonetheless, the meeting broke up amicably enough in an atmosphere of suppressed excitement.

And when his colleagues had dispersed to their various tasks, Markham walked once more to his office window and looked out into the gathering darkness.

Time to turn away from the Bluebell to the world of the unbereaved.

He found himself looking forward to his meeting with retired DCI Jim McLeod.

6. HIATUS

Thursday, 9 January was a fine crisp day with sunshine glittering on the fields and verges that lined the route to Calder Vale. Tranquilized by the mellow landscape, Noakes drove at a more leisurely pace than usual, even grunting in occasional appreciation of the picturesque countryside.

'It's unfortunate that Natalie's dance lessons have had to be postponed,' the DI said carefully. 'But the school will be open again from next week, so hopefully she won't lose out.'

'Yeah, bit of a bummer, that. But she's really looking forward to giving 'em the ole razzle dazzle . . . quite summat when it comes to disco, our Nat . . . really knows the moves.'

Plus a few positions her doting father would never have imagined, Markham thought before adding hastily, 'Is there any particular class she's keen on?'

He would be sure to let Olivia know so she could choose an alternative option.

'Summat modern an' contemporary most like.'

Traditional for Olivia then.

Observing Noakes's proud expression, Markham felt somewhat ashamed of his deviousness, but twelve weeks of class with Natalie Noakes was unlikely to promote sweetness and light at the Sweepstakes.

''Course, finding Shirley's body shook her up good-o. What with her being sensitive like the missus.'

Tough as old boots more like.

'Naturally.'

'*Ackshually*' — the DS swerved abruptly to avoid a squirrel — 'Nat said there's a story going round about the Bluebell.'

'Oh yes? What kind of story?'

'Well, Nat can't be doing with the paranormal an' that kind of thing, but one of her mates said there were a lad died in that theatre thingy where we found Enid.'

'What, in the cellars?' Markham was startled.

'Nah, not down there . . . Hanged hisself on the stage . . . from a rope he hitched to one of them lighting cables.'

'How tragic.'

'Yeah, an' that's not all.' Noakes clearly relished being the purveyor of bad news. 'He left a note saying he was made to do it.'

'*Made to do it . . .*'

The DS shivered extravagantly.

'By the "Ghost Dancer".'

'Oh, *come on, Noakesy*. These places always have their resident bogeyman. Remember that one at the Royal Court on the Baranov case . . . the ghost of a psycho doorkeeper, wasn't it?'

'Well, there *was* a suicide at the Bluebell.' The DS frowned as he negotiated a tight bend. ''Bout ten years ago. Ivor Harrison in Records remembers it . . . Turned out the lad had a history of mental illness an' they hushed it up pronto.'

'There you go then. This Ghost Dancer stuff is just embellishment by teenagers looking for cheap thrills.'

But even as he said it, Markham felt a chill. As though someone had walked over his grave.

Suddenly he recalled a modern ballet he had seen with Olivia at the Royal Court. Something to do with the despair of a spurned lover who was led away at the end of the piece by the 'Man of Death'. In his mind's eye, he saw the two figures transposed onto the Bluebell's stage . . . backlit silhouettes with faces obscured, one behind the other like a shadow.

Noakes's mind was still running on the rumours.

'Prob'ly no one would've thought to bring it up but for Shirley dying like she did.'

And now Enid.

'Nat said folk are talking about the place being under a curse.'

No doubt the tale had given Natalie Noakes a pleasurable frisson, but Markham resolved to keep it from Olivia's ears.

'You gotta admit, guv . . . two bodies turning up one after the other like that . . . an' Enid saying there was some sort of secret. From where I'm sitting, the place deffo looks jinxed.'

'Well, let's keep the Bluebell's backstory strictly between ourselves, shall we? If the DCI gets wind of curses and ghosts, he'll take the case off us.'

'He can't do that now it's murder,' Noakes said with heavy satisfaction, swivelling sideways to look at Markham. 'Enid is murder. Right, boss?'

'*Eyes front please, Noakes* . . . Thank you.' The DI's pulse rate returned to normal. 'Yes, Dimples has confirmed it. Enid was half throttled and then blacked out before she was pushed downstairs. But,' he added sternly, 'the Bluebell's one of our fine civic institutions, so Sidney doesn't want any nasties crawling out of the woodwork.'

'Sidney's a wanker.'

Undoubtedly.

'Try and walk in his shoes, Sergeant. The *Gazette* is gunning for CID right now and we can't afford any more negative publicity.' The DI sighed. 'Stuff about evil phantoms makes it sound like we're on a wild goose chase, so better to "keep it real" at this stage.' He leaned back and put his arms behind his head in an attempt to dispel the tension that any discussion of the DCI invariably evoked.

'If you say so, boss.'

They were now approaching the squat Saxon church of St Bartholomew, its grey flint exterior and stumpy spire gilded by the sunshine. The sight of its ancient graveyard set Noakes off again. 'Nat's mate said a teacher who used to work there saw the ghost one time an' its face was like a skull.'

'Your Nat's "mate" sounds a veritable fount of local knowledge.'

The DS knew the guvnor's sarky tone of old. It meant he was skating on thin ice.

'Jimbo'll be chuffed if this leads back to Mickey Willett,' he said. 'Not chuffed about Shirley an' Enid copping it,' he added hastily in case there was any misunderstanding.

'DCI McLeod will likely be careful about making any assumptions and so should we,' Markham replied austerely before relenting. 'But I dare say he'll be happy there's a link with the Bluebell.'

'He were over the moon when we tied up the Alex Carter case.'

For a moment, the two men were silent, recollecting the investigation that led to them cracking a long unsolved case of child abduction. The upshot was that Jim McLeod had been coaxed out of retirement to assist with occasional cold cases. Not child murders, though. He would never again agree to work on one of those.

'There wasn't owt in the file about Enid being interviewed when Willett went missing,' Noakes ruminated as they approached a line of quaint terraced cottages at the end of a street clinging to the side of Calder Hill. 'But then no reason why she should've been . . . Shirley took over the dance school in 1995 an' her mum didn't move in with her till 2002—'

'A few years after Mickey disappeared.'

'Thassright, guv.' Noakes drew up outside the end cottage, which was painted duck-egg blue and had a seaside feel about it. He cut the engine. 'So most likely Enid had no idea what he was getting up to . . . or whether he was hanging round the school like they said.'

Markham too was thoughtful. 'Enid would have been in her late fifties or sixties then . . .'

'Yeah. Dinner lady at Medway Park. Salt of the earth by all accounts. Moved into the flat when she broke her hip.'

'Mickey's mother Mrs Hernan was Enid's friend,' Markham resumed his train of thought. 'Presumably she talked things over with Enid after Mickey died . . . And whatever she had to say began to prey on Enid's mind . . . led to her becoming suspicious of someone at the Bluebell . . .'

'Enid got sick in 2008,' Noakes said, his face puckered in concentration. 'An Mrs H died in 2010. Both of 'em a bit screwy.' He glanced guiltily at the DI.

'It's all right, Sergeant. I know what you mean.'

'Stands to reason they never went to the cop shop an' fingered anyone for Mickey,' the DS went on sadly. 'Let's face it, who'd have believed 'em by that stage . . . specially with them being on lots of drugs. I mean, even Enid's family thought she'd gone loopy.'

'They were vulnerable and confused,' the DI agreed. 'And maybe afraid for their own safety.' *With good reason.*

'Mebbe Burton'll winkle summat out of the quacks. She's good at that kind of stuff . . . knows the lingo.'

Markham suppressed a smile at the awkwardly expressed tribute. Noakes could be generous when he wanted, and the DI knew a kind of reluctant admiration had sprung up between himself and Kate Burton. On two occasions now, when Burton had been in peril, Noakes had fussed over her like a mother hen, much to the amusement of their colleagues.

Now he replied simply, 'I'm sure she'll give it her best shot, Noakesy.'

'If that bleeding hypocritical oath thingy don' make 'em all clam up.'

Markham reminded himself to save that one up for Olivia. When it came to malapropisms, Noakes surpassed even Doggie.

Clamping down on his merriment, the DI unbuckled his seat belt.

'We'll have to put out feelers with Enid's circle,' he said. 'There can't be many of them, given how long she'd been an invalid.'

'Like that Cathy said, most of 'em are pushing up daisies by now,' the DS agreed grimly. He scowled. 'We should try Dave Gould again . . . Ex-son-in-law an' allus hanging around the flat like a bad smell.'

'We'll need to re-interview the school staff as well,' Markham said. 'I want to know where they all were back in the day when Mickey went missing.'

'Yeah, that's gotta be our best bet cos the alibis for Shirl an' Enid won't be worth jack shit . . . I mean, they'll all say they were tucked up in bed when the two of 'em got whacked.'

'Come on, Noakesy, let's see what Mr McLeod has for us.'

* * *

Jim McLeod was a former prop forward with Bromgrove CID Warriors and had the reputation of being a tough nut. Swarthy and almost piratical with the weathered complexion of an outdoorsman, there was something very winning about his roguish dark eyes and frank kindliness. He received them warmly, while his golden Labrador, Clover, drooled and slobbered a welcome.

'Margaret's out at the WI,' he said, referring to his wife. With a smile in the DS's direction, he added, 'She made extra scones when she heard you were coming.'

The perfect copper's helpmeet, in Noakes's humble opinion.

The low-beamed front parlour was delightfully cosy as ever, with its cheery little fire and big, polished grandfather's clock ticking solemnly away in the corner. Historical prints adorned the walls and old-fashioned round braided mats spotted the dark wooden floor. A round bow-legged table, drawn up to one of three high-backed chintz armchairs, was piled high with pamphlets about old churches and other antiquarian delights, while more of the same jostled for space with quaint bits of china on the bookshelves and cupboards which lined the room.

'Aye, I've not as much time for that sort of thing these days,' McLeod said following Markham's glance. 'Sit you down,' he continued, 'and I'll just fetch the tea.' Nothing loath, his two visitors made themselves comfortable.

Through the diamond-paned window, Markham saw a tiny front garden filled with old-fashioned flowers clustering about crooked herringbone-patterned paths. It reminded him of St Chad's cemetery and the wild plants contending with moss and lichen to shelter those who slept there.

In no time at all, McLeod was back with a tray of tea, scones, cream and (to Noakes's evident rapture) home-made jam.

'You're spoiling us, sir,' the DI observed as his colleague got stuck in.

'No need to call me "sir", Markham. We're all equals now.'

'I can't think of you any other way.'

Noakes nodded vigorous assent.

With eyes suspiciously bright, McLeod got up and stoked the fire while his visitors considerately affected not to notice the upswell of emotion.

Once more firmly in control of himself, the retired DCI returned to his seat, took a hearty draught of tea and buttered a scone for himself. Suitably refreshed, he embarked on the subject that had brought them to his door.

'Mickey Willett,' he said. 'After all this time, I never thought I'd see that case re-opened.' He looked at them steadily. 'And now you're investigating two deaths at that Bluebell place. So, come on, bring me up to speed.'

Much as he had done when a junior officer, the DI gave a succinct summary of developments.

'So it's definitely murder?' McLeod breathed at the conclusion of Markham's account. 'Both of them?'

'Not a doubt of it, sir.' Firelight and shadows danced across the handsome, eager face. 'And we're pretty sure Enid knew something about Mickey's disappearance. Something his mother told her before she died.'

'His old mum kinda lost it after Mickey vamoosed, didn't she, sir?' the DS asked.

'That's right, Noakes.' The twinkle in McLeod's eyes dimmed. 'But she was adamant her boy would never have gone off without a word to her.' A grim smile. 'And she had no truck with the notion of turf wars or some kind of vendetta. Basically, she told Bretherton where to stick it.'

Noakes sniggered appreciatively at that.

Markham too was amused. 'A feisty lady from the sound of it, sir.'

'Well, she had a hard life did Valerie Hernan. And she was nobody's fool.' McLeod sighed. 'The vim was sucked out of her by the end, of course, but I was inclined to believe her when she said Mickey would never have gone AWOL like that. Just wasn't his style.'

'He wasn't a kingpin in some gang or other then?'

'Not a bit of it, Markham. Strictly small-time. Just your average Jack the Lad putting it about.'

Noakes's head came up.

'Yeah, he had summat going with a lass from the Bluebell, right?'

'Mickey was a law unto himself by all accounts, so nobody could be quite sure about his love life . . . But Heathfield Close was his patch, so there must have been some attraction in the vicinity.' McLeod's eyes were remote as he tried to bridge the twenty-odd years that had elapsed. 'He was a good-looking lad . . . like a young Bruno Tonioli . . . y'know, one of the judges on *Strictly Come Dancing*.'

'But not a pansy?' Noakes put in.

Markham shot their host an apologetic glance, but McLeod simply laughed.

'There wasn't a whisper of anything like that and the girls were all over him. From what I heard, he had his pick.'

Ignoring Markham's disapproving glower, Noakes proceeded to regale McLeod with an account of the Ghost Dancer. ''S right up your street, sir,' he concluded by way of justification. 'Being local history an' all.'

'I hadn't heard that particular piece of folklore, Noakes.' McLeod was thoughtful. 'I wonder if there was any foundation for it.'

He subsided into a brooding silence, prompting the DS to say almost timidly, 'I didn't mean to stir up any bad memories or owt like that, sir.'

The other smiled at him kindly.

'There was something about that dance school,' he said. 'Something not quite right . . . Something I couldn't put my finger on.' He got up and put more coals on the fire, as if to buy himself time to think. 'But we didn't find any trace of Mickey Willett . . . It was like watching a cine reel and he just slipped out of shot.'

'I felt it too, sir,' Markham volunteered softly. 'Something wrong with the fabric of the place.'

Noakes was not about to be left out. 'Yeah,' he put in, 'weird as fuck with them churchy bits an' cellars.'

Markham produced a printed list.

'Did any of these names come up in the Willett investigation, sir?'

McLeod scanned the paper carefully.

'Yes to the Goulds,' he said finally. 'But as for the staff . . .' He shook his head. 'I assume those are stage names.'

'Good point.' Markham nodded to his DS. 'We need to check birth details where possible.'

Out came the dogeared pocketbook as Noakes cheerfully wiped away smears of jam with his sleeve.

God in heaven, I need to get him housetrained, thought the DI watching this performance with dismay. *It's like taking a polecat to tea. At least I need to make sure Peabody doesn't offer refreshments at that blasted appraisal.*

The twinkle was back in McLeod's eyes, as though he knew exactly what Markham was thinking.

‘Did you ever speak to Enid, sir?’ Markham was keen to divert McLeod’s attention from Noakes, who had somehow managed to transfer jam from sleeve to hair.

‘No, she never came up in the original enquiry.’ McLeod leaned forward, resting brawny arms on his knees as though bracing himself. ‘It was a mistake,’ he said heavily. ‘She slipped through the net.’

‘Not your fault,’ Noakes said stoutly. ‘You weren’t to know that her an’ Mickey’s mum were pals . . . Anyway, this stuff about a mystery or secret or what have you . . . seems it only came out gradual, like.’

‘Still,’ McLeod’s right leg began to jerk rhythmically, ‘we missed a trick.’

‘Was there a viable suspect in the frame back then, sir?’

McLeod snorted. ‘Bretherton had the hots for Nick Carter, but he was a non-starter.’

Outside, the skies seemed to have darkened. As though the shadow of the man they sought had stepped between them and the sun.

‘How’s this thing gonna work, sir?’ Noakes brought them back to reality with a bump. ‘I mean, with you an’ the cold-case lot doing Willett.’

‘No need to tread on each other’s toes. Just keep me in the loop.’ A sly grin. ‘And we can share intel for the purposes of briefing DCI Sidney.’

Markham remained stoically impassive.

‘No need to look like that, Markham. I know the play-script . . . Pin it on anyone but the nicey-nice respectable brigade . . . preferably some random lowlife with a drug habit.’

The DI burst out laughing. There was something almost painful about the sound to McLeod’s ear.

‘It’s the DCI’s Bushy-Haired Stranger fetish,’ Markham said. ‘And I get it, sir, I really do. *No*’ — with upraised hand to forestall Noakes’s rumbling protest — ‘Sidney’s the public face of Bromgrove at a time when our stock “Up North” has never been lower . . . Is it really surprising he doesn’t want institutions at the heart of the community tarred with criminality and sensationalism?'

'Should be freaking used to it by now,' the DS muttered under his breath.

'Your loyalty's admirable, Markham,' McLeod replied. 'But I'm afraid the dance school's going to be front and centre for the foreseeable future.'

The retired DCI allowed a pause to elapse. Then, 'We're on the same page here,' he said. 'Me and the cold-case team'll re-interview Mickey's known associates . . . at least, those of them who are still around . . . See if we can get a handle on whatever it was kept drawing him back to Heathfield Close.'

An unwelcome image of those shadowy silhouettes from the ballet, one beckoning the other, interposed itself between Markham and his interlocutor.

'Markham . . . Are you all right?' McLeod was concerned.

Noakes was shuffling his feet, a common manifestation of awkwardness when the guvnor 'went off on one'.

The DI came to with a start.

'Sorry, sir. It must be Noakesy's moonshine about ghosts . . . I can't get this idea of some phantom of the ballroom out of my head.'

McLeod regarded him indulgently. 'So long as you don't share it with the top brass, eh?'

'No fear of that, sir,' Markham said robustly. 'They'd have me in Occy Health faster than you can say, *Fab-u-lous, dahling.*'

'That's the spirit.' But McLeod's eyes lingered intently on Markham's angular features, noting dark pouches under the eyes and something attenuated about his athletic frame. 'See you don't let this investigation wear him down, Noakes.' The message was clear.

'You c'n count on me for that, sir.'

And despite Noakes's far from reassuring dishevelment — how the hell did Markham's sidekick get away with looking like a cross between Abel Magwitch and the Fisher King? — McLeod believed him.

Markham felt curiously reluctant to leave the comfortable room with its low, inviting window seat overlooking the unworldly stillness of the country garden, but there was no help for it.

'Better be getting back to base,' he said after some enjoyable chat about station personalities. 'That's if you've quite finished with the scones, Noakes.'

The DS grinned, unabashed. 'They were champion, sir,' he said to McLeod. 'I've never tasted better.' When it came to culinary standards, Noakes was a stickler for exactitude, even at the expense of 'the missus'.

'I'll be sure to convey your compliments to the chef, Sergeant,' McLeod replied, amused.

He escorted the two policemen to the door.

'Keep in touch, Markham.'

'Will do, sir.' They shook hands. 'I'm hoping Kate Burton may have got somewhere with Enid's GP and the district nurses.'

'Burton . . . Burton . . . Ah yes, that extraordinarily earnest DS with the big brown eyes.'

'She's not so bad.' After three scones, Noakes was inclined to be charitable.

'No, indeed. The soul of conscientiousness was my impression.'

'A bit OCD but' — with heavy emphasis — 'she'll learn.'

'With your hand on the tiller I don't doubt it, Sergeant.'

* * *

Back in the car, the two policemen sat peacefully for a few minutes, the gentle influence of Jim McLeod's quaint retreat still on them.

Eventually, Noakes turned to the DI.

'Right,' he said, 'what've we got?'

He counted out names on pudgy splayed fingers.

'There's Shirley's ex, Dave Gould, an' the daughter Cathy. Both likely fed up of her walking all over 'em.'

Contemplating his chipolata fingers as though they could unlock the riddle, he continued, 'Then, we've got Deputy Dawg at Hope.' He pulled a lugubrious face as he recalled Fred Stroud, 'Popping round the flat to have a shag for old times' sake.'

'That's three,' Markham agreed mildly.

'Plus the fairies . . . Clay Clifton an' the German lad.'

'Anton Bhaer.'

'That's the one.' The DS did a mock Nazi salute. 'Heil Hitler!'

Markham's lips twitched. Anton Bhaer was no more of German extraction than Noakes himself, but if it suited his colleague to engage in a little therapeutic xenophobia then so be it.

'Five.' The DI patiently kept the tally.

'An' the dago bird—'

'Robyn DiAngelo. Mediterranean by way of Scarborough, I'd say.'

'Whatever.' Noakes cast a suspicious look in the rear-view mirror as though there was a risk of the suspects creeping up on them. 'Any road, she's the scrawny bint . . . had a snaky way about her.'

'Jealous of Shirley too.'

'The one with the name from the Bible . . . She were jealous too.'

'Bible? Oh, you mean Vivienne Sansom.' Markham chuckled. '*Sansom* not Samson, Noakes.'

'Aye, thass the one,' his colleague said, not one whit abashed. 'Miss Goody Two Shoes. Butter wouldn't melt . . . but she ended up doing ring-a-ring o' roses an' wiping snotty noses all cos of Shirley.'

'Hmm. Yes, that injury certainly put paid to her career as a dancer.'

'An' don' forget,' Noakes had gone into full Leslie Phillips mode, 'she an' Dave Gould had a *thing* going.'

'Vivienne was his protégée, Sergeant.'

'Yeah, an' we all know what that means.'

'We don't know anything of the sort. It's all supposition.'

Nothing daunted, the DS ploughed on with his roll call.

'There's the bitchy mum . . . Ella or Eileen or whatever her name is.'

'Aline Hosking.'

'Any road, we gotta look at all them parents who thought their kids were gonna be Rudolf Neveroff an' blamed Shirley cos it never happened.'

'Thwarted ambition,' mused Markham. 'Yes, that has the potential to cause all kinds of trouble.'

'Or mebbe it's not any of 'em.' Noakes had run out of fingers.

Markham felt a twinge at the base of his spine, as though insects were skittering along the vertebrae.

'Oh?'

'Mebbe he's there but not there.'

'Don't go all oracular on me, Sergeant.'

'I mean ter say, we could've seen him, guv, but not noticed him . . . Like he's jus' there waiting in the wings . . . Lurking.'

It was not a reassuring hypothesis.

'You mean like one of the rubberneckers?' Markham said thinking of the gawpers who had materialized in the vicinity of Heathfield Close.

'Yeah . . . Y'know, the way psychos like to hang around the scene of the crime.'

'I'll get Doyle to check out a few faces.'

'Could even be a student . . . someone who's signed up for classes, same as my girl and your Olivia.'

'That's got to be a long shot, surely,' the DI observed. 'Bearing in mind they're unlikely to have had much to do with Enid.' He stared unseeingly in front of him. 'If she was dropping hints about a secret waiting to be discovered, it's more likely to be someone in the family circle—'

'Or one of the teachers,' Noakes chipped in, 'someone who dropped round to the flat now an' again.'

'Hmm.' The DI shifted uncomfortably in the passenger seat, aware of something which felt like a broken spring sticking into him. 'You may be onto something there, Sergeant.' Meditatively, he steepled his fingertips together. 'I'd rather assumed Shirley kept her work and her personal life separate, but perhaps there was more overlap than we think.'

'Those theatre types tend to hang out together, guv,' the DS said, for all the world as though he possessed an intimate knowledge of the breed.

Wheels within wheels.

'It means we need to go deeper. See who else apart from Fred Stroud and Dave Gould might have been watching rom coms and enjoying takeaways with Shirley. Plus, I want you to get hold of the Bluebell's registers . . . then Burton and Doyle can do a trawl of the clientele.'

'See how many dirty old men are on the books,' Noakes agreed with relish.

'Well, dance and ballet have moved on from when it was all about voyeurs checking out the girls.' Markham gave a short laugh. 'But we may turn up some interesting characters.'

'An' the woofter brigade. All tight trousers an' frilly shirts like summat out of *Pirates of the Caribbean*.'

'*Noakes*.'

'I know, I know, guv. But' — Noakes assumed the air of one making a magnificent concession — 'they're the ones make the best groovers, not the macho types.'

His sergeant did not seem wholly displeased by this fact. And it occurred to Markham that, in dance class at least, the fragrant Natalie was unlikely to be led astray by testosterone-fuelled Romeos on the hunt for trophy girlfriends. From that perspective, 'raving queens' were a father's best friend.

* * *

Arriving back at their temporary quarters in Bromgrove English Language College, Markham was startled to hear raised voices coming from the makeshift incident room.

Kate Burton, looking rather flushed, sat across the table from a man Markham didn't recognize. Good-looking and square-jawed, he was bald on top but wore his silver hair longer and neatly groomed at the sides. He looked to be in his early sixties and exuded an air of authority.

'This is Doctor McKinnon, sir,' Kate said, relieved to see Markham walk through the door. 'He has some concerns about the investigation.'

'Correct.' The doctor spoke in a pleasant baritone with an irascible edge. 'Am I right in thinking that this is some sort of joint enquiry with social services and Bromgrove NHS?' He directed a scorching glance at Burton. 'Because I have the feeling I'm getting the run-around here.'

'In what sense?' Markham replied coolly, sitting down with unruffled calm.

'In the sense that I'm Shirley Bastin's GP and it seems to me you're sniffing round the family and insinuating there may have been . . . frankly, I'm at a loss for how to phrase this . . . some kind of neglect or abuse going on.'

'Abuse of Enid?' The DI didn't turn a hair. 'I very much doubt my officers will have said anything of the kind.' His tone was quiet but steely, his keen eyes steady on McKinnon's face.

Don't fuck with me, buster, Noakes thought with satisfaction as he leaned against a wall to watch the sport. Doyle, meanwhile, squirmed uncomfortably at the foot of the conference table.

McKinnon blinked first.

'It's what was implied,' he muttered. 'Non-stop questions about the medication regime and prognosis. Made it sound as though you think someone did the woman a mischief, either me or one of the family.'

Go on, boss, throw him a bone.

And Markham did.

'There are indications of foul play,' he said levelly, making a snap decision that McKinnon was a man to be trusted.

There was an intake of breath from across the table.

'I see.'

'I hope you do, Doctor.' Markham didn't raise his voice, but each word fell into the room like the measured stroke of a weapon. 'We want to ascertain Enid's mental state before she died and whether she shared anything to make you or her carers think there was something on her mind.'

'What sort of "something"?' The irascible note had softened.

'Something to do with events in the past . . . a secret that someone might have wanted to keep from getting out.'

'She didn't mention anything like that to me.' Well-manicured hands tapped the table. 'But Evelyn Johnson — she's the care-team manager — told me Enid became agitated over an item in the newspaper the other day . . . the *Courier*, I think it was.'

'Did she see what Enid was looking at?'

'No.' McKinnon frowned. 'Cathy or Dave . . . or someone . . . whisked the paper away before Evelyn could see what had set Enid off. So she never got to the bottom of it. Just noticed the old lady muttering to herself and giving these funny little furtive looks round the room as though she thought something was going to pop out of the walls.'

Something or someone.

'What about the domestic set-up? Did she seem nervous of anyone?'

'What, Dave or Cathy?' A quick bark of laughter. 'He's a bit of a sad sack, really . . . She's a howling neurotic, but then Shirley wasn't the easiest person to grow up with . . . hard to be outshone on all fronts by your own mum.'

'Did her behaviour towards either of them undergo any sort of a change?'

'Not that any of us noticed. She was more withdrawn at times, but that's part of the illness.'

'Was there anyone she saw regularly . . . a confidante?'

'Not of late . . . I believe it was a different story when she was mobile and could get around . . . quite the livewire by all accounts.' The handsome features suddenly looked less pugnacious and Markham found himself liking the man much better. 'Until the Parkinson's diagnosis, she never really bothered us at the surgery . . . One of that generation who don't like to make a fuss . . . the stoical type.' He looked over at Kate Burton, a frank expression on his handsome face. 'I'm sorry I came on a bit strong,' he said. 'Shirley's death was a shock. And Enid's death took everybody by surprise despite her health problems.'

Everybody bar one, thought Markham.

The meeting broke up amicably enough, leaving the team to chew things over.

'Sorry, boss. My people-pleasing skills cut no ice with the doc.'

Markham brushed away Burton's apology with a smile.

'Not to worry, Kate. We won him over in the end.'

'He's one of them that allus wants to speak to the organ grinder not the monkey,' Noakes observed.

'Hmm . . . Well, that was an interesting anecdote about Enid being upset by something from the *Courier* . . . I wonder what.'

'I'll check with Evelyn Johnson, sir.' Burton was eager. 'If she can tell us the date, we might be able to narrow it down.'

'Excellent, Kate. Probably something and nothing, but let's follow it up anyway.' He flashed a bracing smile round the table. 'We'll have some tea and then you can fill me in on Doug Callaghan and those accounts.'

The mention of tea created a diversion as he had intended.

It was Thursday, he reminded himself, and the Bluebell would be open again for business on the following Monday. They needed a break in the case, and they needed it soon.

7. APPROACHING STORM

'Right,' said Markham once they were settled with their tea, courtesy of the ever-efficient Mrs Seddon. 'What did you get from Doug Callaghan?'

'Not a nice man,' Doyle ventured, pulling a face.

At that moment, the DI's mobile interrupted proceedings.

Watching the boss's face darken appreciably, it was very apparent to the team who was calling.

'Yes, sir. Quite so, sir. Discretion, sir . . . absolutely.' Markham was doing his finest impersonation of a plank of wood.

'That was the DCI,' he said wearily once the distinctly one-sided call was over. 'Wants a heads-up on our . . . let me see, how did he put it . . . "direction of travel".'

'Oh, for fuck's sake,' Noakes growled. 'You mean he wants a prime suspect as in "The Dodgy Janitor" or "Freaky Psycho".' His pudgy fingers sketched savage air quotes. 'When will he ever change the bleeding record?' The DS produced his most ferocious scowl. 'Right now, the "direction of travel" is shit creek without a paddle.'

'Stow it, Noakesy.' *Before you burst a blood vessel.* 'We'll tell Sidney we're liaising with DCI McLeod regarding the Willett investigation . . . looking at gang warfare or territorial feuds or some such. As per Superintendent Bretherton's initial theory.'

'Will the DCI go for it, sir?' Burton's big brown eyes were magnified to the size of saucers behind her schoolmarm spectacles. 'I mean, how does Enid fit into that scenario?'

'Or Shirley Bastin?' Doyle added.

'We'll tell Sidney the full picture is . . . inchoate.'

Thank God for a guvnor who'd swallowed a dictionary.

'The main thing is to turn attention away from the dance studio . . . talk up neighbourhood grudges and the drugs scene,' the DI continued. 'And it's a fact that Mickey Willett was involved with ravers or whatever they called themselves back then.' Markham endeavoured to keep the cynicism out of his tone, but it leached through, nevertheless. Unconsciously, he echoed what DI Carstairs had said to him at Doggie's. 'Has to be better than upsetting the nice middle-class mummies and daddies by suggesting that someone at the Bluebell is a homicidal maniac.'

'What time does Sidney want us to check in?' Noakes sounded resigned to the inevitable, like a schoolboy anticipating six of the best.

'Five-ish. So we're okay for time.' Markham's smile did not extend to his eyes, Burton noticed. 'Look, it'll be fine, Sergeant. We'll give it the old one-two and blind Sidney with science.'

Noakes looked far from convinced.

Kate Burton cleared her throat.

'What is it, Kate?'

'Clay Clifton came in earlier, sir.'

'Oh yes?' Markham was only too glad to park the subject of DCI Sidney. 'What did he have to say?'

'Wanted to know if they could get into the building . . . There's some kids' shows or competitions coming up and he's worried they're behind schedule.'

'What does he think this is?' Noakes exploded. 'Frigging *Strictly Come Dancing*? We've got a *murder* investigation going on here, so *Mister Spangles* can stick it.'

'The SOCOs were finished, sir,' she said, 'so I gave permission for them to come in and do their practice sessions.' Burton looked anxious. 'Told them it was provisional, mind, and they'd have to up sticks if you weren't happy.'

'An' the parents are okay with that?' Noakes was incredulous. 'With two women having jus' snuffed it in the place!'

'"Stage-door Johnnies", sarge,' Doyle observed sagely. 'That's what they're like. Can't see past the starlight.'

'And nothing official's been said about murder,' Burton added. 'As far as the public are concerned, it's just a family tragedy.'

'Since the SOCOs are finished, there's no reason Clifton and the rest shouldn't be able to get classes back on.' With raised hand, the DI silenced any protest. 'It's a good idea. You can go round casually, Kate . . . Nothing heavy, just checking in, offering reassurance, that kind of thing.'

Noakes was rumbling away like a subterranean geyser.

'Look, it makes sense,' Markham said. 'And Kate's a balletomane so it will look like she's combining business with pleasure.'

Burton turned rosy red with pleasure at hearing herself thus described.

That's right, guvnor, thought Noakes crossly. *Keep digging. She'll only carry that blooming torch forever and a day.*

'If you say so, sir.'

'I do, Kate.' The DI's gaze was remote, introspective. 'It's a case of keeping eyes on the teachers and everyone who comes and goes — parents, students, hangers-on, whoever.' He paused. 'See if anyone shows an unusual interest in Enid or the police investigation . . . anyone you think is maybe a little too keen to know what's going on.'

'Right, sir.' She was visibly re-energized at the prospect of an assignment. Meanwhile, her male colleagues exchanged expressive looks of the too-cool-for-school variety.

'Oh, while I remember,' the DI resumed. 'Before we go on, I need to brief you and Constable Doyle on what we learned from DCI McLeod.'

When he had finished, they looked thoughtful.

'So, the Goulds were around when Mickey Willett went missing, but Mr McLeod's not sure about the rest?' Kate Burton twitched the specs more firmly onto her nose. 'Perhaps one of *them* was in the area when Mickey Willett went missing.'

'If they're local, yes, Kate. It's a possibility.' Markham sipped his stewed tea fastidiously. 'So we need to go behind the stage names and check out people's true identities.'

'Won't they have had to disclose all the names they've been known by on their DBS forms, sir?' Doyle registered Noakes's mystification. 'That's the Disclosure and Barring Service, sarge,' he explained kindly. 'Anyone who works with kids has to fill out the paperwork.'

'Oh aye,' came the laconic response. Clearly his colleague had zoned out in the recent child protection seminar for CID.

'Good point, Doyle.' Markham nodded approvingly.

Like Burton, the young detective looked suddenly lit up from within, such was the respect his troops had for the DI.

'Of course, it's possible some staff may have slipped through the net,' the DI pointed out. 'I suspect Shirley may not have been as rigorous as she should have been when it came to background checks on her staff.'

'First there was the CRB, but DBS checks only started in 2012,' Burton pointed out. 'At any rate, there was room for mistakes.'

'Yeah, jus' think of the Soham murders.' Noakes had roused himself. 'Didn't that pervy caretaker get away with it cos nobody knew he had previous?'

'Correct, Sergeant.'

'You mean, there's folk could have got into the Bluebell on a nod and a wink, sir?'

'Something like that, Doyle.' The DI sighed. 'Strikes me it's the kind of outfit that wouldn't necessarily have bothered with all the red tape.'

Doyle pursued the logic to its inexorable conclusion. 'So someone in the school could be working under a fake identity, sir?'

'It's a long shot, Constable, but we can't rule it out.'

Burton gave her specs another twitch.

'What about this business with the *Courier*, sir?'

'What about it, Kate?'

'Well, from what Doc McKinnon was saying, it sounded like maybe Enid *recognized* someone in the newspaper.' The brown eyes glowed with purpose. 'Might have been someone working under an assumed name.'

'Good luck with that,' Noakes grunted.

'Have you got a better idea, Sergeant?' Markham enquired acidly. 'No, I thought not.'

Collapse of stout party.

Tactfully, Burton changed the subject.

'Doug Callaghan was fit to be tied when I asked about his offer to buy the dance studio, sir.'

'God, yes. Huffing and puffing . . . red in the face and shouty,' Doyle confirmed with distaste.

'What did you make of him, Kate?'

'DC Doyle's right, boss. Not a nice guy.' She shuddered slightly as she recalled the sweaty businessman, all bulging veins and bluster. 'D'you know . . .' She hesitated.

'What?' asked Noakes eagerly.

'Oh, I don't know . . . I just wonder if there was ever anything . . . *personal* between him and Shirley . . . He was like a tinderbox when we questioned him. Defensive like you wouldn't believe.'

'Yeah, 's right,' Doyle confirmed. 'I mean, we were only asking if he'd put an offer in on the dance school . . . *Politely* like,' he added hastily so everyone was quite clear. 'And then the next thing we knew, he was banging on about police oppression and civil liberties. He behaved like we'd accused him of rape or worse.'

'He's *Councillor* Callaghan's better half, remember?' Markham reminded them with a grimace. 'Par for the course as I recall.'

'Bloody awful lefty harridan an' rent-a-gob,' Noakes muttered.

For once, the DI uttered no reproof.

'Interesting that you think he overreacted,' Markham observed.

'What if he *did* slip her one, guv?' The DS was wide awake now. 'Lovers' tiff an' him miffed cos she refused to sell . . .'

'But where does Enid fit in?'

'Mebbe *Dougie*'s the one she was talking about . . . the one with secrets.' Noakes clearly liked Doug Callaghan as a suspect. 'Had a finger in every pie . . . Plenty to lose if stuff came back to haunt him.'

'What about Mickey Willett?' Burton persisted stubbornly. 'What's the connection *there*?'

The DS's underlip shot out. He wasn't going down without a fight.

'Coulda been Willett got in Callaghan's way or summat.'

'*Romantically*?'

'If they were after the same bird back in the day, mebbe Callaghan saw red . . . Or mebbe Willett strayed onto his patch . . . moved in on his territory, that kind of thing.'

Burton looked dubious but dutifully made a note. 'I'll check it out, sarge,' she said to mollify the DS. 'Like you say, there may have been some kind of rivalry.'

Noakes assumed an attitude of Sibylline profundity.

'Twenty-odd years ago, Callaghan would've been in his thirties,' he said. 'Willett was this cocky whippersnapper . . . Who knows what might've gone down.'

Silence fell over the little group. Through the window, the sun looked to have gone in for good. The light had taken on an aqueous, murky quality that Markham associated with thunderstorms.

Was there a storm coming? Was meteorology warning him that more trouble was on its way?

'What now, boss?' Noakes demanded bluntly.

'We'd better get back to the station and rehearse our shtick for the DCI . . . profiles of local hoodlums, etcetera.'

'Sidney's all steamed up about that piece in the *Gazette* saying he's all mouth an' no trousers.'

Which was one way of putting it, certainly.

'So,' Noakes was looking crafty, 'if we make it sound like we're gonna square up to the druggies and headbangers . . . all guns blazing . . . that'll make him look good back at HQ.'

'Got it in one, Wyatt Earp.'

'Eh?'

'Never mind,' Markham said kindly. 'The thing is, we'll be focusing on the Bluebell rather than Bromgrove's 'Wild West', but what the DCI doesn't know won't hurt him. And, as you say, anything that sounds like "muscular policing" is bound to go down well.'

'What about us, sir?'

'Well, Doyle, let me see . . . I'd like you and Kate to get hold of the Bluebell's personnel files . . . I think they're in that office behind reception.' He paused. 'Try to avoid bothering the Goulds, but you may have to ask them if it turns out the filing cabinet's locked.'

'What do we tell them, sir — the Goulds?'

'Just say it's part of routine checks . . . no stone unturned.'

'But we're going to have to tell them this is murder at some point, right?' Doyle persisted.

'Might not be news to one of 'em,' Noakes said grimly.

'Indeed.' The DI's shoulders ached with tension. God, what he wouldn't give for a quick work-out at Doggie's. But there was no chance of that. 'I'll ask Sidney about getting a press release out tomorrow. "Sudden deaths and the police are treating the circumstances surrounding the deaths as potentially suspicious. Thanks to the public for their patience at this difficult time. Important to respect the privacy of the family. Various lines of enquiry being pursued."' His expression intent, he added, 'Not a word about the Willett investigation . . . That's officially down to the cold-case team and DCI McCleod . . . In reality, of course, we'll be working together . . . I'm hoping to hook up with Mr McCleod tomorrow.'

He smiled with genuine pleasure at the prospect of seeing Jim McCleod again, causing Kate Burton's heart to turn over at the softening of those austere features. Suddenly aware of the sardonic gleam in Noakes's eyes, she hastily recalled herself to the business in hand.

'Will there be a press conference, sir?'

'Not if I can help it. A bulletin should keep the journos at bay . . . especially as Gavin Conors and Co. have other fish to fry, working themselves into a frenzy over CID's politically correct approach to crime.' As he clocked Noakes's almost wolfish grin, Markham reflected that at least one member of his team could hardly be accused of 'going soft'.

'Check in with me later, Kate,' he said. 'I'll be interested in your impressions of how Bluebell staff are reacting to all of this.' He turned to the gangling DC. 'As well as those personnel records, Doyle, I'd like you to get hold of Fred Stroud's please. But *discreetly*. Have a word with Mat Sullivan first . . . he'll be able to bypass any nosey HR managers at Hope.'

It was getting darker outside, threatening rain. Time to make tracks.

'Right, Noakes. Time for our showdown at the O.K. Corral.'

Otherwise known as an interview with DCI Sidney.

* * *

An hour later, the two gunslingers reviewed the fallout in Markham's office.

'Could've been worse,' Noakes said. 'I mean, there's no arguing with the doc's report . . . specially not with him saying Shirley was likely murdered an' all.'

'Yes, Dimples really proved his mettle there,' the DI agreed.

'*Bad Doug*,' he practically spat the name, 'didn't 'xactly waste any time having a whinge about "police harassment", did he?'

'I wonder what Callaghan is so keen to hide,' Markham said, idly tracing circles in the dust on his desk. 'Maybe his relationship with Ms Bastin *was* personal.'

'His missus'll have his balls on a plate if that's true.' Clearly it was a prospect that afforded Noakes no inconsiderable pleasure. 'Mebbe it was a love triangle thingy behind Shirley's murder an' Enid's is about summat else — completely separate, like.'

The notion of there being *two* killers at large did not fill the DI with unmitigated delight.

'We need another crack at Mr Callaghan,' he said.

'But he'll jus' whiz straight back to Sidney. *Freaking sneak*.'

The DCI had been even more peremptory than usual.

'I won't have our civic leaders subjected to intrusive questioning, Markham,' he'd honked with a sidelong glance at the Hall of Fame where, ten to one, Callaghan's bonce bobbed alongside all the other celebrity scalps collected by Sidney.

'Just a question of background information, sir. We wanted to know whether Mr Callaghan had put in an offer for the Bluebell.'

'Well, you've had your answer to that, haven't you?'

Actually they hadn't but pointing this out was hardly worth the aggravation.

Now Markham turned to the DS. 'We can try flattery. After all, Callaghan only met Burton and Doyle, which gives me an excuse to go round and apologize for any *misunderstanding . . . junior officers unfortunately over-zealous . . . so sorry to have troubled him unnecessarily and given the wrong impression—*'

'Pass the sick bag.'

'*But while we're at it, perhaps he could give us some useful insights into the Bluebell . . . pillar of the community, superior local knowledge . . .*' Markham ground on remorselessly.

'You make him sound like one of them criminal profiler types,' the DS grumbled.

'Men like Callaghan lap it up. And if he thinks we've ruled him out, he's more likely to talk.' Uncharacteristically, the DI loosened his tie, a sure sign of frustration and that their investigation appeared to be on the skids.

'At least Sidney liked all the druggie stuff.'

'I'll ask Chris Carstairs to see if we can't break down a few doors and haul some local villains in . . . Some of the older ones may remember Mickey Willett.'

'But you don' think this stuff at the Bluebell's anything to do with gang battles, guv?'

'No, I don't, Noakesy.' The long, tapering fingers continued to trace restless circles. 'I know it sounds irrational, but I smelt *evil* in that school . . . a sort of invisible stench that hung in the air.'

'Yeah, them cellars an' that funny pokey patio wotsit where Shirley was sticking out from that barrel . . . an' poor Enid jabbering about secrets an' what have you then getting clobbered.' Noakes shook his head decisively. 'Summat smells off, all right.' He wrinkled his nose, for all the world as though somebody had just shoved a runny brie under it.

Markham's mobile went off, and he put it on speakerphone so that the DS could listen in.

'How goes it, Kate?'

'The personnel records have gone walkabout, sir,' she said without preamble.

'How come?'

'Someone must have broken into the filing cabinet. The lock had been forced.'

'Anything else missing?'

'The petty cash box and some books of press cuttings . . . Oh yes, and some floppy disks of Dave Gould's.' A sniff of disapproval. 'That PC's like something out of the ark . . . I reckon it was the HR stuff they were after. The rest was just window-dressing.'

'What did the Goulds have to say?'

'Looked shocked enough. Said they hadn't heard or seen anything suspicious.' There was a short silence. 'They seemed a bit zonked, the pair of them.'

'And it happened this afternoon, right?'

'Yes, sir. Whoever it was, they were in and out like greased lightning.' Her tone was apologetic. 'I don't know how I missed it, but me and Doyle were sussing everyone out . . .'

'No need to feel bad, Kate. Whoever it was, they struck when the moment was ripe.' A vertical crease appeared between the DI's finely arched brows as he thought hard. 'Get that area secured and call a couple of SOCOs back to take a look.'

It was a lost cause and he knew it. Not only had their killer shown signs of being forensically aware, but the legitimate comings and goings of Bluebell staff would account for any trace evidence found at the scene. Only with blood spatters and the like could the team hope to get lucky. And God forbid it should come to that . . . *Bloodbath at the Bluebell,* it had a ring to freeze the senses.

He became aware of an expectant silence at the other end of the line.

'Sorry, Kate, just wool-gathering.' He rotated his shoulders in an effort to rid himself of the lingering ache, which had only intensified after the interview with Sidney. 'How did everyone seem to you?'

'A bit subdued, to be honest. But that's not surprising really. Robyn DiAngelo and Vivienne Sansom were looking daggers at each other, but whatever was going on they weren't sharing it with us.'

Unbidden, the phrase 'honour among thieves' popped into Markham's mind. He forced it out and tried to concentrate on what Kate Burton was saying.

'. . . Clay Clifton looked ill, sir.'

'As in a guilty conscience?'

'Dunno, sir. But something was definitely bugging him. One of the parents — I think it was that awful Aline Hosking — was on at him in a corridor . . . banging on about some problem with Monica's "turn out" . . . But he just seemed dazed, looked at her like she was speaking Swahili or something. The other teacher—' She broke off and they heard the riffling of papers.

'The Kraut,' Noakes interjected.

Markham shot him a look.

Burton was back on the line. 'Sorry, sir, got it now . . . Anton Bhaer said Clifton was coming down with something but didn't want to let the kids down.'

Plus the Hosking one would have had him on toast had Monica Ballerina missed her chance to shine, thought Noakes.

'Any chance of speaking to Clifton on his own?'

'I tried that, sir.' A heavy sigh. 'But no dice. He *did* look a bit iffy . . . sort of glassy-eyed and clammy.'

There was no doubt of Noakes's verdict. *Likely charlied up to the eyeballs same as all them dancer types.*

'I thought I should give him a bit of a heads-up, sir . . . in case he was holding out on us.'

'No worries, Kate.' Surreptitiously, the DI flexed his scapula. 'What did you tell him?'

'Just said we hadn't closed the file on these deaths and if he knew anything, he needed to tell us pronto.' A pregnant pause. 'Otherwise he could be in danger.'

'How did he react?'

'Not sure he took it in, guv. In the end, I just gave him my card and said he could call me any time.'

'Fair enough.'

Something was niggling at Markham, just within his peripheral vision. But when he reached to grasp the elusive thought, it vanished.

'Hang about there for a bit, Kate,' he said. 'But once the classes are done and you've seen everyone safely off the premises, you and Doyle can call it a day.'

'Righto, sir.' Her voice was flat.

For once, she didn't protest or suggest reporting to CID for a more detailed debrief. The unwonted lethargy made him wonder if her personal life was indeed in some kind of trouble. But the mobile went dead and Burton was gone.

Noakes was wriggling like a bashful schoolboy.

'What is it, Sergeant?'

'You ain't forgotten, have you, guv?'

'Forgotten what?'

'You an' Olivia are coming round to ours for your tea.'

Oh no. He *had* forgotten. And, even worse, he realized he'd omitted to let Olivia know. She would go ballistic.

'Looking forward to it, Noakesy,' he said heartily. 'I've just got to collect Olivia from school.' When the H-bomb would go off. 'And then we'll be with you.' He smiled weakly. 'I hope Muriel won't be going to any trouble on our account. Just a quick bite as we've got "school" the next day.' Thank God it wasn't Friday so they could legitimately plead off staying too long.

* * *

In the event, teatime chez the Noakeses' passed off pleasantly enough.

'Even if Muriel did give it the full Mary Berry,' Olivia chuckled afterwards. 'I mean, don't tell me they usually chow down on shepherd's pie dauphinois and marbled coffee ring cake, followed by coffee and liqueurs.'

'Got to admit it was good, though.'

'Yes, it was. But then, nothing's too much trouble for *Gilbert*.' The last word emerged as an affected shriek.

'Admit it, Liv. She's growing on you.'

'Well, it still felt like I was starring in *Abigail's Party*,' Olivia grumbled. 'All that faux-gentility . . . And as for the name-dropping!'

'It's down to insecurity. And then, she was covering for Natalie.'

'God, yes. Talk about the evil eye!' Olivia punched his arm in mock fury. 'What did I ever do to that girl to make her hate me so much? She barely had a civil word for me. Just sat there glowering . . . Face like a bulldog chewing a wasp!'

'Well, what with you representing Noakes's ideal of Womanhood, she probably gets cheesed off,' Markham teased slyly.

'He couldn't be prouder of them both if they were Bromgrove's answer to . . . oh, I don't know . . . the Kardashians.'

'Muriel's fearsome corsetry doesn't exactly bring Kim Kardashian to mind,' Markham laughed. 'Nor that twinset she was wearing.'

'Anyway, they're both the tops as far as George is concerned.' Olivia linked her arm through his and nestled in closer as they walked along. 'Have you ever noticed, Gil, that "our Natalie" doesn't have a trace of George in her?'

'Can't say I've really thought about it.'

'Typical man.' An affectionate squeeze of the arm. 'But it's true, you know. I can see a resemblance to Muriel, but she's actually a very attractive girl with almost classical good looks under all that Polyfilla she trowels on . . . excellent bone structure for one thing. But,' she sounded genuinely puzzled, 'not an ounce of George.'

'Not necessarily a bad thing, dearest, given that his features are what one might call "lived-in".'

'Maybe it's his unique personality she inherited.'

'As in sheer bloody-mindedness and a genius for driving people round the twist?'

'Something like that,' she gurgled before growing serious once more. 'She'll give them a whole heap of trouble before the day is out, Gil. It's written all over her.'

'I'll do my best to keep a . . . fatherly eye on her.'

'I don't think she sees you in the light of a father figure, Gil.' *More like she wants to snog the face off you, my love.*

Before they could continue this interesting dissection of Natalie Noakes's character, Markham's mobile went off.

'Kate Burton,' he mouthed and Olivia immediately fell silent, watching a shadow fall over the much-loved features. It became more pronounced as the call went on.

'I'll meet you there, Kate,' he said finally.

Ending the call, Markham turned to Olivia. 'Kate had a bad feeling. So she went back to the dance school,' he said.

'Another death?' Olivia's voice was hardly more than a whisper.

'Yes, I'm afraid so,' came the reply.

Their cosy complicity was gone as though it had never existed.

'I'll walk you back to Noakesy's,' he said. 'Noakes and me, we'll get a squad car out to take us to the Bluebell since we're both over the limit. Muriel will order you a taxi.'

'Be careful, my love, please be careful.'

The first spots of rain plopped heavily onto the pavement.

The storm had arrived.

8. NOT SINGLE SPIES, BUT IN BATTALIONS

'*Where is she then?*' Noakes muttered as the two men waited uneasily in the reception area of the Bluebell Dance Studio. Rain drummed heavily on the roof as though nature itself were building up to some kind of dread crescendo. 'Better try her mobile again, guv.'

But there was no answer.

'Why the fuck did she have to go charging in?' Noakes's colour looked dangerously high. 'She *knows* to wait for backup,' he puffed. 'An' after what happened with that freaking snowman the last time . . .'

Markham did not care to remember the climax to their last murder investigation, which had indeed involved Kate Burton in a nasty brush with a piece of snow sculpture.

For all the ideological trench warfare that Noakes waged against Kate Burton, the DI suspected his feelings for her had long since turned paternalistic. Though, of course, Noakes would rather die than admit it.

Now the DS was positively hopping from one foot to the other.

'Mebbe we need to call it in, boss.'

'No.' Markham was looking about him and listening. 'It's only ten minutes since she phoned me . . . I think she's in here somewhere . . .'

'She didn't say who she thought was dead, guv?'

'No, just that she thought there'd been another murder.' Markham's keen eyes probed the dim recesses at the far end of the hall. 'She was whispering. As though she was afraid of being overheard.'

Still the rain kept up its eerie percussion.

'So the killer was still around when she rang you?'

'I think she was taking no chances, Noakes.' The DI lifted his face to the skylight above, like a hunter alert to his quarry's spoor. 'But whoever it was, I reckon he's gone now.'

'*So where's Burton, then?*'

'Let's take it room by room, Sergeant. First the main building and then the annexe.' The DI gestured towards the corridor in front of them. 'You check the rooms on the right-hand side and I'll do those opposite.'

Noakes was out of the starting blocks before Markham had finished speaking.

For the next five minutes, only the sound of heavy footsteps and doors slamming interrupted the rain's rhythmic spatter.

They met again at the end of the corridor.

'Nothing,' said Noakes breathing heavily. 'Jus' pongy classrooms an' sweaty kit.'

'Same here.' Markham thought of his reflection in the long mirrors which ran the full length of one wall in each bare and empty classroom, how it had seemed to mock his impotence.

Noakes's big meaty fists were tightly clenched.

'*If he's done owt to her.*'

'Let's check the annexe.' Markham pushed at the internal fire door. 'Come on, it's through here.'

The two-storey extension was in darkness until Noakes, fumbling along the wall, flipped a light switch.

'Same division of labour, Noakes. You take this floor,' the DI said, making for the stairs which led to the upper level, 'and I'll search upstairs.'

The DI was on the third of six rooms on the top floor when he heard Noakes shout, '*Guv, down here! Guv!*'

Following Noakes's bellows, he located the DS in the annexe's theatre, which straddled both sides of the corridor at the far end.

Scanning the space, Markham could see nothing different from how it had looked when they were called out to retrieve Enid's body. Save for the SOCOs' yellow crime-scene tape, all appeared the same as before.

'Where?'

Noakes pointed towards a cubicle with a glass panel at the rear of the compact little auditorium.

'Thass a one-way mirror, same as down the station,' he said. 'Whoever's in there c'n look out, but nobody gets to see in.' Noakes was flushed and earnest. ''S like in them royal limos an' posh cars they have for VIPs,' he added.

'Or police interview rooms,' Markham added drily. 'What is it anyway?'

'It's the control room,' the other replied, not without a touch of pride. 'I checked with one of the SOCOs . . . Where they do the special effects an' stuff.'

'Wouldn't something like that be soundproofed?'

'This one ain't.' The DS jabbed a pudgy digit at the innocuous-looking little box. 'I deffo heard summat from inside there, boss.'

'Right you are, then.'

Markham stood back, arms crossed, and looked expectantly at Noakes who appeared delighted to be offered this chance of a *Sweeney* moment.

Bloody hell, Markham thought belatedly. What if he has a coronary or something? He only barely scraped through that last fitness test.

But it was too late. The DS was hurling himself at the door of the cubicle like a human battering ram. Again and again he charged before it crashed open with the sound of splintering wood.

Cowering against the rear wall of the cubbyhole, Kate Burton was white with fear, eyes so big in her face that she bore more than a passing resemblance to a terrified raccoon.

Before a word was said, Noakes had crossed the floor and scooped her into a rib-crushing embrace. Then, by way of covering up his emotional reaction, he proceeded to castigate his colleague.

'Why'd you come here by yourself, lass? You musta known it weren't safe.'

'Dunno, sarge. I just felt I had to take another look . . . Something didn't feel right. Like the place was drawing me back.'

Christ! She and the guvnor were peas in a pod with all their mystical hocus-pocus bullshit.

'Bloody daft,' he said gruffly to hide his relief that she was safe and sound.

'How did you end up in here, Kate?' Gesturing to Noakes to take an arm, Markham manoeuvred her out of the cramped space.

'I thought I heard a strange noise coming from this end of the building . . . a sort of *gurgling*. Decided I'd better check it out and—'

Suddenly her eyes widened, so that all the energy in her pert little face seemed concentrated there.

She pointed towards the far right-hand side of the ground-level proscenium stage.

'*What?*' Noakes asked. Then more gently, 'What? There's only a manky ole hamper or picnic box thingy.'

But still she stared. Noakes watched her closely for a moment, his gaze almost tender. Then he went lumbering down the raked aisle towards the wings.

'*Fuck*,' he breathed, bending over for a closer inspection. '*Oh fuck*.'

Markham pressed Burton into one of the tip-up seats. 'Stay there, Kate.'

Then he joined Noakes in the wings.

One swift glance showed him the source of his colleague's consternation.

A hand protruded from beneath the lid of the large wicker basket.

Fuck indeed.

'Open it, Sergeant.'

Gingerly, his colleague complied

Curled up like some ghastly parody of a midwifery illustration, the corpse of Clay Clifton confronted them.

* * *

Afterwards, when all the SOCOs and Dimples Davidson had been and gone, Kate Burton could not stop shaking.

'I should have known,' she repeated, swaying on the tip-up seat. '*Should have known*.'

'Stop beating yourself up, lass.' Noakes's eyes darted about as though he was fearful of being caught displaying such unwonted empathy. 'You thought Clifton were ill . . . coming down with summat like the German lad said. Nothing to say he knew owt about the murders.'

For the first time in living memory, Kate Burton's hand reached out and clutched Noakes convulsively.

'Oh but, sarge, I should have realized it was more than just him being sick.' Another clutch. 'There was something wrong . . . And he didn't trust me enough to tell me.'

'*Get out of it!*'

His colleagues in CID would never have believed that George Noakes, hoary, unreconstructed relict of old-style policing, could react like this. But Markham, aware of chords in the DS's nature that were exquisitely sensitive to certain vibrations, knew better. Lumpen and coarse as Noakes might appear to the casual observer, he harboured chivalric emotions which lay buried in no sealed vault but under the lightest, most easily pierced gossamer.

Now Noakes clumsily sought to assuage Burton's self-reproach.

'You weren't to know,' he said firmly. Then, cudgelling his brains, ''Sides, Clifton could've been upset about summat else.' *Off his face most likely*. 'An' then he ran into the killer by accident . . . caught him out . . . came across him doing summat weird . . .'

Burton didn't look convinced.

'That gurgling noise I heard coming from the stage,' she said miserably, 'was that him *dying* . . . ?'

Noakes and Markham looked at each other. A long, thoughtful look.

No point sugar-coating it for her. She deserves better than that.

'Dimples says the body shifted, so most likely it was air escaping from his lungs,' Noakes volunteered. 'He was strangled, y'see.'

Hearing this, Burton looked even more wan than before.

'Does that mean the killer,' she gulped, 'throttled him while I was poking round at the other end of the building?' Her forehead was beaded with little pinpricks of perspiration.

Markham nodded gravely. 'Yes, it was an opportunistic kill . . . The body was still warm and pliable.' There was something about Clay Clifton's double-jointed flexibility, his dancer's toes eerily pointed even in death, that had made the retrieval of the body peculiarly horrible.

'*Hey, hey*.' Noakes pushed Burton's head down between her knees then awkwardly massaged her slight shoulders. 'It was all over in minutes.' An eternity for somebody with the world turning black behind his eyelids. 'Not even time for him to be afraid.'

Slowly, she sat back up and looked at the two men with an expression of mingled hope and revulsion.

'You reckon he didn't see it coming?'

'The doc said there weren't any defensive injuries.' Now it was Noakes who swallowed hard. 'An' the face . . . well, it jus' looked *surprised*.'

'Surprised' was pushing it, thought Markham, remembering those bulging eyes, their expression of agonized reproach and disbelief.

This was one PM he wasn't going to allow Kate Burton to get anywhere near.

'*Surprised*?' she echoed.

'Yeah, thassright.' Noakes had decided on his script and was sticking to it. 'Like I tole you . . . came at him right outta the blue.'

'It must have been someone he trusted,' she said after a pause.

'Well, he weren't suspicious, any road.'

Markham could see Burton was trembling now.

Shock, he thought and reached for his jacket to put it round her shoulders.

But Noakes was there before him, swaddling his diminutive colleague in a beige parka that had undoubtedly seen better days.

'Ta, sarge.' Normally she would have reacted with fastidious distaste to such garment sharing, but now her big eyes merely swam with tremulous gratitude.

The DI hated to press her, but he knew this was the golden hour.

'When did you last see Mr Clifton, Kate?'

'It must have been around four . . . when he was in the corridor with Aline Hosking. Once he'd got rid of her, I had a quick word about not holding out on us . . .'

'Did you see where he went after that?'

'He said something about going to the staff room to make a drink.'

'Where's that?'

'It's the last room in the main building on the right-hand side.'

The DI looked interrogatively at Noakes who shrugged.

'I went down that way. There was jus' this big empty room — with the mirrors an' that strange pole thing for 'em to hold on to.'

'The *barre.*'

Markham suppressed a smile. Burton's punctilious correction was a sure sign of returning strength.

'Yeah, that's the fellow. *Barre.*' Noakes rolled the word round his mouth as though he liked the feel of it.

'Well, where's the staff room then?' the DI repeated.

The DS scratched his chin.

'There was a sort of curtained-off area at the back,' he said. 'Had a sink in there with a kettle an' a couple of chairs

. . . I took a quick peek . . . Nowt to write home about, though.'

'A case of management cracking the whip,' Markham observed wryly. 'Doesn't do to let staff get too comfortable. If it's too cosy and they're always sloping off for cups of tea, then you're not getting your money's worth.'

Burton pulled a face.

'Staff can make hot drinks in the office behind reception,' she said, 'but maybe the teachers like to get away by themselves for a bit.'

'Away from Cathy Gould, you mean,' Noakes said tapping the side of his nose. 'Somewhere she can't earwig.'

Burton nodded in agreement.

'Did you see Mr Clifton going off with any of the others, Kate?'

'No.' She thought for a moment. 'I got the feeling he *did* want to speak to someone . . . He had that preoccupied look people get when they're gearing up for a tricky conversation.'

'Was that the last time you saw him, Kate . . . on his way to the staff room?'

'I saw him going through to the annexe about forty minutes later . . . But there wasn't anything unusual about that. Various teachers and kids were flitting around jabbering about costumes and routines. There were parents as well.' She caught Noakes's eye. 'We signed everyone in, of course, but it was pretty much bedlam because of this inter-school dance competition they've got coming up.' She smiled weakly. 'Pure *Billy Elliot*, so they were likely wrung out by the end of it all.'

'And you signed everyone out?'

'They were all gone by quarter to seven, sir, and then I reset the alarm.'

She thought hard. 'Someone was talking about giving Clay a lift — one of the girls, I think it was — but he said he'd walk . . . needed to clear his head.'

Or wanted to get away from someone?

'How did he look, Kate?'

'Still pale and groggy, but better than when I saw him earlier . . . definitely more alert . . . bit of a spring in his step.'

Because he had decided on a plan?

'Was it blackmail, sir?'

'I think it may well have been, Kate.' Markham's eyes roamed the little theatre. 'At any rate, he decided to come back here.'

'Mebbe he wanted some rehearsal time jus' by hisself . . . to work out routines an' stuff without every Tom, Dick an' Harry barging in.' Noakes's eyes wandered uneasily to the curtained backstage area with its trapdoor leading down to the cellars. '*Hey, guv*. You don' reckon it was *him* who did for Shirley an' Enid, do you?'

'Returning to the scene of the crime, you mean?' The suggestion startled Markham.

'Well, you know what *theatricals* are like.' The DS cast an apologetic sidelong glance at Burton who appeared resigned. 'Highly strung an' into all sorts.' Meaning deviant sexual practices, drugs and all-round dodginess. 'Mebbe he was superstitious an' couldn't stay away . . . Mebbe it was part of some ritual or voodoo thingy.' A flash of inspiration. 'Like an exorcism.'

Markham bit the inside of his cheek hard so as not to laugh at the images this flight of fantasy conjured up. He had long suspected *The Omen* was one of Noakes's all-time favourites, since it never took him long to come around to the subject of Satanic practices.

But he could see the DS was genuinely trying to be helpful as opposed to riding a hobby horse.

'I'm sure you're correct about those artistic sensibilities, Sergeant,' he said carefully. 'That business at the Royal Court was a real eye-opener and no mistake.' The reference to their investigation into the local ballet company — and the high jinks and murder they'd uncovered therein — elicited a sagacious nod from his wingman. 'But I believe it's more likely that Clay Clifton arranged to meet someone here.'

'To get money, like the lass said?'

'Well, dance instructors aren't particularly well paid, and Mr Clifton struck me as being what they call "high maintenance" . . . Remember, he talked about "having work done".'

'An' that Botox wotsit don' come cheap,' his colleague agreed, happily unaware that his beloved Natalie was no doubt forking out big time for said cosmetic embellishment.

'But *didn't he get it*?' Burton sounded overwrought. 'This was someone who'd killed two women.'

The DI considered this. 'If it was a friend, Clifton might have been sympathetic—'

'Or the killer could have spun him a yarn about what happened being an accident,' Noakes interrupted eagerly.

'Indeed.'

'What if Clay knew something about Mickey Willett?' Like Noakes earlier, Burton's eyes skittered uncomfortably around the theatre, from floorboards to flies. 'Worked out Mickey had a connection to the killer?'

'Then he was taking a very great risk indeed,' the DI said sombrely.

'Something could have crystallized for him,' Burton continued, remembering the pattern of their previous murder investigations. 'He could have remembered something that didn't seem important at the time but came back to him after Shirley and Enid died.'

But what?

'When you called my mobile, Kate, before the phone went dead you said you thought the killer had struck again. What made you so sure?'

'That strange noise . . . The swing doors to the theatre were open, and everywhere was so quiet that the sound kind of carried. Somehow, I knew it wasn't pipes or drains. And I had this sense of someone moving about . . .'

'How'd you end up in the lighting box or whatever it is?'

Now they were coming to it.

The milky pallor was back.

'I just thought I'd better take a look . . . It seemed like a place where someone might hide.'

Burton pursed her lips. 'I was trying to open the door . . . It wasn't locked but felt a bit stiff.'

'You had your back to the stage then?'

'Yes, sir.' Softly, she pounded her fist on the arm of the tip-up seat. 'I should have known better than to turn my back.'

'*Hey, don' start all that again.*' Her fellow DS was having none of it. 'You were — whass the word? *Discombobulated.*' He drew himself up portentously in a manner which suggested a major concession was on its way. 'Coulda reacted the same myself if I were in your shoes.' He smiled almost bashfully at Kate Burton.

'Noakes is absolutely right, Kate. This was spur of the moment and the adrenalin was racing.' Now Markham too smiled at her. 'So, nothing to feel guilty about.'

She drew a deep breath.

'He must have come up behind me from somewhere while I was pulling at the door.'

'What happened then?'

'Just a hard shove and next thing I knew I was locked in.'

'You heard him lock the door?'

'Yes.' She hesitated.

'Go on.'

'Well, that's it really . . . Only I heard a sort of wheezy noise.'

'*Wheezy?*'

'Yeah, sarge . . . Sort of sputtery . . . The kind of noise my gran used to make when she was on twenty rollups a day.'

'*An old person?*'

'Dunno, sarge. But it really creeped me out . . . I waited till I was almost sure he must have gone before using my mobile . . . kept my voice low just in case . . . Then the battery zonked out.'

'You did right, lass.'

'What was he strangled with?' Her voice was very small.

'Some kind of chiffon scarf or headdress,' Markham told her. 'Part of a costume by the look of it. The SOCOs have bagged it.'

'Hey, guv.' Noakes was struck by a thought. 'Which one of them rooms back there is supposed to be the Wardrobe Room?'

'It's round the back of the stage, sarge,' Burton said. 'Nothing special. Just another cubbyhole . . . Cathy Gould showed me earlier.'

'The Goulds were around the whole time today, were they?'

'They drifted in and out, sir. Not much to say for themselves . . . though they weren't happy about the personnel records and other stuff being pinched out of the front office.'

'I'd forgotten about that,' Markham said thoughtfully. 'I wonder if Mr Clifton was responsible . . .'

'Maybe he was looking for something to confirm his suspicions.'

'Indeed, Kate.'

Noakes's eyes narrowed. 'How did Clifton seem around the Goulds?'

'Same as usual, sarge. But then, there wasn't anything out of the ordinary in how he was with any of them.'

'You gotta remember he was a *performer*,' her colleague said. 'Good at hiding his feelings . . . putting on an act.'

It was true, thought Markham. All kinds of signals could have been passing between Clay Clifton and one of the troupe without anyone being any the wiser.

Noakes swallowed an enormous yawn.

'What next, boss?'

The DI fished out his mobile.

'I'm going to organize a squad car so you can escort Kate home, Noakesy.' Markham's eyes felt gritty with fatigue. 'Tomorrow being Friday, we might manage to slip in a press conference without making a great song and dance.'

Good luck with that, guv.

'Then we'll do a briefing next door at the language school for Bluebell staff.'

'They won't like their competition going tits up.'

'They'll just have to lump it.'

Looking at Markham's wintry expression, Kate Burton doubted any of them would care to lock horns with the DI.

'We'll also need to check all the alibis for tonight,' he said firmly. 'Now that it's a triple homicide, everyone's movements need plotting.'

The prospect of an invigorating session with her beloved spreadsheets visibly re-energized Burton, though Noakes was notably less enthused.

'Oh aye,' he said laconically. 'Doyle c'n help with that.' The lad was out with a lady friend and on a promise tonight. But spreadsheets with Burton would put the mockers on any afterglow for sure.

'Oh, before I forget, sir. There's a memorial service or something for Shirley and Enid on Saturday.'

Noakes's face lengthened even more. *Another one of those was all they bloody needed.*

'Where, Kate?'

'Bromgrove Rise Methodist Church.'

'Obviously we'll be there.'

Obviously!

Then Noakes brightened somewhat. Perhaps he could bring Nat. What with her being the one to find Shirley Bastin in a manner of speaking, it was only right she should be there.

He turned to Kate. 'C'mon, lass. Time to get you home.'

* * *

After his colleagues had gone, the DI locked up with the spare keys he had been given and then reset the alarm.

Should they have arranged for the code to be changed, he wondered, before telling himself it wouldn't have made any difference. If not in that theatre, killer and prey would have met somewhere else . . . to the same appointed end.

A sinister consummation ordained by the spinner of years that no one could have prevented . . .

Outside, Heathfield Close was dark and still, but Markham was glad he had elected to walk home.

From being drear and mild, the night had suddenly turned very cold.

Idly, he wondered if that meant snow. Looking back at the Bluebell Dance Studio, he suddenly felt an irrational desire to see the building outlined in white, as if that could somehow mask whatever evil lurked within.

One thing was certain.

The team's troubles were only just beginning.

9. A BRICK WALL

'That's all we need,' Noakes grumbled the following morning as DC Doyle drove him and Markham at speed to Bromgrove English Language College. 'Some daft bints kicking off.'

Markham frowned. 'What did the uniforms say?'

'Jus' that there was this barney going down outside the Bluebell . . . women screaming at one another like banshees an' a couple of blokes trying to calm things down.'

They could really use a female detective, the DI reflected, but he had insisted Kate Burton take the morning off. And to his credit, Noakes had done none of the harrumphing that might have been expected of him. In fact, Markham suspected the old warhorse was actually relieved to know his bête noire was out of harm's way, safely tucked up with her cherished time and motion graphs.

This morning, the DS looked more than usually dishevelled, the haystack hair and five o'clock shadow hardly suggestive of an investigator at the top of his game. Plus, his Arran sweater was on back to front and it looked horribly like a bird had crapped all over his parka.

Given the previous night's discovery, allowances had to be made, but the DI realized he would need to ensure Doyle was front and centre at the press conference to avoid DCI Sidney having a conniption.

The young DC, needless to say, looked dapper as ever with a certain twinkle in his eye that pointed to last night's romantic assignation having come off well.

The day was bitterly cold, with frost silvering the skeletal trees and straggling hedges of Heathfield Close, but Markham was glad of it. The freezing weather somehow cleared his brain and chased away the fug of another restless night in which Clay Clifton's face had floated through his dreams in ghoulish close-up.

Drawing up outside the Bluebell Dance Studio, they appeared to have missed the main event. Now there was only a little gaggle of staff lurking desultorily by the front door, which was guarded by a pimply officer.

'Good morning, Constable. Everything all right?' The DI was very suave.

'Two of these . . . er, ladies . . . had a bit of a disagreement,' came the awkward reply.

'All a misunderstanding,' Dave Gould volunteered.

Markham was struck by how rough and hungover the man looked. Positively a match for Noakes in the dishevelment stakes.

'She had no business implying those things about us.' Vivienne Sansom looked almost ugly as she jabbed an accusing finger at Cathy Gould, delicate features twisted with dislike.

'Stop overreacting,' hissed Robyn DiAngelo. 'It's not all about *you*.'

'If we could just rewind the tape for a moment.' Markham's ironclad courtesy didn't falter. '*What things?*'

'Badmouthing the staff and saying Clay was mixed up in something dodgy . . . that he did drugs and must've had something to do with Shirley and Enid dying.'

It came as no surprise that news of the latest victim had somehow leaked. Markham was only thankful there was no next of kin to be doorstepped, since Clifton was an only child and both his parents were dead.

Noakes's expression was thunderous, and he glared at the young uniform as though he held him personally responsible.

That station's like a fucking sieve.

Cathy Gould, with her runny nose and mottled cheeks, was at something of a disadvantage standing next to the dancers, who appeared chic even in crew necks, scarves and skinny jeans.

Her father seemed to sense this.

'It's been a tough few days,' Dave Gould said pacifically. 'Coping with family bereavements and now *this*.' He put a protective arm round Cathy, though Markham noticed she winced at his touch, as though there was more punishment than kindness in the gesture.

'Viv's being a diva.'

As she delivered this verdict, sultry Robyn DiAngelo regarded her colleague with unmistakeable hostility, a sentiment which appeared to be returned in equal measure. Markham recalled Kate Burton mentioning that the two women had been at daggers drawn the previous day and wondered what had occurred to set them off. He noticed Dave Gould eyeing them warily as though they were made of Semtex: beautifully packaged and utterly explosive.

Before Vivienne Sansom could utter a retort, Anton Bhaer slung an arm across her shoulders.

They make an attractive pair, the DI thought, with those marvellous dancers' cheekbones and a lissom elegance that would make them stand out in any crowd.

'C'mon, Viv,' Bhaer said. 'Let it go.' His handsome face looked suddenly old and withered. 'This won't bring him back.'

Sansom looked as though she meant to shrug him off, then she seemed to think better of it.

'You're right, Ant. They're not worth it.'

Bhaer met Markham's eyes sheepishly. 'Sorry, Inspector. I guess everyone's on a bit of a hair trigger right now.'

'Thass more like it.' Noakes was all paternal approval. 'Why don' you all jus' go have a cuppa or summat?' he advised. 'No point hanging round here getting all wound up.'

'We'll see you back at the language school this afternoon to take your statements,' the DI said with steely politeness. 'Obviously, the dance studio will be closed until Monday.'

'Bang goes the competition,' Robyn DiAngelo retorted acidly.

Everyone turned to look at her and she flushed.

'I'm only saying what everyone's thinking.'

Some things are clearly best left unsaid.

The little group dispersed, leaving the policemen alone.

'Nice one,' the uniform said. 'It was getting a bit nasty before you rocked up.'

Noakes's scowl returned. *That's us, the freaking cavalry.*

'I didn't really get what they were yammering about,' the PC continued, relief making him garrulous, 'but it sounded like the frumpy-looking bird was being snide about one of 'em.'

'That'd be the one who's just been strangled.'

Do keep up at the back.

'Jesus.' The youngster goggled at Markham.

Markham loathed profanity, but on this occasion, he simply shot his open-mouthed, pimply subordinate a compassionate glance.

'Say a prayer for him, Constable,' he said quietly.

That'd be right round the canteen by the time they got back, thought Noakes, well and truly cementing Markham's reputation as a Holy Joe.

Deep down, though, he was proud to be bagman for the DI who was so different from everyone else in CID (a 'legend in his own lunchtime', as he would often joke with DC Doyle.)

Back in the car, Doyle was thoughtful. 'You don't think Clifton murdered the two women cos they'd somehow rumbled him for Mickey Willett, do you, boss?'

'Hmm . . . too far-fetched, Constable.' In the front passenger seat, Markham rubbed his hands vigorously, as the squad car's heater appeared to have given up the ghost. 'And it still leaves the question, *who killed Mr Clifton?*'

'Someone else who knew the secret . . . Someone taking revenge for whatever happened to Mickey . . .' Doyle waited patiently at a roundabout, unspooling his theories. 'Or maybe last night's got nothing to do with Willett, and Clifton was killed cos of something else.'

'You're giving me a headache, lad,' Noakes grumbled.

Doyle grinned amicably at the reproof. 'Sorry, sarge.'

'Don't be too severe on him, Noakes. Remember, you wondered yourself if there mightn't be more than one killer in the mix.'

'Did I?' came a grunt from the back.

'Yes, indeed . . . You thought we might be looking at a love triangle for Shirley's murder and something completely different with Enid.'

Noakes's mutinous expression in the wing mirror seemed to say, *Well, I know better now.*

Mischievously, Markham added, 'And let's not forget what you said last night about Clifton returning to the theatre to carry out some sort of ritual . . . an *exorcism* perhaps.'

'*An exorcism!*'

Doyle was too steady and conscientious a driver to crash the car, but he was certainly catching flies.

'That was jus' to distract the lass . . . keep her mind off things cos of how she were blaming herself,' the DS replied loftily. 'An' anyway' — with increased hauteur — 'black magic don' explain why he copped it. Dimples said it deffo weren't one of them erotic sex game thingummies.'

Markham repressed a shudder as he recalled the staged sex game which had played a prominent role in their recent investigation at the local health centre when a suspect had been discovered dead in what looked like the throes of autoerotic asphyxiation.

Time to stop teasing the DS.

'True, Sergeant,' he rejoined seriously. 'It doesn't bring us any nearer to the identity of Mr Clifton's killer.' He chafed his hands together, but they were still numb. 'And I just don't see his death as a random assault or revenge killing.'

'But you *do* think it all goes back to the Mickey Willett case, boss?' Doyle was nothing if not persistent.

'Yes, I do, Doyle.' Markham spoke with grave deliberation. 'My bet is that Mr Clifton was blackmailing the killer because he'd made the connection between him and Mickey's disappearance all those years ago—'

'And because he guessed Shirley and Enid were murdered for somehow getting too close to the secret,' finished the young DC eagerly.

'That's my best-case scenario, yes.'

'Wotcha gonna tell 'em at the press conference then, guv?' Noakes piped up.

'As little as possible, naturally.' The DI grimaced. 'We'll float the idea of a botched burglary interrupted by Mr Clifton.'

'Make 'em think it were potheads an' nutters?'

'Now you're speaking the DCI's language, Sergeant.' He sighed. 'I want the vultures kept away from the Willett investigation for as long as possible.'

'If we make it sound like CID's coming down hard on the druggies and psychos, the top brass will look good,' Doyle observed cannily.

The DI couldn't deny the truth of this observation.

Let Operation Butter Up commence.

They were drawing into the station car park.

'D'you think Sidney'll sic a profiler on us?'

Markham suppressed a groan at Doyle's enquiry.

'Not if I can help it,' he replied, thinking of the bearded wonder Sidney had produced in their last investigation.

'We keep saying "he",' the young DC suddenly observed, 'but what if the killer's a woman?'

'Shirley an' Enid would've been no contest, 'specially if they were out of it,' Noakes put in. 'An' Dimples said if the killer snuck up behind Clifton, a woman could've done it.'

Markham thought of the female dancers with their sinewy, whipcord-lean physiques. Then there was Cathy Gould with her rodential sideways manner of looking at people and her vicious tongue. From what he had just witnessed, there was a touch of the she-wolf in each of them.

'I'm not ruling anything out,' he told his colleagues. 'As things stand, they're all in the frame.'

* * *

To nobody's great surprise, they found Kate Burton waiting in CID.

Displaying unusual tact, Noakes towed Doyle off to the canteen.

'Back in ten, guv,' he said with a benevolent glance at his fellow DS.

Burton blinked, clearly taken aback at this affability.

Markham beckoned her into his office, giving his radiator the usual futile thump to see if it might rumble into life. Nothing doing, so he plugged in his trusty heater, noting that Burton still looked distinctly peaky.

'Noakesy's desperate to debrief our young friend on last night's amorous adventures,' he said easily, aware that Burton's feminist hackles might well rise at any notion of *her* requiring extra TLC. 'Plus, he'll be wanting to take advantage of the Friday Special.'

She looked as blank as if he were referring to some arcane piece of station lore.

'Fried egg, bacon and tomatoes,' he translated kindly before adding, 'Take a seat, Kate, and tell me how you're feeling.'

'Much better thanks, sir.'

But he noticed how tightly she gripped the arms of her chair. Also, she was back to that thing of sitting on the edge of the seat. 'With her bum half on and half off,' as Noakes put it, 'like she's waiting to take dictation or summat.'

'I wanted you to take some time off, you know,' he said mildly.

'I'm much better out of the house . . . 'stead of brooding, sir.'

Again, he wondered if Noakes was right about there being 'trouble at t'mill'. But something in her wary, defensive posture prevented him asking the question. Inwardly, he reproached himself for not taking the bull by the horns and asking her directly what was wrong, as though this somehow made him a poor boss. And yet, obscurely, he felt he was paying her a compliment by not pushing. As someone who placed a high premium on privacy (one reason why he'd been dubbed 'His High and Mightiness' by the rank and file), he considered it a sign of respect not to pry.

But he was concerned that her career appeared to have stalled.

He really must take the plunge and have her over to the Sweepstakes. Previous invitations had met with a curious reluctance that he was at a loss to understand, though he guessed she was never entirely at ease in purely social situations as opposed to CID jollification down the pub once a case was closed.

Perhaps now she and Noakes were growing closer — 'Peace in Our Time', as Olivia called their détente — the grizzled veteran would be able to get to the bottom of it. Though hopefully without trampling all over her sensibilities with his big size twelves.

In the meantime, she had whipped out her notebook and pen — *dammit*, just like she was waiting to take dictation!

'Oh, no need for that, Kate,' he said.

Reluctantly, she put them down on the desk between them, clearly disconcerted at being deprived of her armour.

'I just want to hear your impressions of the case so far,' he said lightly.

Was it his imagination or did she look relieved that her personal life was off the agenda?

For the next quarter of an hour, they reviewed the investigation, Markham impressed as ever by her lucid and concise manner of summing up developments.

It would be a wrench whenever she decided to move on from his team but listening to her quietly competent exposition made him realize it would be pure selfishness to stand in her way.

'I want you to check out personal details with Noakes this afternoon when we meet up with the Bluebell's staff,' he said.

'D'you think that's why those personnel records were stolen from the office?' she asked eagerly. 'To cover up someone's real ID?'

'That's what I thought to begin with, Kate. But now I'm wondering if it wasn't something more incriminating lurking in there.' He made a moue of distaste. 'I wouldn't be surprised if the Bluebell's management kept details of any . . . missteps or departures from the straight and narrow—'

'By way of insurance, you mean? To keep them in line?'

'Something like that, yes.' Markham was pleased to see the animation returning to her face. 'It may well be that personal details held by the school aren't accurate and they haven't run proper ID and safeguarding checks—'

'But we can get hold of that data no problem and the killer knows that.' The wan cheeks were now flushed with excitement. 'There must be other stuff in there as well that he doesn't want us to know about. Stuff he's afraid we'll find out.'

'*Exactly*.'

There was something inexorable about the DI's expression as he said this. Something that Noakes was wont to describe as 'immoveable force meets immoveable object'. It made her shiver.

Markham mistook her reaction and reached down to turn up the dial on his heater.

'Sorry it's so blasted cold in here today, Kate.'

'I'm sure things'll warm up at the press conference, sir,' she quipped.

The DI raised his eyes to heaven.

'I'm putting you on man-to-man marking there, Kate.' Or should he have said person-to-person? At any rate, she was grinning broadly. 'If you see Noakesy revving up to take a pop at Gavin Conors, for example . . .'

'Don't worry, boss. I'll get between them!'

He laughed at that then, 'Talk of the devil!'

There was the clump of feet directly outside along with an unmistakeable aroma of grease.

The thought of pallid fried egg and bright red bacon made Markham feel as though his gullet and stomach were doing flipflops. From the queasy look Kate Burton directed at her plastic cup of diuretic coffee, she was experiencing similar intimations of nausea.

Noakes, however, was a man restored.

'Nothing beats a full English,' he announced happily, while Markham wondered if there was any chance of passing off the congealed egg yolk on his wingman's tie as some kind of heraldic emblem. Ex-Parachute Regiment, perhaps?

'Right,' he said, with more than a hint of the condemned man about him, 'let's get it over with.'

* * *

'So, in the event, we "got away with it",' Markham told Olivia and their friend Matthew Sullivan as the three enjoyed fish and chips at the kitchen table in the Sweepstakes.

The other two chuckled, recognizing the catchphrase of ghastly Barry Lynch, the station's oleaginous press officer.

'No outbursts from George, then?' Olivia enquired, while picking daintily at her battered cod.

'By some miracle, he stuck to the party line.' Markham's face darkened. 'Though Gavin Conors was his usual snippy self . . . needling away about "loss of public confidence in the police" . . . people not bothering to report burglaries because we're more interested in cyber hate crime, yada yada yada.' He contemplated the chip under his knife as if he wished DCI Sidney could be despatched so easily. 'Luckily, Kate leaped into the breach and began rattling off statistics to show how we're throwing all available resources at violent crime.'

'Did it do the trick?' Sullivan asked.

'Well, she took some of the heat off. But Conors had clearly got wind of the Mickey Willett investigation being re-opened.' Markham pushed away the plate with his supper only half-eaten. 'Which means someone in CID is leaking inside information.'

Like Kate Burton earlier, Olivia shivered at the implacable expression on her lover's face.

'Maybe it was accidental,' she said comfortingly, 'or the journos somehow got onto it because your cold-case people were rounding up local villains, that kind of thing.'

'No, I think it was more than that,' Markham said meditatively. 'Conors asked right out if we had any reason to believe the Bluebell deaths were linked with the disappearance of a local teenager in nineteen ninety-nine.' Getting up to make coffee, he added, 'We gave it the usual . . . "no reason at this stage to think there's a connection", but you could tell Sidney was livid. He brought out the playbook of platitudes, but his eczema gave the game away . . . flared up so badly that by the time we finished, he looked like some kind of crustacean.' He shook his head. 'No, someone's been blabbing.'

'So now you've got a mole hunt to worry about, on top of everything else.' Sullivan was sympathetic.

'Let's just say I hope Sidney gets to them before I do,' came the rejoinder.

The other two exchanged looks.

'How'd it go with the alibis?' Olivia asked.

'Up against a brick wall, Liv.' Markham was fussy about his coffee and set about preparing their drinks with the same elegant precision that characterized all his movements. 'Robyn DiAngelo and Anton Bhaer were having supper together at her place.'

'Marvellous names,' Sullivan murmured.

'Vivienne Sansom — she's the one Doyle says is like Darcey Bussell — was taking a yoga class at Body Works . . . Mmm,' he inhaled appreciatively as a fragrant aroma filled the air. 'And the Goulds were virtuously ensconced drinking cocoa in front of the television.'

'What about Bad Doug?'

Sullivan's lips quirked. '*Bad Doug*? And who might that be?'

'Councillor Callaghan's other half,' Markham grimaced. 'Property developer with a finger in every pie and Sidney's crony to boot.'

'*Ah*.' There was a world of comprehension in that one syllable.

'Strictly speaking, he's off limits, but reliable intel places him at the Black Bull . . . with a blonde at least twenty years younger than his lady wife.'

'Nice work if you can get it,' Sullivan grinned, while Olivia bestowed a mock frown.

The assistant head's double life had caused no end of trouble in a previous murder investigation centred on Hope Academy, leading him to be suspected of having been romantically involved with the assistant head who then turned up dead. But those days were behind him now, and the faintly careworn expression of old was finally gone for good.

A thought struck Olivia.

'What about Fred Stroud?'

'Home on his lonesome by all accounts.' Markham placed a steaming espresso and hot milk in front of their guest. 'Thanks for finding that out on the q.t. for me, Mat. I didn't want to make a big deal of it.'

'No worries.' Sullivan sipped his coffee, while Markham organized drinks for himself and Olivia. Something in his host's expression alerted him to a possible fly in the ointment. And his instinct proved correct.

'It turns out Mr Stroud *did* teach some drama at the Bluebell a while back, when he was doing his PGCE at university . . . Apparently, this was when Shirley Bastin's aunt Rose was running the show.'

'I didn't know that.' Sullivan looked surprised. 'It's not on his CV, but then he might not have thought it worth putting down if it was just a flash in the pan.'

'People don't always bother mentioning casual jobs or stuff that was just short-term.' Olivia shrugged, but she looked troubled.

'The point is, Mr Stroud must have realized it was relevant,' Markham observed levelly.

'Not necessarily.' Sullivan had never been afraid to argue his corner — or that of a colleague. It had made him an invaluable sounding board over the years. 'As far as he knew, when you spoke to him you were just checking out an unexplained death . . . No reason for him to talk about his student days before he even got together with Shirley.'

'Hmm.'

'And it's not as if you'd mentioned this missing teenager case,' Sullivan continued. 'So he had no reason to think you'd be interested in ancient history.'

It was still a loose end. And loose ends made Markham uneasy. Though supposing Fred Stroud was somehow implicated, there was surely no way he could have abstracted those personnel records from the Bluebell.

'D'you happen to know what he was up to yesterday afternoon, Mat?'

'PPA,' came the prompt reply.

By now, Markham was thoroughly conversant with educational acronyms. Planning, preparation and assessment activities.

In other words, free time.

'Did anyone see him?'

'He'd have been in his form room or the drama studio.'

'Could he have left the school site?'

'It's possible.' Now Sullivan looked troubled. 'But we rather frown on it, and anyway people are supposed to sign out.' He put down his cup. 'Could this be significant, Gil?'

'Hard to say at this stage.' Markham was carefully non-committal but inwardly resolved to take Kate Burton through yesterday afternoon once again. Easy, with all the hustle and bustle she had described, for someone to bypass the signing-in process.

'Anyway,' he declared, anxious to dispel the cloud that had darkened their evening, 'enough shop talk. There's the memorial service for Shirley and Enid tomorrow . . . Seeing all the suspects will no doubt fire up my "little grey cells" to some purpose!'

And amid much laughter, the talk moved to other things.

But throughout their chatter the cloud remained. Markham felt as though it would never lift until the Bluebell killer was unmasked.

10. WIDER STILL AND WIDER

Saturday, 11 January saw a continuation of the bitterly cold weather, this time accompanied by mournfully gusting winds.

'Makes me think of Halloween and witches getting ready to ride their broomsticks,' Olivia mused, piece of toast in hand, as she surveyed the dreary day outside. 'You had another restless night, Gil,' she added, watching Markham drink his scalding hot black coffee.

'More weird dreams, dearest,' he said. 'It's like that dance school's put some kind of hex on me. The other night it was Clay Clifton's face . . .'

'And this time?'

'The strangest thing . . . I dreamed there was this person obsessed with returning to the house where they'd been happy as a child . . . so they could relive the golden times . . .'

'Man or woman?'

'I never saw a face . . . It was just this figure . . . But I could sense they'd been desperately unhappy most of their adult life . . . That's why they wanted to possess this place at all costs.'

'Sounds rather a touching fairy story,' she murmured. 'A return to lost youth.'

'But that's where it turned dark,' he went on, with something of the same shadow from the dream touching his face, 'because murder was the only way to get their hands on the house.'

'Ah . . . the owner wouldn't sell?' Olivia was intrigued.

'That's right . . . an old woman.' He shuddered. 'I didn't see her being murdered but I just *knew* that's what had happened . . . The killer pulled it off somehow and no one ever guessed . . .'

'They got the house then?'

'Yes . . . reliving their childhood over and over in this never-ending loop.'

Markham laughed shamefacedly. 'Just one of my crazy dreams, Liv. Like something out of Dostoevsky. God knows what it all means.'

Olivia leaned into him. 'Sounds very Hansel and Gretel-ish,' she said lightly. 'Y'know, the enchanted house under an evil spell. Your mind was running on the Bluebell . . . Shirley and Enid being murdered because of secrets there that someone wants to keep hidden.'

She was relieved to see some of the strain leave her lover's face. Though he rarely opened up about his own childhood experiences, she knew they had left a deep and lasting scar that would never fully heal. This blighted innocence, along with the loss of a younger brother to drink and drugs, gave his tale of a lost domain added poignancy. As though in those night-time hours he'd tried not only to find the meaning in the Bluebell case but also to find his own way back to a vanished realm of unspoiled bliss.

Watching Markham closely, Olivia saw him make a visible effort to shake off the grasp of his nocturnal spectres.

'It's the memorial service for Shirley and Enid this afternoon,' he said. 'Bromgrove Rise Methodist Church.'

'I'll be there,' she said.

'Thanks, sweetheart. Kate's going to have a word with the minister this morning, so he can include prayers for Clay Clifton.'

'What about afterwards?' Her lips quirked. 'George will be disappointed if the thing isn't done properly.'

Markham sighed.

'You mean he'll be hoping for an all-you-can-eat buffet. Well, the language school's letting them do hot drinks and food in one of the conference rooms . . . Some of the parents are setting up in there this morning.' He hesitated. 'I wonder if I could ask a favour, love.'

'Name it.'

'Would you mind giving Natalie a lift? Noakesy's sent a text to say she'd like to go with you.'

'*As if*!' Olivia gave a mirthless chuckle. 'Methinks it's a case of somebody's arm being twisted.'

'Well, he thinks you're a good influence on her, sweetheart.'

'Muriel doesn't,' she retorted flatly.

'She'll sheath her claws if it means prising Natalie away from those undesirables at the Krazyhouse.'

'Great.' A mock frown. 'So that's what I'm reduced to — chaperone patrol!'

'You know how protective Noakes is. In fact . . .'

'What, Gil?'

'He's even more so these days . . . as if whenever he looks at Natalie, he's afraid . . .'

'*Afraid*?'

'Yes. That she'll screw everything up . . . get herself into trouble or something like that.'

'If some of our sixth-formers are anything to go by, she's not exactly one of those flowers "born to blush unseen", Gil.'

'I know, I know . . . I gather Chris Carstairs has dug her out of a few holes.'

'So, George is bound to be disillusioned in the end.'

'It's just this feeling I have . . . The other night when we were round at their place—'

'For "kitchen sups",' Olivia trilled in a deadly accurate impersonation of their hostess.

Markham grinned.

'Right . . . Well, I picked up signs of tension. No,' he went on before she could utter some withering sarcasm about the Noakeses' domestic set-up, 'nothing to do with Muriel carrying on like something out of *Downton Abbey* or Noakesy making sheep's eyes at you. It was the way each of them kept checking out Natalie when they thought the other wasn't looking.'

'Maybe that's because she was being bloody rude, Gil . . . As in making no effort.'

'Hmm. No, it wasn't that.' He gave an exasperated laugh. 'I can't put my finger on it . . . But it was as if they both saw someone else standing behind her and it spooked them.'

Olivia stared at him.

'Now you *are* getting deep.' She swallowed the last mouthful of toast. 'You'll be telling me next it's the *Noakeses'* house that is haunted . . . or Natalie's really one of the undead.' Slapping his arm playfully, she concluded, 'A nice way to start the day!'

'Well, I could be reading too much into it,' Markham admitted.

'*I'll* say you are . . . George isn't exactly Mr Barrett of Wimpole Street!'

'Mr *Who*? Oh yes, now I remember . . . one of those incestuous Victorian fathers who wanted to lock up his daughter . . .'

'That's the one . . . She had to elope in the end.'

Markham knew when he was beaten.

'This case is making me see horrors everywhere. But still,' he stared down at the dregs of his coffee, 'there's something not quite right with them.'

'Tell you what, dearest. I'll see if I can draw Natalie out a bit . . . Most likely it's nothing more than domestic ructions over some spotty nerk or other.'

Gently, she took the mug from him.

'What's your plan for today — I mean before the memorial service?'

'I'm having a quick catch-up with Jim McLeod. I missed seeing him yesterday because of the business with Clay Clifton.'

'Maybe he'll have something for you on the Mickey Willett investigation.'

'To be honest,' Markham pulled a comic face, 'I'm just looking forward to a bitch fest about Sidney.'

Olivia chuckled.

'Will your lord and master be attending the memorial service?'

'No, thank god. He's decided a lowly DI can safely be left to do the honours.'

Olivia pulled a face. 'It'd be different if poor Mr Clifton was a "sleb". Then there'd be no stopping Sidney.'

Markham endeavoured to be charitable. 'He's probably heavily committed elsewhere, Liv.'

'Heavily committed to the golf club, you mean!' she observed sarcastically.

'Plus, it's meant to be low-key. The DCI being there would only attract attention.'

She pursed her lips. 'It's out in the open that Shirley and Enid were murdered, right?'

'Well, we haven't released any details . . . just said their deaths were being treated as suspicious.'

'The *Gazette*'ll want more than that before very much longer.'

'Sidney's specified a "controlled release of information".'

'Good luck with that.'

'Dimples is doing the PM on Clay tomorrow.' Markham looked slightly sheepish. 'I said I'd attend. And afterwards, he's going to review the findings for Enid.'

'*On a Sunday? Oh, Gil.*'

'I'll make it up to you, Liv. We can go for a walk up Bromgrove Rise later. You know you always love it there. Don't you say it always makes you think of *Wuthering Heights*?'

'There'll be plenty of wuthering up there if the weather continues like this,' she replied looking out at the landscaped gardens where clustering elms and shrubs writhed in something approaching a frenzy. 'Our climate is going bonkers . . . Frost one minute and now *this*.' She smiled at Markham. The roguish, generous smile that had made him fall in love with her. 'I'm just glad it's not a school day. Us teachers dread the wind, you know. It always sends the kids a bit crazy.'

He could only hope and pray their hidden killer wasn't affected likewise.

* * *

The exterior of Bromgrove Rise Methodist Church had all the allure of a factory, Markham thought to himself later that day as he waited for his colleagues outside the gable-ended front entrance.

It was a squat building shoehorned between terraced houses on either side, its brickwork a dull red which put him in mind of chopped liver. Not exactly calculated to raise hearts and minds to God . . .

Certainly Noakes was unimpressed.

'Bit of a dump,' he pronounced, slouching over to join Markham and eyeing the architecture with distaste.

The DI was relieved to see Noakes had made an effort with his appearance, no doubt under duress. His Columbo-style mac topped some sort of sober sub fusc which looked reasonably respectable. And the tie wasn't too jarring if you ignored the peculiar motif of what looked like little halberds.

Burton and Doyle joined them on the pavement, the epitome of thrusting young detectives, immaculately suited and booted.

'Good crowd, is it?' Noakes grunted at the boss.

'Fairish,' the DI said. He cleared his throat. 'I think some kind of dance tribute is going to form part of the proceedings.'

Noakes boggled.

'*Dance tribute*!' he guffawed. 'You're having us on, guv.'

Then, as Markham remained impenetrably grave, he let rip. 'You mean there's gonna be prancing up an' down when the vicar's doing prayers?'

The other two looked equally taken aback.

'Don't worry, Sergeant.' The DI's tone was ironic. 'I'm sure audience participation won't be compulsory.'

''S a bit, well, *tacky*, boss,' Doyle ventured. 'I mean, it's meant to be, like, a funeral—'

'Not *Come on down*.' Noakes almost spat the gameshow catch phrase.

'We'll weather it,' Markham said drily. He turned to Kate. 'I'm sure I can count on you to keep these two in order.'

'Absolutely, sir. It's probably just going to be, er, *tableaux* or something tasteful like that.' As opposed to jigging in the aisles. 'The family wouldn't want anything undignified . . . And it's kind of appropriate, what with their line of work and everything.'

Noakes looked as though he needed convincing. As far as he was concerned, 'dancer types' were capable of anything.

Nevertheless, after Burton's fine little pavane of reason and good sense, her fellow DS simmered down sufficiently to walk into church with only a few muttered words of protest under his breath.

The interior of the building was no more prepossessing than the outside, reminding Markham of council chambers down at the Town Hall.

Rows of dark wooden benches were overlooked by a substantial wooden pulpit with twin lancet windows of plain leaded glass on either side. Beneath the pulpit was a low platform where two groups of teenage girls posed awkwardly in tunics and practice skirts.

'No lads, then,' Noakes mumbled as they slipped into their seats at the back. He surveyed the groups of all-female performers. 'Wouldn't be seen dead, I s'pose.'

Burton shot him a warning glance and he subsided.

In the event, as Doyle put it afterwards, it wasn't too 'cringe-making'. The DI even found something touching about the simple patterns traced to the accompaniment of an organ playing Albinoni's *Adagio*. More than the prayers intoned by the elderly minister and a sincere but stilted eulogy by one of the parents, it gave him a sense of hope that the souls of the dead waited somewhere in peace and quietness and rest.

'It's what heaven must be like,' as Olivia put it after the service when they were able to exchange a brief word. At least it fitted the mood of the minister's text: *Blessed are the dead who may rest from their labours.*

As ever when gathered inside a church, the identities of the individual mourners seemed to Markham to be almost rubbed out so that they formed an amorphous mass.

He noticed, however, that Robyn DiAngelo and Vivienne Sansom — chic even in their mourning attire of belted wool dresses, peplum jackets and knee-high boots — sat far apart and studiously ignored each other.

Anton Bhaer, equally chic in a vintage frock coat with military-style frogging, sat with the Goulds, who were restless and fidgety throughout the service. The young dancer was attentive to them, at one point almost propping Cathy Gould up when she sagged against him. Dave Gould's appearance had deteriorated alarmingly in the short time since Markham had last seen him. Outside the church at the end of the service, he looked at the DI and his team as though he was seeing them from a long way away.

'That bloke's got summat on his mind,' Noakes observed once they'd made their way out of the receiving line.

'Like his ex-wife, ex-mother-in-law and one of the teachers being murdered, sarge,' Doyle murmured.

Noakes mimed a clip round the lughole. 'Nah, smart-arse,' he said, 'summat more'n that.' He ran a finger irritably round the inside of his collar as though it was throttling him. 'Didn't pay the daughter any notice neither . . . left the German lad to take care of her.'

'How many times do I have to tell you, Sergeant? He's not German.' Markham sighed, beckoning the team away to a discreet distance. 'They all use professional stage names and that accent's pure Lancashire.'

'Looks foreign to me,' Noakes retorted stubbornly. 'Jus' needs a Panzer to go with his colonel's get-up.'

At that moment, Markham caught sight of Fred Stroud standing with Olivia and Mat Sullivan. His lazy Rhett Butler-esque charm was conspicuous by its absence on this occasion, however, with neither of his colleagues seemingly able to raise a smile.

'No love lost between our Cath and that one,' Noakes commented sotto voce, as he watched the venomous looks a bedraggled-looking Cathy Gould was darting at her mother's former boyfriend. Following his daughter's eyes, Dave Gould too looked less than pleased to see the well-built teacher among the congregation.

'Is there any possibility our teacher friend could have paid a visit to the Bluebell on Thursday, Kate?' Markham asked.

'What, you mean somehow slipped into the building, sir?' she asked, startled. 'Wouldn't he have been teaching then?'

'According to Mat Sullivan he had PPA—'

'Planning, preparation and assessment.'

The DI had forgotten how she loved her acronyms.

'Correct, Kate. So technically he was free . . . Could've snuck out of Hope without anyone knowing he'd gone.'

'What about afternoon registration?'

'They do that after lunch instead of the end of the day,' Noakes put in.

'So, afternoon PPA means nobody had tabs on him.' Her eyes followed Stroud's tall figure as he moved away. 'He's difficult to miss in a crowd, sir, but it *was* absolute chaos that afternoon . . .'

'You think he's the one Clifton planned to meet, guv?' Noakes's gaze too was speculative.

'Maybe they met that afternoon . . . Or perhaps there was a telephone conversation when Mr Clifton was on his break and they arranged to meet later in the theatre once everyone was gone . . . Clifton would have let him back in.'

'Oh yeah, they're all keyholders, aren't they?' Doyle commented thoughtfully.

'Yes, and I plan to keep it that way,' Markham said. 'Our killer's "centre of gravity" is the Bluebell . . . For him it all begins and ends in the school. We have to hope we can corner him there.'

'Like a rat in a trap,' Noakes said with lip-smacking relish.

'I've advised Dave and Cathy Gould to beef up security in the flat,' Markham continued, 'but we'll leave the other buildings alone for now.'

'He's a big bugger all right.' Noakes's mind was still running on Fred Stroud. 'Age-wise, nowt to say he weren't around the same time as Mickey Willett.'

Markham nodded. 'He did his teacher training here, and apparently he was a drama coach at the Bluebell when Shirley's aunt ran the place.'

Noakes's eyes narrowed. 'He didn't tell us that.'

'No, but it all happened long before he got involved with Shirley . . . and remember, we weren't even using the "M" word when we spoke to him at school.' The DI's gaze was abstracted, as though he was revolving multiple options in his mind.

'When'd he tell you this about doing drama at the Bluebell, guv?' Noakes asked curiously.

'I called him yesterday afternoon, left a message asking him to ring me back.' There was something unyielding about Markham's tone. 'I said we were looking at three potential murders and enquired if there was anything he wanted to add to his previous statement.'

'Looks like it concentrated his mind all right,' Doyle murmured.

Noakes scowled. 'That or he thought someone else might tell us.'

'Either way, it makes him a "person of interest",' the DI concluded. 'Not least as our other suspects are alibied for the time of Mr Clifton's death whereas he has no one to vouch for him.'

'Wotcha want to do about him, guv?' Noakes asked.

'Covert surveillance courtesy of DI Carstairs.' Markham smiled thinly. 'It wouldn't do to let the DCI know we're looking in the direction of a long-serving teacher at Hope.'

'God, no.' Doyle whistled. 'He'd go into orbit.'

'Quite.'

'There's that awful woman,' Burton said suddenly.

'Which woman?'

'Aline Hosking . . . The mother who's always bending their ears about her equally poisonous brat.'

The sudden flare of emotion was unusual for Kate Burton. Feeling Markham's eyes on her, she blushed.

'Sorry, sir. She reminds me of my mum's best friend when I was little. I had to call her "Auntie Pat" . . . Anyway, she had this nicey-nicey way of going on, but she was a complete bitch underneath it all . . . Always talking her horrible Eithne up when we did ballet after school while making me feel like I had two left feet.'

Noakes was sympathetic. 'Know the type, luv. There's a couple of friends of the missus make me feel like that . . . all soft an' smarmy but sticking the knife in 'bout us not being as posh as them.'

The DI did his best not to laugh as the two sergeants smiled awkwardly at each other and shuffled their feet. At this rate, they'd be doing therapy together!

'Should we be looking at Ms Hosking more closely, Kate?' he asked, watching the hard-featured bottle blonde as she zeroed in on Anton Bhaer, who seemed decidedly uncomfortable with the encounter.

'Well, she definitely wasn't on good terms with Shirley. And I get the feeling she does a lot of trouble-making . . . I heard one of the other parents call her the world's biggest stirrer when they thought she wasn't listening.' The DS flicked the fringe out of her eyes. 'But it's hard to see where she'd fit into the Mickey Willett scenario.'

'She could've been around,' Doyle said with a swift appraising glance. 'In her forties now, so would have been early twenties then.'

The DI became aware the team was attracting a certain amount of attention.

'I think we should get off now,' he said.

'To the eats?' Noakes had the look of a man ready to do justice to whatever spread awaited them back at the language school.

'We'll show our faces,' Markham said, 'out of courtesy.' He eyed the DS resignedly. 'But go easy on the canapés and cakes,' he said. 'Don't want them thinking we've no idea how to behave.'

'I c'n have a catch-up with our Nat,' the other said happily.

Doyle looked somewhat apprehensive at these words, doubtless recollecting close encounters of a not altogether comfortable kind with the fair Natalie at various police shindigs.

But Doyle could take care of himself, Markham reflected. And with Noakes on guard duty, his daughter was unlikely to put the moves on the young DC.

Actually, he thought, watching Natalie tag along behind Olivia and Matthew Sullivan, the girl was by no means unattractive and there was something positively graceful about her gait. Were it not for the sulky look on her face and the cleavage-baring blouse, her appearance might almost be said to possess a certain distinction. It would be interesting to see how she fared in the dance studio when the school re-opened next week.

* * *

The rest of that weekend passed uneventfully, the formaldehyde horrors of Clay Clifton's PM effectively banished by a long bracing ramble with Olivia through the undulating stretches of furze and gorse that criss-crossed the sandy paths of Bromgrove Rise. Watching the waving grasses reminded Markham of the young dancers' softly circuiting movements at the memorial service. But there was nothing discordant or disturbing in the memory, and on Sunday night he slept well.

* * *

Monday, 13 January dawned bright and crisp, the gusting winds gone as though they had never been.

The Bluebell Dance Studio presented a cheerful enough prospect when Markham parked outside it, with dancers of various ages, shapes and sizes trooping through its doors.

It almost looked as though Clay Clifton's murder was proving good for business, the DI reflected before reproaching himself for such a cynical thought.

He sat there enjoying the procession of students until he became aware of Kate Burton rapping insistently on the car window.

He snapped back to reality and jumped out.

'What is it, Kate?'

'Robyn DiAngelo hasn't shown up for work, sir.'

Cold dread in the pit of his stomach.

'She hasn't phoned in, which they're supposed to do if they're sick so Cathy can sort cover.'

'Have you got an address for her?'

'Yes, sir.'

'Get in,' he said. 'And while you're at it, give Noakes a call and tell him to meet us there.'

What was it he'd said about the Bluebell being the epicentre of this case?

Now he was hideously afraid the ripples were spreading outwards.

11. RUNAWAY TRAIN

When they arrived at Robyn DiAngelo's terraced property in Quarry Street close to the town centre, Markham felt a sensation of ice, sending chills up and down his spine as he took in the gaggle of uniforms and SOCOs.

Noakes detached himself from the group and came over to join them.

A distant, almost stony quality came into Markham's voice. 'I take it the news isn't good, Sergeant.'

'She's dead, guv,' Noakes came right out with it. 'Battered to death with a portable *barre* thingy . . . She had a practice space in the garden shed . . . Looks like the killer went in there an' undid one of the steel tubes . . .'

Something throbbed across the DI's right cheek. Like a welt, it stood out livid against his olive complexion. Burton watched, fascinated. It seemed to her almost as though an invisible finger was sinking its nail into the DI's skin.

In fact, Markham felt something akin to despair, as though events were moving too fast for him. Like an express train that he couldn't jump off.

None of the suspects in the case resembled the archetypal serial killer, slipping with hunchbacked malignancy through the dark.

But the hunchback had come for Robyn DiAngelo, breaking through the outer mask as though a homicidal rage had rent the fabric of the killer's psyche.

Which of the Bluebell family was harbouring a twilight interior realm of hidden horror? Which of them had a personality so distorted, a scale of values so warped that human life counted for nothing in their eyes?

'Let's take a look inside, Sergeant,' was all the DI said, however.

'Dimples is upstairs, guv. The vic were having a kip when it happened.' Noakes's usual expression of slit-eyed bolshiness softened. 'Jus' never woke up, poor kid.'

'Any signs of burglary? Sexual assault?'

'Nowt like that, boss.'

So, Robyn DiAngelo was killed for what she knew, thought Markham. Something she chose not to tell the police.

* * *

Markham had been expecting a minimalist and streamlined décor, but the dancer's two-bedroom house was chintzy and cluttered, suggesting that she was at heart an old-fashioned girl.

'Next of kin?' the DI enquired, as they climbed the narrow stairs which led to the first-floor master bedroom.

'Dad died a few years back. Mum's in the Hydrangea Care Home. Rheumatoid arthritis . . . There's a sister, but she's on holiday in the States . . . sent a postcard,' Noakes replied succinctly.

They found Dr Davidson and DC Doyle in the master bedroom, which looked out onto the street.

The latest victim did indeed look as though she was sleeping, dark hair spilling across dusky pink pillows. Though when the pathologist gently tilted her head to one side, a mass of blood and brain tissue showed that her head had been stoved in.

Seeing Kate Burton swallow convulsively at the sight, Markham felt the usual pang. No doubt it was horribly un-PC and backward, but a strong protective instinct made him want to shield her from such grisly realities. Not that she would thank him for it, of course.

As though by common consent, the group moved over to the window, Dimples gesturing to the SOCOs who promptly wheeled screens around the bed.

'How is it, Markham, that I never ask your mob to gown up like the rest of us?' the pathologist enquired drily, gesturing to his own portly paper-suited physique. 'I'm sure we're breaking every rule in the book.'

'What the DCI don' know won't hurt him,' Noakes retorted with ferrety glee. 'An' any road, we ain't got time to be fannying around with disposable coveralls.' He blew out his cheeks contemptuously. 'Like we work in Greggs or summat.'

'Given how you rate their butties, would've thought you'd be up for that, sarge,' Doyle murmured mischievously.

The DS affected not to hear.

''Sides,' he continued, gesturing at a stocky figure busily taking photographs, 'Bri ain't going to snitch on us.'

'There's the little matter of contaminating the crime scene, Sergeant,' Dimples said heavily.

'Let's face it, doc,' Burton spoke up stoutly, 'like you always say, DNA transfer and cross-contamination mean it's anyone's guess at this stage.'

'Not entirely "pearls before swine" then, m'dear,' the pathologist boomed. 'Glad to know *someone's* taken my lesson to heart.'

Burton was clearly somewhat taken aback by her own temerity.

'That's not to say luminol won't give an idea how she died,' she said hastily.

'She got her head smashed in,' Noakes said grimly. 'An' we're gonna nail the fucker who did it.'

'Quite.' Though privately Markham felt they had never been further from identifying the killer.

'We gotta catch 'em in the act,' Noakes persisted, 'jus' like we allus do.'

At that moment, there was a commotion in the doorway heralding the arrival of two paramedics with a stretcher.

'Let's go downstairs,' the DI said. 'It's getting crowded up here.'

The red-wallpapered front living room was cosy but old-fashioned, with a glass cabinet on one wall displaying a collection of Lladró ballet figurines that had Noakes puckering his lips.

'Looks like she was majorly into the Russians,' Doyle said, scrutinizing titles on the cream bookshelves that ran from floor to ceiling on either side of the vintage fireplace. 'Baryshnikov, Nijinsky, Makarova, Nureyev—'

'Mighta known she'd have the hots for ole Rudolf Neveroff,' Noakes observed cheerfully before scowling as he observed the scene from the sashed window. 'Doyle, get rid of them gawpers outside, will you? It's not a bleeding free-for-all,' he muttered, 'with that poor lass upstairs barely cold.'

'While you're at it, Doyle,' Markham interposed smoothly, 'ask Dimples if we can have a rough time of death.'

The young DC had the look of Daniel venturing into the lions' den.

The DI laughed. 'The doc won't be pinned down, I know, but it's worth a shot.'

Doyle clumped out of the room, somehow more gangly than usual in the doll's house inhabited by Robyn.

On a low coffee table in front of the red two-seater damask sofa was a copy of the *Radio Times*. Markham noted that Robyn DiAngelo had circled her choice of programmes for an evening at home: *Pointless*, *Richard Osman's House of Games*, *Michael Portillo's Great British Railway Journeys* . . . Sadly, he glanced across at the television on its oak console. Just an old-fashioned girl beneath the vampish makeup and edgy outfits. No doubt planning a TV dinner after a day spent trying to turn clodhoppers into gazelles . . . a dinner she would never live to eat . . .

'Give them an inch and they take a bloody mile.' Noakes was glowering out of the window. 'Like it's a frigging soap opera. *Go on, get out of it*!'

'Take it easy, Sergeant,' Markham admonished him. 'You'll only give yourself a coronary . . . It's always the way with something like this.'

'Let's go into the kitchen,' Burton suggested. 'That way when the photogs turn up, they won't see us.'

'Good idea.' Markham led the way into the hall.

At that moment, the two stretcher-bearers appeared at the top of the stairs with their light burden in its body bag. The three detectives bowed their heads in respect as Robyn DiAngelo left her house for the last time.

Then they moved into the little galley kitchen, perching awkwardly on breakfast-bar stools. Through French windows standing ajar at the far end of the room, they could see a narrow strip of garden bordered by a flagged path leading to the garden shed.

Doyle reappeared.

'Dimples said nice try. He thinks she was killed some time last night.' Gingerly, he seated himself. 'SOCOs say our man was in and out like a ghost.' He gestured to the French windows. 'Jemmied the doors there and did the business in a matter of minutes.'

Methodical, clinical and forensically aware.

'D'you think she suffered?' Kate Burton's voice sounded rusty.

Noakes's eyes were kind as he took in the pinched white face, which at that moment had the distant look of someone worlds away.

'She won't have known a thing, luv.' He waved his pudgy fingers like a conjuror. 'It were all over in seconds.'

'We need to know Ms DiAngelo's precise movements since yesterday,' Markham said.

'Well,' Burton gathered herself with an effort, 'the last time *we* saw her was at the buffet after the memorial service.'

Noakes sniffed. 'Didn't think much to that . . . all them veggie things . . . spinach an' sushi . . . an' *black bean burgers*, for god's sake.'

'They're *dancers*, sarge,' Doyle grinned, 'health-conscious and all that.'

Another portentous sniff. 'Yeah, but they could have looked at the bigger picture . . . I mean, not everyone likes bird food.'

'We realize the veganistas are your least favourite people, Sergeant.' *And heaven knew there was plenty of competition for that top spot*, thought Markham. 'But if we could return to the matter in hand.'

'Yeah, right.' Not at all abashed, the DS parked his grievances about the bill of fare. 'DiAngelo an' the other scrawny one jus' picked at the grub.' He allowed himself the mandatory mental eye roll at such finickiness. 'They were still looking daggers an' then DiAngelo told the German lad she had to be somewhere else an' pushed off.'

'Think carefully, Noakes.' The DI fixed him with a level stare. 'Can you remember her exact words?'

The other thought hard for a moment.

'She said she had to get off cos she was meeting up with a friend.'

'Nothing about where this was?'

'Sorry, guv.' Noakes's hangdog features creased with the effort of remembering. 'I *think* she said something about a mate going abroad an' it was their last chance to see each other . . . summat like that.'

'Anything else?'

'Jus' that she'd check in with the Kraut when she got back.' Noakes looked slightly embarrassed. 'I weren't really concentrating, to be honest, boss.'

Too busy siphoning off any stray sausage rolls, or whatever the vegan equivalent might be, thought Markham. Aloud, he mused, 'We'll need to find out if she got back to Mr Bhaer or any of the other Bluebell staff after she saw her friend off or whatever it was they were doing.'

'D'you think the meeting with this friend's got anything to do with why she was killed, sir?' Doyle asked.

'Well, it looks as if something could have occurred between the memorial service and last night which made Ms DiAngelo a threat to the killer.' The DI contemplated the tiny back garden as though for inspiration. 'Either that or he already had her in his sights and was just waiting for the right moment to strike.'

It was a sobering thought. The predator stalking his prey at leisure before pouncing.

'What if she learned something and confronted the killer about it?' Burton was intent on her scenario. 'Maybe she told him she'd go to the police—'

'She could've given him the chance to turn himself in,' Doyle interrupted eagerly, 'or maybe even clear out altogether . . . leave the country or something like that . . .'

Now Noakes ran with it. 'Yeah . . . He could've strung her along . . . pretended he was dead sorry an' all that . . . then snuck back later that night to finish her off.'

'Robyn was in bed when she was attacked,' Burton mused. 'No sign of a struggle . . . so she must have been taken by surprise . . . Assuming there *had been* a confrontation with the killer, she was content to sleep on things and leave the police out of it . . .'

'In that case, he must have been sufficiently plausible and unthreatening that she lowered her defences,' Markham added.

'D'you think whatever she found out was connected to Mickey Willett, sir? Could she have been blackmailing the killer?'

'That's the million-dollar question, Doyle.' The welt on the DI's face had faded, but there was a haggardness about his expression that spoke of intense frustration. 'The secret, assuming there was one, could just as easily have related to any of the other victims — Shirley, Enid or Clay . . . And as for blackmail,' he thought of Robyn DiAngelo's vulpine little face on the pillow upstairs, all trace of avarice and earthiness wiped away in the moment of death, 'it's possible, of course . . .'

'Maybe the secret didn't relate directly to the killer,' Burton said hesitantly. 'Maybe it was about someone else . . . Or it could have been something she wasn't sure about—'

'And she asked the killer what she should do,' Doyle finished her sentence.

'Chuffing Nora.' Noakes's hair was now standing wildly on end as he alternately raked it and rubbed his chin in a comical two-step of unmitigated dismay. 'You two ain't 'xactly narrowing things down here! Don' tell me we're back to there being more'n one nutcase an' all that caper. *Jeez*.'

'I can't see a common thread.' The DI spoke as though to himself. 'But I'm sure there is one . . .'

'An' it all leads back to Mickey Willett,' Noakes said hopefully.

Markham nodded slowly. The missing teenager padded round the periphery of his subconscious with the subtlety of a cat, but try as he might, he could not grasp the phantom.

He came to a decision.

'Let's do a search of the house,' he said. 'Ms DiAngelo was a proud homeowner by the looks of things, so it's not as though we'll have to sift through all kinds of rubbish.'

Noakes was restive. 'What sort of stuff are we looking for, guv?'

'Anything that sheds light on her private life.' Markham stood up and the others clambered down from their bar stools. 'There's a little writing desk in that back room . . . Looks like she used it as a dining-cum-study area, so that's probably the best place to start.'

'Doyle and I can take that,' Burton said promptly to the evident dismay of the lanky redhead.

Noakes gave the younger man a sly wink behind her back. *Good luck*.

'Right, guv, reckon you an' me are on wardrobe duty.'

For the next twenty minutes, Robyn DiAngelo's house was silent save for the sound of drawers and cupboards opening and closing as the DI's team conducted their fingertip search.

Then there came the shout, 'Down here, boss!'

'What you got?' Noakes was out of breath and dusty from his fruitless rummaging through the upstairs regions.

'She had a fling with Dave Gould,' Doyle declared triumphantly, handing over a wodge of letters that still held traces of the dead woman's distinctive musky perfume.

Markham looked questioningly at Kate Burton.

'That's right, boss.' She shrugged her shoulders as though to say, *There's no accounting for taste*. 'Lasted around six months till he took up with someone else at the Bluebell.'

'No prizes for guessing who.' Now it was Noakes who was exultant. 'Has to be the one who looks like Darcey Whassername.'

'Vivienne Sansom.' Burton nodded. 'It would certainly account for the bad blood between them.'

'He's not exactly love's young dream,' Doyle put in, wrinkling his nose fastidiously.

'I suppose it's the familiar cliché,' Markham observed. 'Young women falling for the older boss.'

Burton was thoughtful. 'He was divorced from Shirley, so it's not like they were breaking up his marriage.' The pungent scent from the letters was making her feel slightly sick. 'He had no reason to mention it to us—'

'Apart from the fact that someone went an' clobbered his ex-missus an' sort-of mother-in-law,' her fellow DS interrupted darkly.

Burton shrugged. 'Sounds like things were quite free and easy between Dave and Shirley.'

'She still might not have liked him shitting on his own doorstep.' Noakes's louring expression remained unchanged. '*Dirty old man*. If my Nat ever—'

'Interesting that he didn't see fit to mention his romantic entanglements.' Markham cut his wingman off at the pass, only too aware of Noakes's prodigal daughter's sexual liberality. 'But perhaps understandable.'

'Shows he's got his secrets.' Noakes was not to be silenced.

'Like Fred Stroud keeping shtum about teaching at the Bluebell,' Burton pointed out. 'Didn't want to volunteer stuff in case it backfired.'

'You don't see Gould for Mickey Willett, though, do you, boss?' Doyle sounded doubtful. 'He'd have been, what, forty-odd when Mickey went missing . . . wouldn't have run with the same pack.'

'Could've been a Jimmy Savile scenario,' Noakes suggested.

'What, you think Gould's a *paedo*?' The DC was startled. 'Anyway, Willett was nineteen.'

'Coulda been Gould was after one of the other youngsters that hung round the Bluebell — one of them hipsters — an' Willett interfered somehow . . . got in Gould's way . . . queered his pitch.'

'Hmm.'

The DI contemplated the letters. There was something infinitely poignant about the way they'd been squirrelled away like a lovesick young girl's stash. Once again, he recalled Robyn DiAngelo's dead face, which had somehow lost the insolence it possessed when she was alive, seeming to be touched with more delicate, purer sentiments. Maybe that was the dancer's true face, he thought sadly, vowing in that instant to ensure he never forgot it.

'It puts Gould and Vivienne Sansom in the mix,' Burton said.

'You really think Little Miss Muffet coulda done this?' Noakes was open-mouthed.

'Why not?' She uttered the challenge with a touch of defiance. 'They were love rivals . . . And it wouldn't have required unusual strength.'

'Sort of thing a dancer would think of too,' Doyle said somewhat reluctantly, 'using a dance pole to attack her.'

'Knew where to find it an' all,' Noakes admitted.

'What about Cathy Gould?' the DC asked suddenly.

'What about 'er?' the older man grunted.

'Well, she could have resented DiAngelo for stepping into her mum's shoes. Or' — with a flash of inspiration — 'maybe she was frightened for her dad cos DiAngelo had something on him . . . something he didn't want to come out.'

'She ain't got the bottle.'

'I dunno about that, sarge.' The DC stuck to his guns. 'She may have a face like a wet weekend, but types like that can surprise you . . . Remember the Newman . . .'

Noakes shuddered as he recalled the startling conclusion to their investigations at the psychiatric hospital when the unlikeliest of suspects threw aside the mask of normality.

'Don' even go there, lad,' he muttered.

'It's a good point, Constable.'

The tall redhead blushed delightedly at this praise from the DI while Noakes looked on sardonically.

God, he's getting worse than Burton. The freaking Gilbert Markham Fan Club. They'll be setting summat up on Facebook next.

But despite these dire reflections, something indulgent came into Noakes's expression as he observed his younger colleagues.

'We can't rule anyone out at this stage,' Markham continued. 'Physical unattractiveness and a downtrodden appearance are no barometer of inner resolve.'

Noakes's bushy eyebrows shot up.

'Might as well say it coulda been Bad Doug or that batty mother,' he muttered.

'Well, Aline Hosking gets a few mentions in the letters,' Burton said apologetically. 'Looks like she's been a thorn in the flesh of teachers and management alike . . . Banging on about reporting them to the British Dance Council or some such.'

'On what grounds?' Markham asked quickly.

'God knows.' Burton pulled an expressive face. 'The letters don't say . . . From what I've seen of the woman, I think it was all about them not giving her precious daughter the right opportunities.'

'Daft bint with more money than sense.'

Burton looked as though she was strongly inclined to agree with Noakes's verdict.

'Nothing in there about Doug Callaghan or Fred Stroud, I suppose?' Markham's tone was resigned.

'Not a dicky bird, sir.' Burton hated to confirm it.

Which didn't mean either or both mightn't have crossed paths with Robyn DiAngelo.

His three subordinates were watching him expectantly.

Time to saddle up.

'I need to speak to Ms DiAngelo's mother,' the DI said simply.

'I'm with you, guv.' No way was Noakes letting the guvnor go through that ordeal on his own.

'Thanks, Noakesy.' Markham's voice was tight, 'After that, it'll be time to brief the DCI.'

His number two flinched, anticipating the wall-to-wall carnage of a set-to with Sidney.

'Me and Doyle will check in with Mr McLeod and the cold-case bods.' The DI tried to sound optimistic, despite the fact that nothing useful had emerged from the weekend conference with his old boss.

At that moment, Burton felt she would do anything to make Markham's countenance less bleak. 'We're bound to turn up some unsubs common to both investigations.'

Normally Noakes would have bridled at what he privately scoffed at as 'FBI bollocks', but on this occasion, it was clearly a case of any port in a storm.

'You do that,' he said with satisfaction. 'We gotta keep Sidney thinking we're looking at the local scrotes.'

'Is it time to call another press conference?' Doyle sounded apprehensive.

'No way,' the DI replied earnestly. 'I don't want *anything* out there at the moment.' Soberly, he added, 'And remember, careless talk costs lives.'

'Thass a quote.' Noakes was decidedly pleased with himself. 'They used to say that in World War Two, innit?'

'Indeed, Sergeant.' Markham was amused despite himself, then turned grave. 'But seriously, someone in CID is leaking and,' the sudden steeliness of his tone made them jump, '*I just won't have it.*' He smiled at the team to take the sting out of his words. 'So, if you catch anyone sounding off, be sure to let me know.'

And he'll have their guts for garters. To Noakes this seemed a reasonable quid pro quo. He rather relished the thought of witnessing one of Gilbert Markham's legendary verbal disembowellings.

'We'll get on to the alibis too, sir,' Burton said gallantly.

Should be worth sweet FA, Noakes told himself. *They'll all have been tucked up for the night like good little boys and girls.*

'Sir . . .'

'What is it, Kate?'

'Oh, I don't know, boss . . . could be a dead end.'

'What could?'

'Dave Gould has an allotment the other side of Medway Park,' she said. 'Likes to spend his afternoons there.'

'Oh aye.' Noakes smirked. 'An' you reckon Alan Titchmarsh is gonna spill his guts over a chat about runner beans.'

'Could be worth a try,' she continued falteringly. 'Away from the dance school, there's a chance he might open up.'

'You reckon he's hiding something, Kate?'

'Hard to say, sir. But *something's* bugging him.' She wheeled round on Noakes. 'You said it yourself at the memorial service, sarge . . . about him looking like he had something on his mind.'

'Oh aye.' As an endorsement, it lacked conviction.

'Go for it, Kate.' The DI forced enthusiasm into his voice. 'We need to throw everything at this one.'

She beamed. 'I'm on it ASAP, boss.'

Doyle's expression seemed to say, *Leave me out of it.* Like Noakes, he clearly didn't think there was much to be gained from tracking down Shirley Bastin's ex-husband among the tomato plants.

* * *

When it came to ritual disembowellings, Slimy Sid was second to none, Noakes thought an hour and a half later as he and Markham sat in the DI's office.

Markham too was reflecting on the evisceration.

It had proved even more harrowing than their interview with Robyn DiAngelo's mother, who'd accepted the news of her daughter's murder with a stoicism belied by her trembling hands and lip. Never had Markham been more thankful for his DS who wiped away the woman's tears with a gentleness that would have astounded any casual acquaintance of CID's resident grizzly bear.

Like a demented samurai, Sidney had slashed away at them giving no quarter.

'You mean to tell me you've got *nothing*, Markham? *Absolutely nothing*?'

Fruitless to attempt to propitiate the angry god.

'*Four murders*,' came the cobra's hiss, 'and not a single arrest to show for it.'

'I'm convening an emergency meeting with Mr McLeod's team first thing tomorrow, sir.'

Narrowed eyes greeted this announcement.

'You're convinced there's a link then?'

'I'm sure these deaths are somehow connected to Mickey Willett's disappearance, yes, sir.'

Markham thanked God for Kate Burton's diligence as he pushed her latest 'criminal tracker' across the table.

Sidney looked suspiciously at the tracker. 'You're following up these *leads* as a priority?'

'Even as we speak, sir.'

Clearly mollified at the prospect of some grungy no-hoper's imminent arrival in the custody suite, Sidney had let them salaam their way out of his office. But not without a parting shot.

'Watch that *flair* of yours — eh, Markham? Good solid policework's what we need now. None of your famous *hunches*.'

Just thinking of it made the DI grind his teeth. He had started the day convinced a breakthrough was imminent. And now it was back to square one.

Noakes sensed the guvnor's depression. Like his nemesis Kate Burton, he wanted nothing more than to give the boss a lift.

'What about that piece in the *Courier*?' he said unexpectedly.

'Sorry?'

'You know, guv. The one Enid was reading . . . the one that got her all upset.'

'Oh right.' Markham shook his head as if to dispel the fog. 'Wasn't Kate going to check with the community care team about that?'

'She said it were no dice with the head nurse or whatever she calls herself,' Noakes rejoined. 'Couldn't say what date it might have been.' Craftily, the DS added, 'But it's gotta be recent . . . We could allus have a gander down the Central Library.' With a distinct note of pride in his tone, he added, 'They've got all the newspapers on them microfiche wotsits . . . I've used 'em before, boss, when we cracked the Ashley Dean case.'

'So you did, Noakesy.'

For want of a better idea, the DI was prepared to give it a go. Afterwards, they could pay Doug Callaghan a visit.

'Lead on, Macduff.'

They exchanged smiles of pure complicity.

Burton could have her sodding runner beans, Noakes thought. He was willing to bet the newspaper would be the thing to give him and the guvnor first dibs on the killer.

Outside, the day grew imperceptibly darker.

The sands of time were running out.

12. A SLIVER OF LIGHT

'How d'you mean, something was wrong with George?'

Olivia prodded the spaghetti she was cooking for their supper to see if was sufficiently al dente before draining the pan and spooning the pasta onto plates.

Turning her attention to the tomato sauce and mozzarella cheese, she added, 'Didn't you say the old dragon from community records was off sick? I'd have thought that would be bound to cheer him up.' She flashed Markham a grin. 'That and the fact the library's got its own Costa.' She located two wine glasses and a bottle of Pinot Noir. 'For medicinal purposes,' she grimaced. 'Last lesson today was bottom set Year Eleven. Felt like I'd lost the will to live.'

Markham nodded sympathetically.

'Let's eat in here, Liv.'

Without further ado, they sat down in the kitchen to the simple evening meal.

'You're right — Miss Todd wasn't there,' he continued. 'It was some nice young trainee who, by happy coincidence, turned out to be a friend of Natalie's.'

'George should've been in clover then.' She chewed a forkful of spaghetti appreciatively before continuing. 'So, what was bugging him . . . Costa's paninis not up to scratch?'

'That's just it,' he replied slowly. 'I like the Central Library . . . And Noakesy's got a bit of a thing for that Edwardian Reading Room. You should see him tip-toeing round, taking it all in reverentially as if he's in church . . . Though come to think of it,' he chuckled reminiscently, 'I seem to recall him telling Kate Burton it was like an aquarium one time when they were in there doing research.'

'Very apt simile.' The English teacher nodded approvingly. 'With it being so still and echoey, there *is* something of an underwater feel to the place.' Wryly, she added, 'Judging by her A-level results, I suspect Natalie wasn't equally spellbound.' With an impish look, she imitated Muriel Noakes's shrill falsetto. '"*Didn't do herself justice . . . Teachers uninspiring . . . University vastly overrated.*"'

Markham laughed. 'Natalie's what they call a late developer apparently.'

Olivia choked on a gulp of wine. 'Not when it comes to the opposite sex she isn't, Gil!'

'Hmm. That's as maybe . . . At any rate, she'll always be Noakes's "rose without a thorn".'

'Personally, I find her a prickly specimen.' Olivia sighed. 'To be honest, it was a relief when I heard tonight's classes at the Bluebell had been cancelled . . . Oh, I'm sorry, Gil.' She bit her lip in compunction. 'I sound callous after what happened to that poor woman.'

'No need to apologize, sweetheart.' Markham took a long draught of wine. 'At least it was quick and she didn't see it coming.'

'You've had a bummer of a day,' she said gently.

'Well, it was Kate Burton who had to break the news about Ms DiAngelo to the staff at the Bluebell.' His lips were tightly compressed for a moment. 'I say "break the news", but the bush telegraph had been busy, so they already knew a body had been found in Quarry Street.'

'Poor Kate.'

'She's going to brief me on everyone's alibis tomorrow, but the fact that the murder took place at night means they'll most likely be thin on the ground.' He sighed. 'Same old, same old.'

'No other leads then?'

'Kate intended to track Dave Gould down in his allotment — apparently he likes to chill out in the afternoons over the sweetcorn and artichokes.'

'Very Monsieur Zen.'

'But the daughter said he'd taken off without telling her and she didn't know when he'd be back . . . Sounded quite miffed about Daddy Dearest keeping her in the dark.'

Olivia sniffed. 'Cathy Gould's a cold fish and no mistake. Shirley had real pizazz by all accounts, but in this case the apple fell a long way from the tree.' A thought struck her. 'Hey, maybe now they'll sell up.'

'I wouldn't count on it. Bad Doug's blandishments haven't got him anywhere as yet.'

'*Bad Doug* . . . Oh yes, now I remember . . . you mean the property developer guy.' She took another mouthful of pasta, relishing the flavour. 'This spaghetti isn't at all bad, Gil, even if my cooking is what dear Muriel would call "rustic".'

'It hits the spot tonight, Liv, that's for sure.' But she noticed he was toying with his food.

'No joy with Mr Callaghan then,' she said lightly.

'Well, he's a slimy character and I wouldn't be surprised if he's up to all kinds of dodgy dealings, but I don't see him as a killer . . . He hinted at there being something nasty in the Gould family woodshed.' Markham looked troubled. 'Could just have been sour grapes . . . getting his own back because they persuaded Shirley not to sell to him . . . but' — listlessly, he twirled the pasta round his fork — 'I'd like to have located Dave Gould . . .'

'You think he's not on the level?'

'Kate said something wasn't right . . . and she's quite shrewd when it comes to picking up those kinds of vibes . . . It's why she wanted another crack at him.'

'Talking of vibes,' Olivia said softly, 'you still haven't told me what was amiss with George.'

'Well, as I said he likes that library . . . We've probably got our own newspaper archive somewhere in CID.' He pulled a face. 'But any chance to jump over the wall, if you know what I mean.'

'Especially if it takes you out of Sidney's orbit.'

'Exactly.'

He was making steady inroads on the Pinot Noir, she noticed, but there was still a mound of spaghetti on his plate.

'We can't stall Hissing Sid forever, but we've got zilch at the moment.'

'And you got nothing off the microfiche?' Olivia put down her spoon and fork with a sigh of satisfaction. Time to get her second wind. 'What were you looking for anyway?'

'Shirley's mum Enid saw something in the *Courier* that upset her.'

'What kind of thing?'

'Difficult to say.' Manfully, Markham scooped up some more pasta, washing it down with a hefty glug of wine. 'Could be a red herring, but one of the care team noticed something was a bit off, so we wondered if there might be a link to her murder.'

'You mean a story about the Bluebell?'

'That's right . . . But all we turned up was the odd bit of PR about kids winning competitions and a couple of pieces about rising stars back in the day . . . naff titles like *A Trip Down Memory Lane* and *Where Are They Now?*' Markham sounded thoroughly dispirited. 'You know the kind of thing . . . cub reporters' stuff.'

'Eat up, Gil. There's jam roly-poly and custard for afters . . . not home-made, I'm afraid.'

'Sorry, sweetheart. This is great but—'

'I know, darling, I know . . . Have some of the garlic bread at least,' she clucked, pushing another plate towards him and clearing away the remains of the spaghetti. Then, returning to the table, 'So what put George's nose out of joint?'

'It was more that he went very quiet.' Another swig of the Pinot Noir. 'You know what he's like . . . I can usually count on a Doric chorus from him when it comes to a civic trawl — "Outraged of Bromgrove" — but he suddenly went very subdued.'

Olivia whisked the untouched plate of garlic bread away, returning minutes later with steaming plates of the nursery stodge that was normally a sure-fire favourite with her lover.

Markham attacked Aunt Bessie's offering with greater vigour than her own spag bol.

Oh well, horses for courses.

'D'you ever wonder, Gil . . .' She was uncharacteristically hesitant.

'Wonder what, love? God, this jam thing's good.'

'Glad to hear it.' Then, almost under her breath, 'Well . . . I mean, I wonder if Natalie is truly George's daughter . . .'

'*What*?' Markham dropped his spoon with a clatter and looked at his partner wide-eyed. 'What makes you say that?'

'It hit me at the memorial service,' she replied. 'Don't you remember me commenting that I couldn't see an ounce of George in her.'

'Yes, but that's a long way from deciding she's not his child . . .'

'I don't mean she's not his child, Gil.' Olivia was nettled. 'Obviously she *is*, in every way that matters . . . It's just *biologically* . . .'

'I'm sorry, dearest. I didn't mean to doubt you.' Markham held out a hand, which his lover clasped without a moment's hesitation. 'Now I think about it, I see what you mean . . . It was just a bit of a shock, that's all.'

'There's a certain refinement there, Gil . . . something bred in the bone . . . but not a trace of George.' She gave his hand a tender squeeze before she moved away to brew their coffee. 'I've often wondered about Muriel and George. There's something so fiercely protective and watchful about his attitude . . . as though he's determined to make amends to Muriel for something that went wrong . . . something that happened long before we ever knew them . . .'

'And you think being in the library, seeing that young trainee and those pictures of talented dance kids triggered something . . . ?'

'Who can say, Gil?'

She set an aromatic beverage in front of him, helping herself to hot milk as he contemplated his own black coffee.

'Maybe you're right, Liv,' he said at last. 'Noakes looked as if he'd had a jolt, certainly. Could've been he was thinking about Natalie — missed opportunities, asking himself where it all went wrong . . .'

''Course Natalie's still so young,' she said bracingly, concerned at the worn look on Markham's face. 'Plenty of time for her to get tired of that loser she hangs out with at — what do they call it? — the Krazyhouse. If George plays the overbearing father, she'll only stick to the dreary dropout like superglue.'

'Hmm . . . reverse psychology. I'm sure you're right, love.' He eyed the empty bottle of red as though debating with himself whether to open another. With a sigh, he decided he'd better not. 'It's funny you know, I've somehow never thought of Noakes and Muriel ever being *young*, but of course they must have been once.'

'I know what you mean.' Olivia stirred her coffee meditatively. 'But it's not that much of a stretch to imagine an unplanned pregnancy.'

'But *Muriel* . . .' Markham looked as though it would take a lot more Pinot Noir for him to get his head around the idea of Mrs Noakes kicking over the traces.

'It happened to a cousin of mine,' his lover continued. 'But she completely reinvented herself later. You should see her now . . . pillar of the WI, scourge of the permissive society and all that.'

'There's none so righteous as a reformed libertine,' he chuckled.

'Well, I don't know about libertine, but she was definitely what my dad called a bit of a goer.'

'Even so . . . *Muriel Noakes*.'

'I could have got it all wrong, Gil. I'm almost sorry I said anything . . . It's just that there was definite tension in the air when we were over at their place, plus seeing Natalie and George side by side at the memorial service got me thinking.'

'But assuming he knows about Muriel's, er, youthful indiscretion, why would he suddenly have a fit of the glums looking at cheesy pics of the Bluebell's hoofers?'

'Maybe Natalie's just being more than usually stroppy right now,' Olivia's tone suggested she considered this a distinct possibility, 'and seeing all those shiny-faced little tykes upset him. If he's worried about keeping her on the straight and narrow, or afraid of the past somehow repeating itself, he might be more than usually sensitive to other folks' "happy snaps".'

'Or maybe he was thinking back to when Natalie was an angelic little girl and comparing it with how things are now.'

'Humph. If you ask me, Gil, that one has always been a handful.'

Seeing her lover's troubled expression, Olivia decided it was time to change the subject.

'Talking of vibes,' she said, 'Fred Stroud's been out of sorts . . . like a bear with a sore head.'

'Noakes calls him Yogi Bear.'

'Well, there was nothing easy-going or cuddly about him today. He really barked at the kids. It was the first time I've ever seen him go for them like that.'

Carefully, Markham asked, 'Could you imagine him ever losing it in his personal life — with a woman?'

'You mean could he be a killer?' Olivia's tone was pragmatic. She took her time before answering and then her reply was unexpected. 'I've just been reading a book about Ted Bundy,' she said. '*The Phantom Prince*.'

'Oh yes?' Markham was intrigued. 'Noakesy's always bending my ear about the guy. Crops up regularly on that True Crime channel he's addicted to.' He frowned. 'The serial killer, right?'

'That's the one. His sometime lover has just brought out another book about her life with him . . . how he was a Grade-A boyfriend most of the time and a sort of adoptive father to her little girl.'

Thoughts of Noakes's troubled expression came momentarily to mind.

'And she and her daughter never guessed a thing, right?'

'That's it.' She shivered. 'He even nipped away from the little girl's christening party to find a victim.'

'Appalling.' Markham's expression was bleak.

'The point is, on the surface he was a real charmer. Exactly the kind of wholesome all-American boy any parent would want for their daughter.'

'But nobody ever really knew him.'

'He was illegitimate . . . thought his mother was his sister and lived with his grandparents to start with . . . Could well have been abused by his grandfather who was a porn addict — the whole family was pretty pathological — but Bundy buried his childhood experiences fathoms deep so nobody realized how disturbed he was.' She shivered again. 'Fred Stroud has a look of Bundy sometimes . . . the American jock. And you feel you could never really get close to him.'

'We're keeping tabs, Liv.'

Her eyes widened.

'You're looking at Fred as a suspect?'

'All secret squirrel otherwise Sidney'll kick off.'

'I see.' She shook herself, aware of Markham's constraint. 'Right, enough of the morbid talk. I'll make us some more coffee and then we can slob in front of the telly. You go on through, Gil, and I'll see to it.'

Nothing loath, Markham went into the living room and across to the bay window. It was dark outside, with just his hollow-eyed reflection confronting him through the glass.

For a moment, he stood immobile, thinking ahead.

He'd show those 'happy snaps' from the *Courier* to Kate Burton at tomorrow morning's briefing. Better be sure to do it away from Noakes, though.

Then he needed to hook up with Jim McCleod, see if the cold-case team had anything for him.

It was essential to run Dave Gould to ground. Doyle could drill down into witness statements at the Bluebell while Kate headed back out to that allotment. Funny, Gould didn't look like anyone's idea of a gardener but perhaps it was an idyllic alternative to all the fuss and feathers at the Bluebell.

Outside the wind was beginning to pick up, whistling around the building's eaves with that strange mournful sobbing.

A pair of arms stole round his waist. Gratefully, he turned back to comfort and the light.

* * *

Tuesday morning was grey and overcast to match Markham's mood.

Seeing Noakes and Doyle, heads together, engaged in some sort of post-match analysis at the latter's desk, he forbore from interrupting them. Instead, he quietly beckoned Kate Burton into his office.

The question of alibis for Robyn DiAngelo got them nowhere. As Noakes had predicted, the potential suspects all claimed to have been virtuously asleep in their beds and there was nothing to say otherwise.

'Dimples says time of death was between eleven and midnight, sir, and none of them admitted to having been anywhere but home sweet home at that time of night.'

There was an uncharacteristic edge to her voice which made Markham look at her closely.

'Everything all right, Kate? I mean, with *you* and not the case.'

'Didn't sleep too well, boss.'

Had she slept alone, he wondered, before giving her a reassuring smile.

'Well, I definitely know that feeling, Kate. Just as long as there's nothing else you want to tell me.' Seeing her look uneasy, he continued, 'Did you get anything from the house-to-house?'

'One of the neighbours thinks she saw a woman going into DiAngelo's house.'

'She's quite sure it was a woman?'

'To be honest, no, boss. Whoever it was had a hoodie on . . . just something about the way they moved suggested a woman.' Burton sighed. 'The old dear wanted to be helpful but I'm not sure she's reliable.'

'What time did Ms DiAngelo's mystery caller arrive?'

'Early evening, half six-ish.'

Markham leaned back in his chair and closed his eyes as though picturing the scene.

God, the guvnor looks rough, she thought. *Death skimmed over.*

Strangely enough, she felt better for knowing the DI too was at the end of his rope.

'Maybe this was the cards-on-the-table confrontation between Robyn and the killer,' she suggested. 'It didn't go the way the killer wanted, so later that night . . .'

No need to finish the sentence.

'I need you to get over to that allotment of Dave Gould's,' Markham said. With a brave attempt to lighten the atmosphere, he added, 'Maybe down among the cabbages and carrots he'll open up.'

'It'll more likely be a compost heap,' Burton said ruefully, gesturing at her immaculate trouser suit. 'And I'm not exactly dressed like an allotmenteer!'

'Think you may have coined a new word there, Kate.'

At least his feeble attempt at wit produced a wan smile.

'Before you go,' he slid the pictures from the *Courier* across his desk, 'I'd like you to take a shufti at these for me.'

She raised her eyebrows interrogatively but, as in all matters, she considered the evidence gravely and deliberately.

'That one,' she said eventually, pointing at one of the grainy images. 'The lad second from the left on the back row.'

Markham squinted hopefully before shaking his head.

'What about him, Kate?'

'Oh, I dunno, boss.' She ran her hand over the pictures as though trying to communicate telepathically with their subjects. 'Only, it feels like I've seen that face somewhere else.'

'Someone from the Bluebell?'

Suddenly, she looked self-conscious.

'Can't be sure, sir.' She ran a hand over her face as though trying to reboot her memory. 'It was just I spoke to someone on Mr McLeod's team. He mentioned something about Mickey Willet having been seen with another boy . . . dark-haired, something monkey-ish about his features . . .'

'*Childlike*?'

'Yeah, not childlike exactly . . . kind of puckish was what he said . . . almost like a changeling.' Again, that nervous wiping of her face. ''Course kids' faces change, so he might look totally different now. Only,' her fingers lingered over the sheet of pictures, 'he's the dead spit of—'

She broke off, embarrassed.

'Take no notice of me, sir. I'm burbling . . . Not enough sleep, seeing phantoms everywhere.'

You and Olivia both, the DI thought.

'You got a name for me, Kate?' Striving for a note of raillery, he pressed, 'Come on, don't hold back.'

The DS hesitated. 'I'll have a clearer idea once I've spoken to Dave Gould, sir.'

Markham looked at her steadily. It was his policy not to press his subordinates. To give them the time and space to draw their own conclusions.

But time was no longer on their side.

'Get off then,' he said. 'But call me the minute you've finished with Gould, understood?'

'Will do, sir.'

'By the by,' he slipped in casually, 'any idea what's eating DS Noakes these days?'

She looked genuinely surprised.

'You mean more than the usual, sir?'

He chuckled. *Noakes contra mundum* just about summed up his wingman's philosophy in life.

'Can't say I've noticed anything, sir.' A pause. 'D'you want him with me for Dave Gould?'

'God forbid. I'm pretty sure "allotmenteers" are right in contention for the top spot on Noakesy's *most hated* list.'

He was pleased to see she allowed herself a tiny smile.

'Okay, Kate, off you go. I'll be expecting to hear from you.' She could hear the ripple of anxiety underneath the attempt at humour. 'Tell Pinky and Perky to get their backsides in here, will you?'

'Righto, boss.'

At the door, she turned to look back at the DI, but he was already nose-deep in reports. Time enough to raise her suspicions once she'd spoken to Dave Gould.

Like a ghost, she slipped away.

13. TIGHTENING THE SCREWS

Dave Gould belonged to the Medway Park Allotments Association or MPAA. 'Sounds like a virus,' Noakes had sniggered.

But Kate Burton was rather impressed by the vista of neatly strimmed paths and beds. With a feeling of relief, she guessed the blue tarpaulins that dotted the slopes covered the gardeners' compost heaps.

A sudden wave of nostalgia rolled over her at the recollection of her dad's allotment and the internecine warfare he waged against local birds and squirrels. As a child, she had watched fascinated as he booby-trapped his domain with nets and cages. She grinned as it occurred to her that this was the kind of thing Noakes would enjoy — full-on hostilities against vermin with no quarter given.

She wondered what was up with the old warhorse. He'd seemed all right debating the footie with Doyle but, come to think of it, before that he'd looked rather tired and beaten-up with less of his trademark willingness to take on all comers.

She sighed. Noakes looked exactly how she was feeling.

Colin was like a polite stranger these days, the euphoria of their engagement long gone. It couldn't be that he'd guessed her feelings for Gilbert Markham, because she'd gotten that well under control . . . *or had she?*

For a moment, she stood stock-still, oblivious to the tranquil order of the well-ordered plots.

Let's face facts, she told herself. The most her boss was ever going to feel for her was a sort of avuncular interest and she'd schooled herself to hide the tell-tale signs of her infatuation with him. Though Noakes still shot her the odd knowing look. But she still took an acute pleasure in observing Markham when he was unaware of her scrutiny — like someone dying of thirst who knew the well to which she crawled was poisoned but went ahead and drank regardless. However, she was careful to ration these poignant draughts and lost no opportunity of reminding herself that it was Olivia Mullen's image which filled Markham's horizon to the exclusion of all else.

Hey, maybe *Noakes* was a fellow sufferer. His goofy admiration for the boss's partner was no secret in CID, though few of his colleagues ventured any open raillery.

But on reflection, no. For all his worship at Olivia's shrine, it was clear that Muriel held ultimate sway over Noakes's heart, however baffling their bond might appear to outsiders.

She would give it one last try with Colin. In many ways they were ideally matched (as though by mail-order catalogue, her mum was wont to say) and she hated the thought of writing off the last two years. There *had* to be something between them worth salvaging, surely.

A sudden noise made her start guiltily.

Shit. Get a grip. You're supposed to be checking out a suspect, not carrying on like some soppy teenager.

She looked around nervously, but there was no one to be seen.

With it being winter, she presumed there wasn't much doing on the horticultural front. She thought back to her dad . . . as far as his tasks went, digging in manure (or 'black gold') and checking out the shallots was pretty much it for this time of year.

At the far end of the gently sloping terrain was a row of a dozen or so garden sheds. Presumably somewhere to shelter from the elements and have a brew or, she shuddered delicately, use whatever compost toilet set-up passed for the facilities round here.

She made her way towards the little wooden huts along parallel grass avenues, admiring the early splashes of colour and bramble-free paths. It was a marvel that the place appeared immune from vandalism or worse. With its broken padlock, the gate at the entrance didn't exactly offer effective security and there were no signs of CCTV or other devices.

Maybe folk were just more civilized round here, she thought, noting with approval the wheelbarrows and storage boxes ranged neatly along hedges. Or maybe this little paradise was simply Medway's best kept secret. She liked the modest scale of the place. Just a few greenhouses and polytunnels. There must be something very satisfying about growing your own fruit and veg, to say nothing of escaping the concrete metropolitan wilderness once in a while. One of the boss's favourite quotes came into her mind. *God Almighty first planted a garden.* Ruthlessly, she beat down thoughts of Markham.

Idly, she wondered what happened when 'allotmenteers' fell out. She vaguely recalled her dad and his beloved committee being up in arms against a hoarder whose plot ended up looking like a rubbish dump. And then there was the fellow who went round nicking other people's strawberries.

Probably a microcosm of society if it came to that.

Now she was outside the little row of huts. Feeling somewhat foolish, she called out, 'Mr Gould . . . Mr Gould, are you in there? It's DS Kate Burton from the police . . .'

She was about to turn away when she noticed the door of the fifth shed along stood ajar.

In that instant, she felt an overpowering sense of repugnance quite at odds with her previous sensation of being at one with nature, as though an evil miasma seeped out from the shed towards her.

Clenching and unclenching her fists, she walked forward and pushed open the door.

It was as though Eden had been polluted, she thought, taking in the sight of Dave Gould's crumpled body tangled in vegetable netting next to his mower.

Somehow the devil had infiltrated this little green oasis and God was nowhere to be seen.

* * *

'Fractured spine an' ribs plus bruising on his face . . . Dimples says the killer knocked him out before strangling him.' Noakes took in the way Kate Burton's teeth wouldn't stop chattering and added gruffly, 'He were unconscious at the end . . . never came round before being choked.'

'Time of death?' Markham's question sounded almost curt.

'Doc says around seven o'clock this morning, give or take.' For once, Dimples had given him an answer on this, jettisoning his usual complaint of medical *lèse-majesté*.

The team were sitting in the largest hut which, with its Formica table and sagging canvas chairs, looked to be where the allotments committee held its meetings.

Outside, the miniature estate teemed with forensic officers and uniforms preparing to track down allotment holders. A fine drizzle fell on hastily erected cordons and waterproof sheeting as the place was transformed into a hive of activity.

Inside their hut, the mood was sombre.

Noakes, as ever, was uncomfortable with silence.

'We're not talking wrinklies falling out over their onions,' he said. 'He came for Gould.' Then he turned to his fellow DS. 'You reckon you know who it is, don'tcha?'

She might have known Noakes would realize. Nothing got past him.

'Anton Bhaer,' she said simply.

'*What*!' burst from Markham and Doyle simultaneously.

It was clearly not the answer they'd been expecting.

Noakes, however, just watched her steadily, eyes intent on her face.

'The German lad,' was all he said.

'Scunthorpe,' she corrected automatically.

'But why him?' Doyle asked in bewilderment.

'It was what I got from one of the cold-case team.' She ran her fingers through her fringe as though by this means she could marshal her disordered thoughts. 'He turned up the description of a lad Mickey Willett used to hang out with . . . good-looking, a bit lantern-jawed with these deep-set black eyes. The witness said Willett called him "monkey boy" . . .'

'*Monkey boy*!' Doyle continued to boggle at her.

'Well,' Burton was getting flustered, 'maybe cos he was cute as a monkey or something like that.' More ruffling of her fringe. 'It was what the witness said about how this boy moved. Fluid . . . almost acrobatic . . . Like a dancer.' Burton willed herself to stop fidgeting. 'Suddenly Anton Bhaer's face came into my head and I couldn't get it out.'

'It doesn't exactly sound like Anton, though.' The DC sounded profoundly sceptical.

'I wouldn't get too hung up on that,' Markham said as Burton looked across at him gratefully. 'A puckish demeanour might account for the nickname.'

'Mebbe not.' Something gleamed in Noakes's eyes. 'But that dark hair an' the whey face are creepy for a fella his age . . . he's famished-looking an' all . . .'

'Was there anything else, Kate?' the DI pressed her. 'I take it this witness isn't still on the scene.'

'No, sir. Died a while back.' She looked despondent before brightening slightly. 'But there's the photo you showed me . . . you know, when you were trying to work out what it was upset Enid.'

Markham was instantly alert, his stillness mirrored by the other two.

'The snap from the *Courier*,' she continued, 'with those teenagers from the Bluebell. I could swear it was Anton Bhaer right there on the back row. He stood out on account of his good looks.'

'Where's it leave us, though?' Noakes began to pace up and down the cramped space like a caged tiger. None of them had ever seen him so pumped up.

'Sit down, Noakesy, before you bring the place down on us.'

The other thudded back into his seat.

'Robyn and Anton were friends,' Doyle began. He turned to Noakes. 'She gave him an alibi for Clifton. And didn't you say you heard her planning to check in with him when she got back from seeing her mate off?'

'Thassright.' The admission sounded as though jerked out of him.

'It doesn't matter that they were friends — he could still have killed her,' Burton said. 'Say she confronted him that afternoon . . . maybe about something she'd just discovered. He could've found a way of pacifying her and buying some time . . . then come back later and taken that pole from the shed . . .' It was a dancer's choice of weapon, she thought.

'You think all the deaths stem from Mickey Willett's murder, boss?' Doyle asked.

'I'm sure of it.'

The DC frowned. 'What was his motive for killing Willett, then?'

'Who knows . . . Quite possibly sex,' came Markham's reply.

'Swings both ways then,' Noakes muttered under his breath.

Doyle shuddered, though the day was relatively mild for the time of year and it was stuffy in their musty potting shed. 'D'you think Willett's still there . . . You know, at the Bluebell?'

'They dug up the garden when he went missing,' Burton said quickly, 'what with him having last been seen hanging round Heathfield Close.'

'What about the cellars?' It was almost a growl from Noakes. 'That bit underneath the theatre jobby where we found Enid.'

She jumped slightly. 'Wouldn't they have checked out the buildings along with the garden, sarge?'

'Cathy Gould were yammering on about her Aunt Thing—'

'Rose,' Burton amended.

'That's the one. Well, she said Rose were up to all kinds of shit . . . wanted to extend the cellars.' Noakes pulled a face. 'Prob'ly hoping to get her mitts on one of them council grants for regional development or whatever they call it.'

'What came of that?' Markham's voice was like the crack of a whip.

'They had student types an' local youngsters an' whatnot volunteering in there,' Noakes replied. 'Lots of BS 'bout archaeological interest . . . But the cellars backed onto Heathfield Primary or a water course or some such, so that were the end of it.' His mouth stretched to its full extent. 'No spondulicks.'

'D'you reckon Bhaer was one of 'em,' Doyle asked eagerly, 'the student volunteers?'

The DI turned to Burton.

'According to his CV, he was out in Australia on a student visa after finishing sixth form.' She raked her fringe again. 'But before that in the summer . . .'

The summer of 1999 when Mickey Willett went missing.

'*Jesus*,' Doyle breathed aghast. 'You mean, Willett's somewhere in the cellars? After all this time . . .' He broke off. 'You okay, boss?'

In the gloom of the hut, Markham had turned the colour of bleached bones.

Suddenly the DI was transported back to his own student gap year and a visit to the Capuchin Crypt in Rome . . . that underground cemetery, decorated with the bones of thousands of long-dead monks, waiting for the Last Trump to sound. At the time, he had thought irreverently that the mosaic of skulls and tibias looked more like some gigantic Thorntons Toffee exhibit than any ecclesiastical memento mori, but now those same ranks of desiccated remains seared his eyeballs with the force of a demonic revelation.

'Kate' — she sat up straight at the urgency in his tone — 'I want you and Doyle to check with Cathy Gould and the council about any works at the Bluebell . . . specifically, any activity in the cellars.' The DC too was now all ears. 'Also, I need you to check out that photo with staff at the *Courier.*' His voice was granite-hard. 'I want to know everything about the lad in the back row.' Like Noakes's, his eyes held a peculiar gleam. 'If he's our man, I want it watertight.'

Noakes's voice was strangely hoarse. 'You reckon it's him, guv.'

'I don't know, Noakesy, I just don't know. But it's our only lead.'

'Who's going to break it to Cathy Gould, sir? I mean, about her dad?'

'Leave that to me, Kate.' The DI visibly braced himself. 'Go ahead with those checks. Quick as you like. Say nothing about Dave for now.'

Pray God it wouldn't leak.

'We'll break it to Cathy very shortly,' he reassured her.

Another notification of death to be faced.

Burton and Doyle got to their feet, the latter's height making the hut seem suddenly impossibly small.

The gangling DC looked excited. *This is it.*

Burton was warier. It was all circumstantial at this stage, she thought. Diddly-squat, as Noakes might say.

'What do we do about the dance classes, sir?' she turned back at the door of the shed.

'Say they should go ahead as normal, Kate. Everything as normal.' He air-quoted with self-loathing. '"It's what they would have wanted."'

'I get you, boss.'

'We need to lay a snare,' the DI said. 'Lure Bhaer into it somehow.'

'You think he'll bite, boss?' Doyle towered over Burton as they stood in the doorway.

'It's possible he may lose it,' the DI answered, 'if he thinks we're closing in.'

And with that, they were on their way.

* * *

Markham and Noakes sat in the gloom of the potting shed in contemplative silence, the soft hiss of winter drizzle faintly audible outside.

The sharp, acrid scent of hyacinths was in the air, as though to remind the two men of that spring renaissance Dave Gould would nevermore behold.

'You can't trust the Huns,' was all Noakes said.

Markham refrained from correcting his subordinate, well aware that it would be futile.

It struck him for the first time how curiously washed-out Noakes looked. This case had somehow aged him more than any of their previous investigations.

'You gonna put surveillance on him, guv?'

'No need, Noakesy. As far as I know, he's got classes all today and this evening. So we know where he is.'

'If he killed Willett . . . cos they had some pervy thing going . . . coulda been he wanted to keep 'im close . . .'

'Yes, Sergeant.' Markham sighed heavily. 'I wonder now if it wasn't Anton who courted Shirley with a view to her transferring the dance studio to him.'

Noakes considered this. 'Not Bad Doug Callaghan?'

'Well, they likely both wanted an option on the premises for their own reasons.'

'But you think Anton put the moves on Shirley cos he wanted access to Willett's grave site?'

Markham's brow furrowed. 'Well, it makes sense for a killer wanting to eliminate the risk of Willett ever being found.'

'Why'd he kill 'er then?' Noakes demanded, scratching his chin.

'Maybe she knocked him back . . . Or he realized there was no chance of persuading her to transfer the Bluebell to him.'

'What about Enid?'

'Enid might not have been "all there", Noakesy, but she was a friend of Mickey Willett's mother Valerie Hernan, remember.'

'Oh yeah.' Something unfathomable kindled in the sergeant's eyes. 'So you think mebbe Val said summat which got Enid wondering about Anton.'

'Precisely.' Markham stretched his long legs out, almost toppling a pyramid of ceramic pots. 'She might have sensed something off-key about Anton — something Val said sparked a memory — or maybe she even saw him do something dodgy round Shirley.'

'Like what?' Noakes was doggedly intent.

'Feeding her tranquilizers or sleeping pills . . . whatever was calculated to make her pliable.'

The DS nodded slowly. 'An' then Enid shot her mouth off, so he killed her.'

'It's all speculation at this stage, Sergeant.'

The DS's eyes glittered in the gloaming.

'Clay Clifton musta twigged, guv.'

'Pure conjecture, Sergeant.'

'Hear me out, boss.' Again, that hoarse intensity.

'Mebbe Clifton got wind of Enid's fixation with the Willett case an' picked up on summat . . . All of 'em at the Bluebell traipsed in an' out of the flat at some time or other—'

'You mean the old lady said something that made him suspicious about Anton?'

'Yeah . . . Like she sensed summat weren't right with the lad, boss, an' let it slip.'

Markham picked up the thread. 'And then Clifton got confirmation of his suspicions from another quarter—'

'If they were both homos, guv, one of Bhaer's boyfriends could've split.'

'Split how, Sergeant?'

'Passed on summat he got from pillow talk, guv.' Noakes's intensity filled the shed. Markham had to admit, it was compelling. 'Gave Clifton stuff he could use for blackmail.'

'Enid was upset by that photo from the *Courier*,' Markham ruminated.

'Cos it showed Bhaer large as life an' twice as natural,' riposted Noakes. 'An' she were convinced he'd done for Mickey Willett. If she were wittering on about the pic an' Clifton got wind of it, then bingo!'

'What about Robyn DiAngelo?'

The DI's finely tapered fingers beat out a rhythmic tattoo on the dusty Formica table.

'The lass met up with some friend an' then next thing she were dead.' Now Noakes too was rapping the table. 'What if there was some skeleton in the Kraut's cupboard an' she found out about it?'

'What sort of skeleton?'

'Oh I dunno, guv . . . Diddling boys, fiddling girls . . . Who cares?' The DS tilted his canvas chair back at an alarming angle. 'The point is, he didn't want it coming out . . . leastways not while we were sniffing round Mickey Willett an' asking all kinds of awkward questions 'bout Enid an' gay-boy Clifton.' Again, that strange glittering distinctness of the eyes which turned Noakes into a species of imp or goblin in the half-light. 'So he killed Robyn.' A contemptuous snort. 'But didn't have the nous to make it look like a botched burglary.'

'Something could have spooked him so he didn't hang around . . . Or perhaps he hoped we'd start looking at ex-boyfriends.'

'Yeah.' Weirdly, Noakes was almost capering in his chair. 'But he couldn't even manage that, could he?'

'Manage what?'

'Couldn't make it look like it was about sex.' The DS spoke with a strangely joyous satisfaction. 'At least, not sex with a woman.'

'This isn't Top Trumps, Sergeant,' Markham said with unusual asperity. 'We're not handing out marks for forensic subtlety.'

'No, guv, 'course not.' The DS shook his salt-and-pepper mane. 'But it means he's coming apart at the seams, don' it? Like he's panicking?'

The DI shut his eyes.

God, I hope not.

He contemplated his unusually animated wingman.

'What's got into you, Noakesy?' he asked curiously. 'You had all the oomph of a pig's bladder before . . . and now look at you.'

'He's a wrong 'un, the Kraut,' the DS replied doggedly.

'How many times do I have to tell you, Sergeant? He's no more German than you or me. Bhaer's most likely a stage name.'

'Nasty sneaking son of a bitch.'

'Undoubtedly, but let's try to keep national allegiances out of it, shall we?'

The storm clouds didn't lift and, as if to match Noakes's black mood, outside the rain came down with rattling ferocity.

The DS contemplated his balled fists.

'What now, guv?'

'Back to the station and wait for Kate to check in.'

Dodging the DCI into the bargain.

'Then we need to break her father's death to Cathy Gould.'

'Fuck.'

'Indeed.'

Noakes's massive shaggy head tilted sideways as though he was sniffing the air of the allotment.

'Why'd he kill Dave Gould, boss?'

'God knows, Sergeant.'

'Gould an' Robyn had an affair, didn't they?'

'Correct.'

'So mebbe she asked his advice 'bout whatever it was she found out?'

'That's a distinct possibility, Noakes.'

The SOCOs hadn't found Robyn DiAngelo's mobile telephone. He had a sudden intuition that Noakes was right and the dead woman made a final call to her ex-lover.

'Why the fuck didn't Gould come to us?' Noakes had picked up a pruning knife from somewhere and was agitatedly whittling away at his thumb.

'If you gouge yourself on that thing, no way am I going to patch you up.'

The whittling stopped.

'I think he was likely going to share his suspicions with us,' the DI continued. 'But fate intervened.'

'Yeah, but why wait? I mean,' the DS looked wistfully at the pruning knife, 'the fucker had already killed his ex an' mother-in-law plus two of his staff.'

'There's the thing, Noakesy.' Markham's voice was sad. 'Mr Gould chose to play God and paid the price.'

'Cos he couldn't face the truth or he was worried Bhaer might be innocent?'

'Yes, something like that.'

Noakes looked round the shed with its pots full of compost and the little green watering can next to the door.

'He won't ever see 'is hyacinths come up,' was all he said.

* * *

Back at the station the atmosphere held a certain febrile anticipation.

'Word has it you're close to an arrest, Markham.'

Jim McLeod plonked himself down in the chair opposite the DI while Noakes lounged by the window.

'Not sure about that, sir. Though we may have something.'

The rain was coming down in sheets now, making the three men feel they were enclosed in their own Perspex bubble.

'Sounds promising,' McLeod said at the conclusion of Markham's recital.

'We owe it to the cold-case unit, sir. They came up with that witness statement in the first place.'

The retired DCI broke into a smile of singular sweetness.

'Talent makes its own luck, Markham,' he said gruffly. 'You and your team deserve the credit for this.' He rolled his eyes skyward. 'I can only imagine the pressure you're under.' A grin split his craggy features. 'Sidney's out pressing the flesh in Birmingham,' he added. 'A conference on Restorative Justice.' Noakes mimed being sick behind Markham's back. 'So at least you can get on without, ahem, any back-seat driver.'

There was a knock at the door and Kate Burton appeared in the doorway, closely followed by DC Doyle.

'I'll let you crack on.' McLeod nodded affably at the two newcomers and took his leave. 'Good luck.'

'What news, Kate?' The DI's eagerness was ill-concealed as they sat down.

'You were right, sarge.' Burton's smile was so radiant that Noakes blinked, as though momentarily dazzled. 'The Bluebell *did* have work done in the cellars round the time Mickey Willett went missing.'

'An' Bhaer,' Noakes leaned in, 'was he in on it?'

'No one called Anton Bhaer,' she replied, then, as her colleague's face fell, 'but BCVS—'

'That's Bromgrove Charity and Voluntary Services,' Doyle translated.

'They have a lad called *Tony Barr* applying to get involved with the Bluebell restoration project.'

'What about the time frame?' Noakes's voice was a guttural whisper.

'Summer of nineteen ninety-nine — when Mickey Willett went missing,' she replied exultantly. 'It fits, sarge, it fits.'

'Where's Bhaer right now? Have we got eyes on him?'

'Take it easy, sarge.' But Doyle too was clearly cock-a-hoop. 'He's doing his usual thing. Classes are running today same as usual.' He bit his lip guiltily. 'None of 'em know about Mr Gould yet. No sign of the daughter . . . holed up in the flat with a cold or something. God' — he broke off in consternation — 'there was that neighbour said she saw a woman calling on Robyn DiAngelo . . . You don't think Bhaer had, well, an accomplice . . . ?'

'I think it was Bhaer the neighbour saw.' Markham spoke decisively. 'He's slight and fine-boned, like a woman, and had his hoodie up . . . so he could easily pass as a female.'

'What're we waiting for?' Noakes lumbered away from the window. 'Let's get the bastard.'

Markham raised his hand with such authority that the pachyderm was halted in his tracks.

'We can't go in all guns blazing.'

'Why the fuck not?'

Burton had never before heard Noakes speak to his boss in such a tone.

But Markham faced him down.

'What've we got, Sergeant? You tell me, what've we got?'

'Sweet FA as things stand,' Doyle piped up.

'We know he did it.' The DS was mulish.

Seeing that Noakes looked ready to punch someone's lights out, the young DC sat well back in his chair. 'Yes, but we need to catch him in the act.'

'An' how're we bleeding well gonna do that?'

'First of all, we give the Bluebell staff a briefing this afternoon.'

The DI's authoritative tone stopped Noakes in his tracks.

'What sort of briefing?'

'*The police are confident of making an arrest shortly . . . a witness has come forward . . . promising developments . . . connection with a previous investigation.*' Markham's smile was chilling. 'We stand there looking delighted with ourselves and make out we've got everything practically sewn up . . . whatever it takes to unbalance him.'

'Whatcha think he'll do, then?' The DS wanted more.

'I think he'll wait till classes are finished for the day and then go down to those cellars—'

'What, you mean dig up Willett?' Doyle swallowed hard, his expression appalled. 'God, that's sick.'

'I'm with you, guv,' Noakes was nodding. 'He'll want to get rid of the evidence.'

'I think it's more than that.' Burton's eyes were remote, as though gazing deep inside herself for answers. 'You see, Mickey Willett is just as important to Anton — sorry, Tony Barr — as when he was alive.'

Now Noakes too was looking queasy.

'Like one of them necrophiles,' he muttered. 'You know, like the one who said he were killing for company.'

'Hey, I know that one.' For a moment, Doyle forgot his nausea. 'The civil servant bloke who strangled all those drifters and kept the bodies in his flat.'

This elicited a weak smile from Burton, as though two hitherto unpromising students had suddenly shown unexpected potential.

'That's right,' she replied and paused, as though debating with herself whether some reference to her beloved *Diagnostic and Statistical Manual of Mental Disorders* might be in order. The internal struggle was brief, however, and all she said was, 'Mickey's remains are a treasure he can't bear to relinquish . . . It's often the way with serial killers who have this compulsive relationship with their trophies.'

'You're not telling me he did that with the others . . . Enid and the rest.' Doyle gulped. 'Took . . . *bits* of them to keep.'

'More than likely,' she said. 'It's all about power and control.'

'But Mickey was the first.' Markham was equally phlegmatic. 'The lover who tried to get away, perhaps.'

'That's right, sir.' She seemed pleased they were on the same wavelength. 'So *that* was special.'

'Mebbe he was at the same game in Australia,' Noakes said grimly.

'I wouldn't be surprised,' his fellow DS said owlishly.

'Anton — Tony — wasn't able to take Mickey with him when he went abroad, though,' Doyle pointed out.

Noakes was ready for this. 'Yeah, but he had the secret knowledge of where the body was.' Mentally, the DS rifled through his *True Crime* rolodex once more. 'Like Ian Brady when he wouldn't say where that poor little lad with the specs were buried on Saddleworth Moor . . . like the bastard got off on knowing but not telling.'

'That's a good comparison, sarge,' Burton said approvingly.

With a flare of amusement, Markham noted how the pedagogue in her just wouldn't be repressed.

She continued, 'Tony Barr was able to possess Mickey absolutely in death and no one else could get to him.'

If I can't have you, nobody can.

'Thing is,' Doyle began then came to a full stop.

'Go on, Constable.' Markham's tone was warm and encouraging. For all the horror of this investigation, it was heart-warming to see his team wrestling with the knotty complexities together.

'I'm thinking about the cellars, boss.' Like Burton, the DC seemed to be looking inward. 'Don't remember any sign of the floor having been dug up or anything like that . . .'

The DI recalled that monastic crypt and the Capuchins' shining skulls.

'I'd hazard a guess we should be looking at the rear wall,' he said quietly. 'Once we've cleared away some of the clutter down there, I think it's likely the brickwork in that area may yield some clues.'

'You reckon he shoved Willett into a hole in the wall then, boss?' Doyle's voice sank to a whisper. 'How the hell did he manage it without anyone noticing?'

'It was a chaotic field dig . . . volunteers an' Indiana Jones wannabees fucking about down there . . . an' the weirdy aunt rocking up from time to time when she felt like a break from the ballerina bit.' Noakes furled and unfurled his horrible tie as an aid to cogitation. 'Security was probably crap too . . . he waited an' watched an' then.' An expressive flourish of his pudgy hands concluded the picture. 'Mebbe had the body in a suitcase or a wheelie bin . . .'

'*Jesus.*' Looking at the DC's stricken face, Markham forbore to reprove the profanity.

'So he creeps back down there tonight,' Noakes said venomously, 'but we're waiting for him, right?'

'Sounds like a plan, Sergeant,' Markham replied.

'What if he doesn't take the bait?' Burton asked. 'I mean, what if he sees through it?'

'He won't — provided you act your little cotton socks off,' Noakes retorted grimly.

The DI was gentle. 'Think you can do it, Kate?'

'You mean give the spiel about an arrest being imminent and all of that?'

'Exactly.' Markham steepled his fingers in characteristic meditative pose and smiled at her. 'I think you've got the requisite poker-playing skills.'

'I'll do my best, sir.'

'Excellent.'

Noakes was visibly chafing at the bit. 'Are we gonna let Cathy Gould in on the secret, guv?'

'Better not.' Markham was crisply decisive. 'This is a third bereavement for her.'

'She'll be all over the place,' Burton added softly.

'How're we going to get away with, well, hanging around like spare parts, sir?' Doyle was worried. 'I mean, isn't he likely to twig something's going down?'

'We'll offer our condolences to Cathy Gould and then hold our briefing. After that, Noakesy'll sound off about needing a brew and refreshments.'

Burton and Doyle met each other's eyes.

Shouldn't take too much acting.

Printed in Great Britain
by Amazon

49996099R00132

'We'll ostensibly adjourn to Costa,' Markham continued, 'but in reality, mount surveillance from around the corner at the primary school.'

Noakes headed for the door with unusual alacrity.

'I'm on that,' he assured the team and disappeared into the outer office.

The DI's expression was thoughtful as he watched him go.

Aware of the other two waiting for instructions, he snapped back into operational mode.

'Right,' he said, 'let's give it ten minutes and then we meet in the car park.'

Something about his wingman continued to niggle.

'Hook up with Noakes, will you please, Kate?' he said casually. 'Better if we stick together.'

'Righto, sir.' She and Doyle headed for the outer office.

* * *

The rain had finally stopped, but pewter skies pressing down on the station made Markham feel that nature was full of foreboding, holding its breath in anticipation of the last act in the drama.

He pressed his hands to his temples as though to cool the raging tumult of his thoughts.

Right, he said to himself, *let it come down.*

14. THE FIGURE IN THE WALL

When Markham drew up in front of the Bluebell on the afternoon of Tuesday, 14 January, everything seemed pretty much as normal. No signs of any unusual activity and, more importantly, no newshounds lurking. For a wonder, the news blackout had worked, and Dave Gould's murder was evidently not yet known at the dance school.

As he got out of his car, the DI was relieved to note it was getting colder once more, though the sleety rain had temporarily abated. The skies still had that angry swollen look, but everything felt somehow sharper, cleaner. Or maybe it was just the adrenalin that was making his nerve ends tingle.

A crunch of wheels and Burton pulled up alongside him with Doyle in the passenger seat.

'Where's Noakes got to?' Markham asked. 'I thought you were all going to come together.'

'He shot off to do something before I was able to catch up to him,' she said with a hint of exasperation.

Shot off? Didn't sound like his number two, who was built for comfort not speed.

'Did he say what was so urgent?'

No answer from his subordinates.

God, this was no time for Noakes to pull his infamous 'gotta-see-a-man-about-a-dog' routine.

'Here he is, boss.' Doyle sounded relieved as a dreadful grinding of gears announced the arrival of their colleague.

'What happened to you then?' The DI decided to play it cool, noting the DS's unusually flustered demeanour.

'Got taken short.'

'Not sickening for something, I trust.'

Not now when we're baiting the trap for a multiple killer, was the subtext.

The DS had the grace to look sheepish.

'Sorry, guv. The ole Delhi belly.'

Hmm. For some reason, the old reprobate couldn't look him in the eye, but there was no time to dwell on whatever shifty dodge he'd been up to.

He addressed the team.

'When we get in there, Noakes and I will take Cathy Gould and break the news about Dave.'

The DS's face lengthened perceptibly, but he did not demur.

'Kate, I want you and Doyle to do a circuit of the place.' He glanced at his watch. 'It's coming up to half past four so, according to their timetable, afternoon sessions should be finishing shortly.'

'What do we tell the staff?' Doyle asked.

'Just say there's going to be a short briefing in the theatre.' Muscles tensed along the DI's jawline. 'That's when we'll make the announcement about Mr Gould—'

'An' you do your Larry Olivier bit to make psycho-man think we're onto him,' Noakes told Burton who took a step backwards, startled by her colleague's vehemence.

'I'll do my best,' she said earnestly. Then, 'It might help if we suggested they cancel tonight's classes. You know, we can tell them it's out of respect for Dave Gould . . . but really—'

'Make him think the coast's clear an' then he'll walk right into it.' Noakes clearly liked the idea.

Doyle agreed. 'Yeah . . . if Barr's got the place to himself, he'll most likely decide it's now or never.'

'How can we keep tabs without him clocking us?' Burton smoothed the front of her Nehru jacket with hands that felt suddenly clammy.

'We head off for our loudly trumpeted pit stop at Costa, leaving staff to deal with any students and then lock up.' The DI contemplated the facade of the Bluebell thoughtfully. 'I'm betting our man will ensure he's the last one on the premises . . .'

'But he won't actually leave,' Doyle said.

The DI nodded grimly. 'That's right. He'll secrete himself somewhere in the building and wait till he's sure of being unobserved.'

'Only he won't be, will he, sir? Unobserved, I mean.' Burton asked anxiously.

'There'll be two uniforms outside the school on static guard duties,' the DI replied. 'I want to give the impression the focus of our enquiries has shifted to the allotment and manpower is firmly concentrated out there for now.'

'Away from the school.' This was Noakes.

'Exactly, Sergeant.'

'What if he smells a rat?' Doyle needed reassurance.

'He won't.' Markham spoke with more confidence than he felt. 'At the briefing, Kate can finish off by talking about there being a uniformed patrol outside. *A visible presence to reassure the public* . . . that kind of thing.'

'Foot patrol as opposed to anything high-powered.'

'Precisely, Kate . . . Make it sound like Neighbourhood Watch rather than a CID stakeout.'

'Their friendly local Plod,' Noakes chipped in. 'Nowt threatening.'

'Correct. With the emphasis on checking *perimeter* security . . . That way he'll feel confident of being undisturbed.' For all his inward qualms, the DI appeared perfectly in control of the situation.

Burton's mind was running on timings. 'When will we move in, sir?'

'Not until we've given him enough rope to hang himself,' Markham told her.

'What about backup?' Doyle sounded wistful, as though he would have relished having all the bells and whistles.

'*No*.' The retort came out like gunfire. Then Markham smiled at the crestfallen young DC to soften the rebuke.

'We keep this between *us*,' he said firmly. 'No blues and twos, no radios, no damned loudspeakers or ambulances.' He looked at them steadily. 'We owe it to Mickey Willett and the others who've died to bring Tony Barr out of there in one piece. So there'll be no heroics.'

Doyle considered this. 'You reckon he'll come quietly, boss?'

'If we can convince him the police just want to *understand* his side of it and he's headed for a cushy berth like the Newman or Ashworth rather than Wormwood Scrubs, then I think it's game on.'

'I still can't get my head round it being Anton Bhaer,' Doyle burst out.

Noakes glared at the younger man. 'Keep your voice down, nitwit.'

'Sorry, sarge . . . But it's bleeding *surreal*.'

Markham took pity on him. 'The killer's been acting a part, Constable. Playing out the role of a normal person onstage in front of his audience . . . showing people what he thinks they want to see . . . trying to keep his dark side hidden.'

'But the dark side keeps getting stronger,' Burton took up the baton. 'So he becomes even more secretive . . . compartmentalizing his life for fear he might slip up.'

'The trouble with compartmentalization is that it can be very destructive . . . Life narrows to a game of chess where you have to stay mentally two moves ahead of the opposition to ensure success and keep the inner demons away.'

Was it Burton's imagination or was there some hidden personal significance behind the DI's words?

But she'd have no chance to dwell on the conundrum.

'D'you think there's other people he's killed, sir — more than the ones we know about?' Ignoring Noakes's scowl, Doyle felt compelled to ask the question.

Markham treated the enquiry with the grave courtesy he invariably showed to even the most junior officer.

'I don't know enough about the pathology,' he said, 'but it's possible.'

Doyle let out a faint hiss.

Markham continued, 'With Mickey Willett's murder, once he stepped over that final boundary — or whatever was protecting his shaky identity — then he could have started to lose control over his sickness. It could have escalated fast.'

Noakes felt as though this entire conversation was giving him the bends.

The dark side . . . pathology . . . shaky identity . . . sickness. Anton Bhaer or Barr or whatever he called himself was just one evil fucker and that's all there was to it.

As though aware exactly what his wingman was thinking, the DI flicked an invisible speck of dirt from his own immaculate pinstripe.

'C'mon,' he said and then, in an attempt to defuse the mounting tension, 'standing out here won't "butter no parsnips" as they say down your neck of the woods, Noakesy.'

Duly admonished, they followed behind him.

It was getting colder, but Markham welcomed the drop in temperature, which braced and fortified him like a draught of wine.

The little red-brick building ahead looked so unprepossessing. It was the last place one would imagine to be the lair of a twisted killer, but Markham felt sure he was looking at the heart of the spider's web.

On the threshold, he halted momentarily, unnerved by the plangent strains of a piano sonata coming from somewhere inside the building.

The DI prayed that the road along which he and the team were headed would have no figurative exit ramps for their killer and that they would be able to remove the mask from Anton Bhaer's face forever.

Then he passed through the front door.

* * *

Three quarters of an hour later, the team reassembled in the back office behind reception, its door firmly closed on comings and goings in the foyer.

'You did well,' Noakes told Kate Burton with an air of grim satisfaction. 'Sonny boy won't have sussed the plan.'

'It was difficult to behave normally round him,' Doyle observed with a shudder. 'How could he sit there along with all the others pretending to be shocked at the news about Dave Gould when all the time . . . ?'

The spectacle of 'Anton Bhaer' consoling his unsuspecting colleagues had indeed been chilling since he had been revealed as a madman with a carefully crafted outer shell.

'None of them know him,' Burton said slowly. 'The person in front of them is just a mirage.'

'He's a dancer, remember,' Markham pointed out, 'a *performer*. That makes it easier for him to create a fictional outer life and retain control . . . it's up to him when he unleashes the beast within and when he reels it back in.'

Never keen on philosophizing or what he privately designated 'that criminal profiling shit', Noakes returned them to the matter in hand.

'You reckon he'll not be able to keep away from the cellars then, guv?'

'He's off-balance now thanks to Kate's smokescreen,' Markham replied. 'I think the reference to "a previous investigation" will act like igniting fuel, propelling him forward.'

'Cos he thinks he's gonna lose control over what's left of Willett?' Noakes's expression was eloquent in its disgust. But there was something else there too, the DI thought observing his sergeant closely, something reminiscent of a big-game hunter who had tracked his quarry for long distances with only one goal — to finish it off at the right moment.

'What you have to understand, Sergeant,' Markham said, 'is that if we're right about him, the bond he shares with Mickey Willett is of almost mystical significance . . . far more important than any bonds he might share with the living.'

'That's why the Bluebell matters so much to him,' agreed Burton. 'It's kind of sacred ground.'

'You sound almost, well, *sorry* for him, sarge.' From the way Doyle said this, it was clear the DC was in Noakes's camp.

But Markham was pleased to see Burton held her ground.

'I suppose in a way I do,' she countered. 'It must be exhausting living a lie . . . having to hide what's really going on inside.'

Chuffing Nora, next thing we know, she'll be suggesting a group hug or a couple of verses of 'Kumbaya', thought Noakes.

However, he held his peace. Allowances had to be made, though that psychology degree had a lot to answer for.

The hubbub outside appeared to be subsiding as the remaining staff dealt with stragglers and shooed students away.

'Think we shoulda cut Cathy Gould in on the plan?' Noakes asked the DI. 'What if she barges in on him or summat?'

Markham considered this. For all that there was something creepy about the woman, her situation was pitiable. After all, she'd just lost her entire family at one fell swoop.

'I think that's unlikely, but let's not take any chances.' He turned to Doyle. 'Constable, I want you to arrange for Ms Gould to stay elsewhere tonight, please. Her GP's with her at the moment but see if you can rustle someone up.'

'Try one of them nosy mums,' Noakes said sourly. 'They'd flipping love it . . . getting to hear all the juicy details first-hand.'

'She's hardly in a fit state for that,' was the DI's tart response. 'I'm not sure she's even fully taken in the fact of Dave's death or made any connection with the other murders.'

'Yeah,' his number two conceded. 'Sounded almost like she thought some vagrant or a random whack job did it.'

Doyle departed on his errand.

'It's funny,' Burton said as the door closed behind him. 'Going round the classrooms before, watching people learning how to waltz and samba, everything felt so *normal* and *nice* . . . even with everything that's happened here . . .'

'An' someone buried in the basement,' Noakes added with lugubrious relish.

'Did you notice,' she went on distractedly, 'Bhaer had an inhaler?'

Her fellow DS looked at her as if she were mad.

'So what?'

'Well, you remember that wheezy noise I heard the night we found Clay Clifton. I know what it was now . . . someone with asthma.'

'Well spotted, Kate,' the DI said quietly.

'Anton's — sorry, Tony's practice bag was open,' she explained, 'and I saw the inhaler on top.'

'*Hey*.' Noakes was struck by a thought. 'Mebbe *he's* the Ghost Dancer.'

Now it was Burton's turn to do a double take.

Her colleague duly filled her in on the tale of the boy who hanged himself in the theatre leaving a note to say the 'Ghost Dancer' had made him do it.

'How horrible,' she said when he had finished. 'I never heard anything about that.'

'Nor did we.' The DI was firm. 'There *was* a suicide but as for the rest of it — pure fantasy.'

'Our Nat' — a curious shadow crossed Noakes's face before he went on — 'she got the story from someone who knew all about it.'

Hardly an unimpeachable source, but Burton diplomatically kept her counsel.

There was a knock and Vivienne Sansom put her head round the door. The pert allure had vanished, and her complexion was putty-coloured. Markham guessed she was tormented at never having been able to make it up with Robyn DiAngelo before her rival was murdered.

'It's just staff left now, Inspector,' the teacher said, sounding like a sleepwalker.

'Thank you,' he said quietly, 'we'll be there in a minute.'

'Right,' he turned to his colleagues. 'When we get out into the hall, Noakes, I want you to do your piece.'

'As in saying time for us to get a brew an' snacks?'

'Correct.' The DI eyed his wingman shrewdly. 'Make lots of noise about how Costa's round the corner and we could stop off there for supplies en route to the station.' Wryly, he added, 'I'm sure you'll be thoroughly convincing.'

As she heard this, Burton suppressed a smile. Method acting at its finest!

'Kate, I want you to set up the static patrol in their hearing,' Markham continued. 'Make sure they get the idea it's just a couple of uniforms to deter thrill-seekers or anyone hanging round outside . . . stop local teenagers making a nuisance of themselves, reassure the neighbours, that kind of thing.'

'Got it, sir.'

'I'll talk about going to the allotments this evening.' The DI felt a fresh surge of adrenalin at the thought of what lay ahead. 'Let him think he's got the Bluebell to himself.'

'Do we wait to see the staff clear off, sir?'

'No, Kate. Better if we leave them to it . . . Our man's bound to find a way of staying on the premises . . . He'll probably come over all chivalrous and offer to lock up.'

Noakes's mouth twisted. 'Proper little gent,' he sneered.

'What about the uniforms?' As ever, Burton wanted everything watertight. 'Do we fill them in?'

'Better not,' Noakes counselled. 'Otherwise they might get a fit of the lone rangers an' screw everything up.'

'Well, ignorance is bliss, I suppose.' The DI weighed it up. 'And if Barr decides to check them out, they'll be more convincing if they don't know what we're really planning.'

'You think he'll nip out for a chat?' Noakes sounded incredulous.

'Quite possibly, yes.' Markham's face was unusually serious as he added, 'He may need to feed whatever entity lurks inside him, but his cunning side will be on high alert.'

'He might even try to pump them for information,' Burton put in.

'Who knows what a sociopath will do when cornered.' With that, the DI gestured to the door. 'Come on, we need to get moving. Hopefully Doyle's sorted a berth for Cathy Gould. No harm if he mentions it casually . . . should help to lower Barr's guard.'

* * *

Costa was closing when they arrived, but the manager readily gave them a table and the all-important refreshments before tactfully retreating to do a stock take.

Unusually, Noakes seemed disinclined to gorge on the muffins and shortbread provided for them. For some reason, this case more than any other had really gotten under his skin, Markham reflected.

Outside, darkness had fallen and the street was deserted. The detectives' reflections, taut with anticipation and strain, looked wanly back at them from the shopfront window.

Their exit from the Bluebell had proceeded according to the script and now it was just a waiting game.

'How long do we give it?' Noakes asked for the umpteenth time, a vein jumping near his temple. 'It's coming up to eight now.'

Instead of swatting him away, this time Markham nodded.

'I think we can risk it,' he said. 'Radio the uniforms please, Doyle, and tell them to meet us in front of Heathfield Primary . . . Tell them not to rush, just routine checks, right?'

Pale with excitement and trepidation, the DC hastened to comply.

Ten minutes later saw them in front of the school awaiting the arrival of the foot patrol.

'Here they come,' Noakes rumbled.

The fresh-faced duo visibly snapped to attention on spotting Markham.

'Good evening, Inspector.' The taller one was obviously surprised to see him but recovered well. 'Nothing doing at the Bluebell to speak of.'

To speak of.

'What d'you mean?' Noakes was bullish.

'Well, it's just one of the teachers in there right now . . . stayed behind to sort costumes for some show they've got coming up.'

'Oh, and your Natalie, sarge,' his colleague said brightly. 'Figured it was okay to let her in seeing as she's practically one of us.' His voice tailed off uncertainly as he took in Noakes's expression. 'Hey, are you okay sarge?'

In the light from the streetlamp, Noakes had turned deathly white.

'What the fuck is my girl doing in there?' he demanded hoarsely.

'She turned up around ten minutes ago . . . said something about wanting to switch classes and was there anyone she could speak to . . .'

'*Jesus.*' Noakes was remembering that it was his big idea to keep the uniforms out of the loop. And now his daughter was in there with . . . '*Jesus.*'

The portly figure began to shake as the two officers looked at each other in consternation. Something was clearly very wrong.

'It's all right, Constables, you haven't done anything amiss.' Although his heart was in his mouth, the DI kept his tone level. 'But now I need you to do exactly as I say.'

Minutes later, having briefed them as succinctly as possible, he stood outside the Bluebell with his team, noting uneasily that no colour had returned to Noakes's complexion. He still had the ashy pallor that had so alarmed their colleagues.

'We know where the fucker is,' Noakes ranted distractedly.

Kate Burton laid a restraining hand on his arm as he swayed unsteadily.

'In them cellars digging up a skeleton . . . an' my baby walked in on him . . .'

'This only happened in the last ten minutes or so, Noakesy.' Markham kept his voice calm. 'He won't have decided what to do with her.'

Please God.

* * *

In the event, they found the killer where they had expected to find him.

Hearing their approach — with Natalie Noakes's life at stake there was now no benefit in subterfuge — Bhaer had realized the game was up and waited for them next to a small grated aperture in the bottom of the far wall. Markham saw the gleam of fragile milky-coloured bones and in that instant knew they had found Mickey Willett's last resting place.

But Noakes had eyes only for his daughter, tied to a clothes rail next to the killer. Beneath the Oompa Loompa spray tan, her sweat-streaked face was the colour of lard. Irrationally, the DI was struck by how the girl's features, bleached with fear, showed the outlines of an unusually delicate bone structure beneath.

'It's over. There's nowhere to go.'

Noakes's voice was so thick with hatred that Markham barely recognized it. His wingman's face was contorted too, as though he had been scorched by an emotional bolt of lightning.

The man they had cornered looked steadily back at them. The DI noticed the pupils in his remarkable black eyes had narrowed to pinpricks in one of the eeriest transformations he had ever witnessed.

But the murderer did not utter a word.

At the subsequent enquiry, Markham could hardly say how events unfolded in the next few moments.

All he knew for certain was that the DS lunged forwards, eluding Burton's restraining arm. There was a glint of something sharp and metallic as he flung himself on the man standing motionless against the cellar wall.

The two figures fused and remained silhouetted in an embrace which might almost have been loverlike.

Save for the crimson jet that sprayed upwards between them and Natalie Noakes's terrified screams, which seemed as though they would never end.

* * *

A week after the conclusion of the Bluebell investigation, Olivia and Markham sat in the Grapes.

Like the Bluebell School, their favourite pub had a fantastical Brothers Grimm feel to it, being a lopsided, arthritic old building with absolutely no pretensions to Cool Britannia status, adorned as it was with a variety of nautical odds and ends that would not have looked out of place on-board a mid-nineteenth-century clipper.

Its landlady Denise, blonde and busty with carefully lacquered beehive and a voice that could strip sandpaper, adored Markham. 'Gil's very own pocket Venus . . . Babs Windsor to the life,' Olivia was wont to tease, but she too loved the pub's quirkiness and its cosy firelit back parlour, which gave her a feeling of battening down the hatches and keeping the world at bay.

Now she asked bluntly, 'What's going to happen with George, Gil?'

'Nothing much,' her lover answered. 'He'll say he thought he saw Barr reach for a weapon . . . danger to life and limb and all the rest of it.'

'Do you believe that?' she asked softly.

'It doesn't matter what I believe, sweetheart.' Markham gulped down his quadruple G&T like it was lemonade. 'That's his line and everyone's sticking to it.'

'Kate told me she saw George holding a photograph afterwards,' Olivia said slowly. 'Something he pulled out of his pocket at the last moment . . . She said he was clutching it like some sort of talisman.'

'Burton shouldn't be discussing operational details with you, Liv.'

As if by magic, another G&T appeared on the table in front of him, Denise whisking away in a waft of Chanel No. 5 before Olivia was even aware of her presence.

'*Come on, Gil. This is George we're talking about.*'

Olivia reached for her lover's hand and gripped it tightly. 'Kate said it was a photo of a young man who was a dead ringer for "Anton Bhaer" or Tony Barr or whoever the hell he was.'

'I don't know anything about a photo,' Markham said doggedly.

'Of course you don't, dumbass,' she squeezed his hand. 'Kate got rid of it. Pronto.'

Olivia took a long draught of her own drink.

Then she continued, 'I reckon when George saw that picture in the *Courier*, he recognized Natalie's father cos he'd found an identical snap at home . . . some hidey-hole Muriel had placed it in for safekeeping.'

'What're you saying, Liv?'

'That George killed him as payback for seducing Muriel.'

'We'll never know for sure.'

And you'll never ask, she thought to herself. Plus, you'll always wonder if George secretly *wanted* to destroy the man who was Natalie's biological father . . . so he'd never face the risk of a rival for her affections.

Could this secret erect a barrier between her lover and the man who was indispensable to him? Only time would tell.

'How did everything fit together?' she asked lightly, moving to safer ground. 'C'mon, Gil, you can spill the beans now.'

It was the right note to strike. The cloud on Markham's brow lifted.

'It would appear Tony Barr was bisexual and killed Mickey Willet when they were both youngsters. We'll likely never know why, but he buried Mickey in the cellars.' He raised the refill to his lips. 'Afterwards Barr left Bromgrove, and by the time he came back he'd reinvented himself — new name and backstory.'

'But he couldn't stay away from the Bluebell.'

'That's right . . . drawn there like a moth to a flame. Besides, it's where he'd kept Mickey . . . His own special secret.'

'Why'd he kill Shirley Bastin?' she asked, realizing the conversation had turned cool and logical now they'd moved away from the subject of George Noakes.

'I think it most likely happened in an explosion of rage after she repelled his advances and he realized there was no chance of her ever making the dance school over to him,' Markham said.

'And Enid?'

'Everyone else was thoroughly hoodwinked, but I think the old lady rumbled him . . . She'd known Mickey's mother, you see, and likely picked up titbits about the boys' lifestyle . . . That's why the picture from the *Courier* bugged her—'

'As in brought it all back?' Olivia ventured.

'That's right.' Markham speared a plump olive from the plate of tapas in front of them. 'On a deep subconscious level, "Anton Bhaer" bothered her, and he became anxious her ramblings might awaken suspicion and threaten his carefully constructed new life.'

'D'you think she challenged him?'

'It wouldn't surprise me . . . She may even have caught him slipping Shirley sleeping pills or some other medication to make her compliant.'

'What about Clay Clifton?' It was the first time Markham had opened up about the investigation and Olivia relished the chance to discuss it. 'Was he trying to blackmail Bhaer?'

'We think so,' her lover replied, helping himself to some goat's cheese. 'Could be something Enid let drop made Clay suspicious and he made the connection with Mickey Willett . . . We've tracked down an ex-boyfriend of Anton Bhaer who was also a friend of Clay's . . . Apparently, he told Clay that "Anton" had nightmares when they were together as well as a horror of confined spaces.' His voice steady now, Markham added, 'In the end, it was a case of putting two and two together.'

'Why didn't Clay go to the police?'

'I think Anton/Tony probably convinced him Mickey's death was a *crime passionnel* and what happened to the women was accidental.'

'You couldn't argue what happened to Robyn DiAngelo was accidental, though.' Olivia was indignant.

'No indeed.' Markham pushed the shared platter towards her. 'C'mon, Liv, get stuck in.'

To please him, she toyed with some Serrano croquettes.

'Robyn trusted Anton and even gave him an alibi for Clay's murder,' her lover continued. 'But after meeting a friend from the dance school, she began to have second thoughts.'

'This was the friend she was seeing off on holiday, right?'

'Yes, that's the one . . . She knew Tony Barr from their early days at the Bluebell and confided in Robyn that he'd sexually assaulted her when she was very young—'

'So you think Robyn tackled him about it?' Olivia asked eagerly.

'Most probably, yes . . . She could have challenged him about "skeletons in his closet" and asked if Shirley had realized what he really was.'

'And he couldn't afford to have it come out . . . not with the police sniffing round Mickey Willett and running a treble murder investigation into Shirley, Enid and Clay.'

'Right again.' Markham smiled the meltingly tender smile that invariably made her heart do somersaults.

They moved onto the focaccia and ate contentedly in silence for a time.

'I think before Tony Barr ever stretched out a hand to murder his first victim, he was somehow a victim himself, Liv.'

'Uh-huh.'

'A victim of his own internal devices . . . No matter how monstrous he turned out to be, the first life to be destroyed was ultimately his own . . . There must have been some fracturing of his personality . . . something that went horribly wrong.'

'We'll never really know, sweetheart,' Olivia said gently. 'And finally he killed Dave Gould.' She jabbed at a stray pepper. 'For the love of God, why did *that* poor man have to die?'

'It's likely Robyn shared something with him.'

'Something about what she'd learned?'

'Most probably.' Markham sighed. 'But Dave agonized over what to do with it and ran out of time.'

He helped himself to some roasted radicchio, savouring the bitterness.

It was undoubtedly Barr who stole those personnel files from the back office of the Bluebell, though they'd drawn a blank with Cathy Gould who steadfastly declined to be drawn on their contents.

Barr could have bluffed his way through any enquiries as to his name change. So there must have been something else in there to compromise him . . . Markham would have given a great deal to know what that was. Possibly Cathy Gould intended to hold it over Barr, only to be foiled at the end.

'D'you think Cathy Gould guessed?' It was uncanny how Olivia seemed to read his thoughts at times.

'If she did, we'll never be able to prove it.'

'Maybe she'll sell the studio now if the price is right.'

'Not to our friend Mister Councillor Callaghan at any rate.'

Olivia paused, the cured ham halfway to her mouth.

'How come?'

'Let's just say some awkward questions have arisen as to the Callaghans' involvement in the golf course development scheme.'

'*Ah*.'

'Looks like even the DCI's got dragged into it.'

'Now that *is* good news.' Olivia visibly perked up.

'Oh, you know Sidney. He's like Teflon . . . Nothing ever sticks.'

'If you *were* to come across anything, Gil, it'd help get George out of the brown stuff.'

'The thought had crossed my mind,' he admitted.

She knew better than to push.

'Fred Stroud's had enough of Bromgrove,' she said inconsequentially. 'Can't say I blame him after being suspected of multiple homicides.'

'Understandable,' he agreed. 'I believe Vivienne Sansom's moving on as well. A fresh start all round.'

'It'd be good if the Bluebell stayed in business as a dance school for a while longer.' Olivia smiled. 'When I first went in there, I had this strange sense of oppression, of something negative . . . but it's lifted now.' She added almost casually, 'I've told Natalie we should forget the fuddy-duddy stuff and register for Zumba fitness.'

'I reckon she'll like that,' Markham said simply.

After they'd left the pub, walking along hand in hand in the crisp night air, Olivia said thoughtfully, 'Everyone was fooled by him, weren't they, Gil?'

No need to ask who *he* was.

'We never picked up a hint of the real Anton Bhaer or realized there was anything out of place.' She shivered. 'Perhaps in the final analysis, none of us is ever fully knowable.'

Markham thought of George Noakes. The only man he had ever counted on as being a 'sure thing'.

Then he looked up at the stars taking over the night sky, forming their own enigmatic pattern in the vault beyond.

Who could say on what path he and the team — his family — were bent?

All he knew was, it was a journey they would make together.

THE END

ALSO BY CATHERINE MOLONEY

THE DI GILBERT MARKHAM SERIES

Book 1: CRIME IN THE CHOIR
Book 2: CRIME IN THE SCHOOL
Book 3: CRIME IN THE CONVENT
Book 4: CRIME IN THE HOSPITAL
Book 5: CRIME IN THE BALLET
Book 6: CRIME IN THE GALLERY
Book 7: CRIME IN THE HEAT
Book 8: CRIME AT HOME
Book 9: CRIME IN THE BALLROOM

FREE KINDLE BOOKS

Please join our mailing list for free Kindle books and new releases, including crime thrillers, mysteries, romance and more.

Thank you for reading this book. If you enjoyed it please leave feedback on Amazon or Goodreads, and if there is anything we missed or you have a question about then please get in touch. The author and publishing team appreciate your feedback and time reading this book.

We're very grateful to eagle-eyed readers who take the time to contact us. Please send any errors you find to corrections@joffebooks.com